THE BLOOD

NANCY JACKSON

WILD
IDEAS
PRESS

Hardback ISBN: 978 0-578444-11-6
Paperback ISBN: 978-1-710573-36-7
eBook ISBN: 978-1-386684-40-4
Audible ASIN: B07R7DK28V

Published in the United States
Wild Ideas Press
Edmond, Oklahoma

Book Cover Design by
Angela Westerman of
AK Organic Abstracts
AKOrganicAbstracts.com

This book is dedicated to my family, my husband Rick. And to my children Ben, Lacey, and Kendon, their spouses, my grandchildren, and great-grandchildren. My quiver is truly full!

To my friend Linda who encouraged me to write this book. Thank you for your constant applause and your brutal honesty. For both of those I thank you!

To Angela Westerman who creates my original book covers and graphics. Thank you for 'getting me'! Look her up and hire her for yourself at AKOrganicAbstracts.com

CONTENTS

CHAPTER 1

The blood drew her. The richness of the red, the thick fluidity, the touch. She was drawn to the blood.

But the blood never lasted. It changed color and dried up. The feeling faded as the blood faded.

She sat back on her haunches and watched as the blood created a red river running away from the body. The dirt was causing it to weave and wind in an erratic pattern. Amazing how just a grain of sand could disrupt the flow and change its entire course.

It would take a while to dry tonight. It was cold here and the moisture in the air would help keep it hydrated. But it never lasted long enough.

Why did she need the blood? She often thought about this. Why was it that the only thing that helped her feel whole and alive was the blood? It had to be wrong, releasing human blood, but she felt as though her survival depended on it. The need raged deep within her.

She touched the blood and brought her fingers up to look at them. It still felt warm on her skin, but it dried soon after touching it. So she dropped her hand and gazed at the pool on the ground.

The little rivulets had ceased. Soon the blood would separate and the yellow liquid would appear, and that was just not acceptable. She would leave before that happened because she could not bear to see it. She could not bear to see the blood broken and separated. It had to be alive and whole so she would feel alive and whole.

CHAPTER 2

The rumble of Ike's 1964 Harley Panhead roared into the parking lot of the Darkside bar. Kicking it into neutral, he let it roll to a stop along the side of the bar near the backdoor.

Ike slung his leg over and off the worn black leather seat of the bike and stood looking around at the neighborhood as he tugged off his fingerless gloves. The instinct to survey his surroundings had been with him since his biker days in Nevada. After thirty years of that life he'd grown jaded and tired and wanted out of the biker club, but the old habits had stayed with him.

Leaving the biker club, he'd come to Oklahoma for asylum and found he liked it here. It was peaceful and quiet and he could work and live without the constant fear of arrest or death.

As usual, it was quiet in the neighborhood, so Ike turned to unlock the backdoor of the tavern. The Darkside Tavern was on the far northeast side of Kachina, Oklahoma and had sprung up in the era of prohibition. A man and a woman named Cantor had lived in the house that was now the bar. It was a stately two story home built with a white clapboard exterior. There was an entrance to their basement at the backside of the house where a hill sloped down at least two stories.

Inside their basement they had creatively built false walls and hallways to a speakeasy that the cops knew existed, but had never found. Patrons had named it Darkside because to get to the speakeasy you had to go to the dark side of the house where there were no lights to guide you to the entrance.

When prohibition ended, the owners moved the establishment to the first floor, and the couple continued to live upstairs. They tried to make it a reputable place with fine dining, a nice bar and entertaining.

But it never caught on. The reputation of the speakeasy held its ground and those with class refused to enter the new establishment even though most any night of the week a year earlier they could have been caught secretly underground. Appearances were everything.

No matter what the couple tried, they could not bring the Darkside to the status they desired. They had changed the name to Cantor's Fine Dining and Ale but it didn't matter. Everyone still referred to it as the Darkside.

After several years of trying, the Cantors stopped fighting it and just let it drift back into the Darkside. It was a bar. Just that simple. So be it.

The Cantors had long since died and new owners had taken over. Ownership had changed many times. And it was now Ike's.

As Ike lifted a crate of liquor from the floor of the back storage room and carried it to the front, he chuckled to himself as he thought about the random mix of clients he had come to know through the years.

There were bikers, cowboys, ranchers, and all sorts of people who had the guts to get a drink and play there. The common thread to the Darkside clientele, was that none of them wanted anyone else to know what they did or where they did it. On that, they could all agree.

It was often the first stop for the occasional down and outers. They would hit on hard times and need to drink away their grief in a dark and dirty hole where no one would know.

The bottles clanked as Ike lifted them from the box and placed them on the glass shelf attached to the mirrored wall behind the bar. Ike himself no longer drank. It was ironic, he thought, but his health had suffered from it and he needed to keep a clear head to run this business and to stay aware of his surroundings.

He had no family left, so he watched over the

customers at the Darkside; they were his family now. Many just needed a place to go where they could hide for a while. Others came here to do the things they should not, could not, do anywhere else. Ike didn't judge. He had no room to judge because he had done it all at one time or another.

Maybe that was why he felt so protective of them. When they were at their lowest point and at their most vulnerable, he was there watching after them and they never even knew it.

It was still early in the day and he had cleaned up the night before; so, once the bottles were all stocked, he went to his office and began working on his bookkeeping. Living in this place was definitely a trade-off. The peace and quiet for a large bankroll.

"Hey, Ike," a voice rang from around the corner.

"Hey back at 'ya," Ike greeted Heather, his part-time employee.

Heather rounded the corner to stand against the doorframe of Ike's office. "Did you hear about the murder?"

Her words startled Ike. "What murder? Where?" Murder in Kachina had never happened since Ike had lived here and he couldn't recall anyone ever mentioning there ever being one here.

"Kim, the dispatcher at the police station called me this morning and said that a body had been found over at the old warehouses by the train tracks."

"Who was it?" Ike asked. His concern caused him to shift his office chair around to face her, fully engaged.

"Don't know. That's all Kim knew. A call came in and they headed out to go look. She said she would call me when she knew more."

Ike's mind was racing, wondering what it was all about and if any of his slightly colorful customers had anything to do with it.

"Thanks, Heather. Can you let me know when she calls you?" Ike asked.

"Sure thing. I just stopped in this morning to pick up my check. I'll be back at five o'clock."

Ike had the check ready and handed it to Heather. When she left, Ike turned back to his bookwork, but his mind couldn't disengage from the thought of murder here in his small town.

THE CLATTERING of the hairbrush on the wood floor startled Senna's already jangled nerves. She took a deep breath, closed her eyes, and willed herself to calm down. When her breathing slowed, she unclenched her fists. With a controlled whoosh of breath, she opened her eyes.

Her upbringing had led her to a life of strict rule-making in order to bring structure and maintain control. But this morning she was late and her anxiety did nothing to help her get back on track.

She was thankful for her daily routine where the night before she would lay out her plain and simple clothing and prepare her lunch. Grabbing lunch out of the fridge the cool rush of air emphasized the hot flush of anxiety she was feeling.

She hurried out the door and turned to look back, assuring herself that her tiny house was in order and that everything was in its place.

The sun was shining, and she could hear the birds with their songs. On any other day she would have enjoyed her walk to work, but the anxiety of being late pushed her forward with intent, as she half walked, half ran to work.

As she reached to open the door to the library, she noticed her watch. She was right on time. Relief replaced the anxiety, and she opened the door, glad to be on time.

"Good morning, Andrea," Senna greeted her co-worker as she walked through the door. Senna thought to herself, *always be sweet and polite,* Momma would say.

"On time, but barely," Andrea teased. "I never thought I would see the day you cut it so close!" Andrea beamed.

Andrea had worked with Senna for three years now. They had met at the local community college, both taking the same English classes.

For Andrea, the position at the library was a low-stress job which provided her time to pursue her dream of becoming a novelist.

She wasn't sure, but she thought Senna would be comfortable to work the rest of her life at the library.

When Andrea had first met Senna at school, she didn't know what to make of her. She was quiet and withdrawn, but there was something she couldn't quite put her finger on, that drew her to Senna.

Sitting next to her in class day after day, Senna and Andrea had developed a comfortableness, if not a friendship in the traditional sense of the word.

They had never gone shopping or out to eat like girlfriends do, but through time, she and Senna had bonded. Senna always declined offers to go places and do things, but Andrea kept trying.

Andrea thought Senna was sweet, innocent, and endearing and enjoyed being around her. She sensed that Senna must have experienced an abusive childhood which had wounded her to the point that not even she realized just how severe it had been, or her need to overcome it.

"Yes, I know. I didn't hear the alarm this morning," she replied. She was embarrassed and ducked her head as she spoke. Familiar shame crept in for almost breaking one of her rules.

"It's okay. It happens to everyone. We're all human. You've never been late, so if you had been, it wouldn't have been a big deal."

Senna nodded and gave a half smile in acknowledgment, but it betrayed what she felt inside. She was scared that she had come close to breaking a rule. It felt useless to try and break free from her father's words—which had taught Senna that rule breakers were worthless—and she didn't want to be worthless.

Soon, the routine of the library and the work helped to soothe and comfort her. Senna breathed deeply to take in the familiar smells of the books. She felt at home here.

The library was not a busy place and Senna took comfort knowing she could organize the books and order them without being disturbed. The library was a peaceful place, and Senna yearned for peace of any kind.

Senna loved the books, and she loved reading. The stories would sweep her away into a life she felt she would never know. She loved the feel of the books with their crisp yet subtle pages, and their leather-bound covers.

The new books were so fresh and alive, just beginning their new journeys into the world and into many hands. The old ones, too, with a history that had nothing to do with the story within, but of where they had been and the homes and hands that had held them.

"Miss can you help me find a book?" asked a lady. The voice jarred Senna out of her deep thought.

"Yes ma'am, I certainly can!" she replied. She enjoyed helping others even though personal social interaction often made her uncomfortable. "What book were you looking for?"

"I am doing research on blood and was not sure

where to start. Is there a medical section or would it be in a science section?" the lady asked.

"Are you writing a research paper or do you just need general information?"

"Neither. My father is ill and I'm not sure he has been diagnosed correctly. I've tried Google, but it was so overwhelming; and, honestly, so much of it seems like utter junk. It's hard to decide what's true and what's not." Senna noticed the lady's face was lined with concern for her father. When Senna's father had died, she had felt almost nothing.

"The medical books are grouped in the science section and they are here. If you don't find what you need, let me know and I'll see what else I can find for you." Senna gave the lady a genuine smile. One thing that always made her feel good was helping people.

"Thanks, I appreciate it." The woman said as she turned to peruse the books on the shelf, her finger already sliding along the titles while she read each one.

Back to sorting and returning books to the shelves, Senna's mind floated away as she felt the joy of helping the new client fade and sadness creep in. A thought of Mother and Father from out of nowhere caused a pain so severe it plunged through her gut.

The faces she saw when she thought of them were stern and severe. She frequently wondered how they had come to be that way. Mother had a soft side. Father was always stern. There were times when she knew Mother did not agree with what Father had said or done and Senna would see worry and compassion on Mother's face. But Mother never spoke up.

She thought of how her mother's softness would take over when they were alone and how she would wrap her arms around Senna making her feel warm and whole. But so often, it was fleeting as her father would come walking back in. He always wanted to make sure Mother wasn't undoing his stern reprimands by being soft on Senna. The punishment would be severe for them both.

The anguish of working so hard to be good and fearing she would fail, constantly encompassed her as a child. Not only did she feel the need to abide by everything Father demanded of her, but she also felt compelled to anticipate what new rule he would bring down upon her in a moment's notice.

Many of his demands were taken from the Bible, or his twisted version of it. They went to church each Sunday and sat through a long service. Senna remembered her starched dresses itching her as she tried to sit still and feeling the stone cold stare of her father when she didn't. That stare was always followed with painful punishment later at home.

Senna would often read the words to many of the songs they sang and thought they should bring comfort and hope, joy even, but they were always sung with such a sense of duty and never with joy. If an outsider were to look in, they might think they were all being forced to this ritual of singing against their will.

The sermons were the worst, Senna thought. They were never about the love of God or His mercy and compassion, which the songs spoke of. They were harsh and were delivered with a fiery fist from the pulpit. Senna often thought the preacher could have been her father delivering those messages because she had seen his fiery fist on many occasions.

In short, her home had been a home of sadness. A sadness that was tinged with an anger that lurked somewhere off in the shadows. It was everywhere.

As Senna finished putting the returned books away, she also pushed away the dark thoughts of her childhood. The woman who had asked about books on blood had chosen a few, and Senna helped her check out. She took a deep breath and worked to ignore her lingering sadness and tried to focus on finding joy in her work.

The lady was about thirty, maybe a bit younger; no, maybe a bit older. Senna couldn't tell. She didn't recognize the name on her library card either. Senna noticed she was fit and beautiful. Part of Senna longed to be beautiful like her, but plain was safer, it was her comfort zone.

Senna gently slapped the last book closed and handed the stack to her with a smile. "Here you go, they will be due back on the twenty-fifth. You can slide them through the return slot or just bring them in. If you wish to check them out for a longer period, bring them in and I will reset the due date. You are allowed one reset for each book."

"Thank you," she said with a smile and turned to go.

Senna watched her and noticed that she seemed happy and she wondered what that felt like.

"Did you know that lady?" Andrea asked.

Senna shook her head. still looking toward the door where she had exited. "No, I didn't. I know it is a small town, but there are still so many people here that I don't know."

"I've lived here a long time and don't remember ever seeing her," said Andrea.

Both Andrea and Senna continued to work the rest of the morning. Senna had recovered from the stress of being late and found herself laughing with Andrea while working.

Later, noticing it was time for lunch, Senna clocked out and told Andrea that she was leaving. It really was a beautiful day, and Senna was glad she finally had time to notice it. The springtime air was warm but with a hint of coolness. The wind that was typical for Oklahoma was on good behavior and had relegated itself to a light breeze.

Senna walked across the street to the park and sat on a cast iron and wooden bench that faced the swings and play equipment. She enjoyed this spot where she could watch the mothers out with their young ones who were not yet school age.

She unwrapped her sandwich and sat watching them before even taking a bite. The mothers talked and enjoyed each other's company, barely watching their children playing nearby.

Senna thought to herself, *this time was about them and meeting friends rather than bringing the little ones to play. What if someone tried to take one of the kids? What if something happened to one of them when they weren't paying attention?*

And just then something did happen. A little boy slid sideways off the slide and fell face first onto the ground below. Senna jerked and started to jump up to help when she saw the mom was up in an instant, almost before he hit the ground.

Senna pondered, *how could the mother be so engaged with the other mother and still know what was going on with her child?* It intrigued her, and she felt bad for misjudging the mother.

The mother crouched down to where the little boy was and after looking him over; she squeezed him as if she did not want to let him go. She talked to him with love in her voice and in her eyes. She wiped his tears, dusted him off, and helped him over to the swing where she began to push him.

Senna marveled that there were no harsh words to command him to shake it off and get up and get on with it. The mother had expressed no irritation because he had interrupted her conversation with the other mother. There was no reprimand for falling off the slide, and they didn't immediately leave to go home amidst angry words and a sour attitude.

Senna had only experienced that kind of love when she had been able to stay with her grandparents—her mother's parents—for very brief periods of time during the summer school break.

Senna remembered that compassion had radiated from her Gran's and Grandpa's home. It often made her uncomfortable though. The compassion drew her like a moth to a flame; but just like a flame, she feared it would singe her, so she tried to keep her distance emotionally.

Senna had felt their love, it was tangible and unwavering. But the question, didn't her parents love her with discipline, moored itself in her mind. Didn't teaching her to be disciplined, to be good, show that they loved her? The sharp contrast of the two was irreconcilable for Senna.

Her father's rules were so ingrained in her that while at her grandparents' home there was never a need for her to be reprimanded. In a strange way, the rules had grown to comfort her. Father's constant reprimands created firm boundaries.

In the freedom of her grandparents' home, it felt as if there were no boundaries. It was unsettling to Senna. As long as she followed the rules, she knew she was okay, that she was right, that she was worth something.

But altogether, it felt as though something was missing. Even though she followed the rules and did everything her father asked, she felt no lasting joy or happiness. She often believed it had all left her feeling dull and flat. Helping others at work was the closest she had ever come to joy.

Senna tried to remember if she had ever felt the joy she saw on those little ones' faces on the playground. She had been that young once. Had she laughed with abandon the way they did?

She shut her eyes and leaned her head back to catch the sun full on her face. The warmth felt good. She could hear the brush of leaves as a breeze blew through the trees and she smelled the fresh floral scents of spring. This was happiness, wasn't it?

MURDER IN KACHINA, Oklahoma had never happened in its modern day history. No one on the police force had ever experienced a murder. There had been all manner of domestic violence and accidental deaths, but not murder.

At the police station, all was chaos. No one felt equipped to handle this murder, but no one wanted to say it. The chief of police in Kachina, Darren Webb had called the OSBI, Oklahoma State Bureau of Investigation, and asked for help when a body had been reported around noon.

At one p.m., Randy Jeffries and Carrie Border, who had been with OSBI for ten and eight years, respectively, walked into the Kachina station. They had seen a lot in their few years. Oklahoma may seem like a *Little House on the Prairie* kind of place to many, but the truth is the crime rate is high. With the intersection of I-40 and I-35, human trafficking and all that comes with it may be as high or higher than in any other state. It is the U.S. crossroads for illegal guns, drugs, and humans.

"Busy place," observed Carrie as they stepped into the squad room.

"Yep," replied Randy. He was looking around the room to see if any one person stood out as if to be in charge. Finally he looked at the woman manning the front desk and asked for Darren Webb.

Randy had been married to his wife for five years and they had two little ones. His wife Sandy was a kindergarten teacher and there were many nights they didn't talk. How could he share with her the horror he experienced every day? Would she take it back to her class, knowing that, despite her best efforts, someday some of those sweet babies would grow to do or be the victim of these horrific occurrences?

Carrie dated a lot. She could not get close to anyone; didn't want to get close to anyone. Loving her job, she had never been willing to put anyone before the love of her life. It didn't feel like she needed anyone. Possibly, she was in denial about being lonely, but she refused to even consider it.

She loved working with Randy because being married made him safe. They were best friends and could talk about the things he couldn't take home.

Darren rushed up to the front with a hand extended as if to get the pleasantries out of the way and on to the business at hand.

"Thank you so much for coming. Let's get right over to the scene. If you'll follow me in your car, I'll show you the way." And just like that, he was out the door and headed down the stairs.

"Let's go," said Carrie, scurrying to catch up with Darren.

The crime scene was at a warehouse on the southwest side of town just north of Crown Rock Park which sat on the top of Crown Rock, a flat, red sand rock mesa, and the tallest point around for miles.

A railroad still ran from east to west through the south edge of town. Warehouses sat close to the railroad depot on South 22nd Street which was the last street before heading out of town. It was the perfect place for businesses to load and unload their cargo.

The trains did not carry people anymore, and the depot was only for the railroad staff to document arrivals and departures, loading and unloading. It was only open when they knew a train was coming in or leaving. No need to pay someone to sit there and do nothing when a train was not expected.

"There," said Carrie pointing to a place off to the side where they could park without being in the way. As Randy put the car into park, a flurry of red sand dust swirled around the car.

"Pretty secluded," said Randy standing just outside the car. He stood with his hands resting on his hips. "But it is still technically in town and not the most secure location to hide a murder."

"Warehouses seem pretty abandoned," replied Carrie. "Late at night in a small town, I doubt there was anyone anywhere near here."

There were three large warehouses in two rows for a total of six warehouses. A couple of them were unoccupied. Some were subdivided, holding offices and cargo.

Randy and Carrie entered the area where the crime tape indicated, and saw that Justin Thatcher lay with his throat cut. He was in the dirt on a concrete slab next to the most remote warehouse. He laid on his back with his eyes closed. His blood had pooled out onto the concrete slab which ran along the front of the empty warehouse.

"What are you writing down?" asked Carrie. She rarely took notes, but Randy was always taking extensive ones. Her mind really was like a steel trap and once it went in, it never left. She had learned early in school to just listen carefully to what the teacher was saying and it would stay with her much better than if she was distracted by trying to write it all down.

"Drawing a little sketch of the scene and my thoughts about the area," replied Randy. He turned and walked toward the body.

"Do you see what I see?" Randy asked Carrie. "Or rather what I am not seeing?"

"Not sure. What am I supposed to *not* be seeing?"

"Almost no footprints. I am guessing the few we see are from the witness or first responders. They look very fresh. I'll wager that any tracks left in the dust earlier have been swept away by the wind," said Randy.

"Look at that cedar branch over there. It wasn't broken, it was cut. Killer could have used that to sweep away their prints," Carrie motioned to the branch laying off to the side.

Randy and Carrie had experience in working with FBI profilers and were studying the scene from a psychological perspective as well as the physical evidence which they could see. This was one body, though, and that could mean many things; it could be a drug deal gone bad; it could be a hit; there seemed no sign of a struggle, so a fight gone wrong didn't appear to be the reason.

"He isn't a large man," Randy commented. "He looks about five feet, eight inches tall and is slight in build."

"Appears he was dressed to go out. His Wranglers are not faded and are creased. He has a nice shirt on too.

Ranchers around here don't dress that nice to work," responded Carrie.

"What do you think?" Randy asked Carrie as they squatted as close to the body as they dared without disturbing it.

"I don't see a struggle. So, was he brought here? Was he drugged? I don't even see drag marks because whoever did this took the time to get rid of them."

"I don't see tire tracks either. How did they get here?" asked Randy as he turned his head to look from another angle.

"That appears to be one long solid, steady slice into his neck too. Would a first timer have been that steady? Took force, so had to be a man, right?" Carrie looked at Randy as she asked. His eyes were squinting against the sun and his dark hair was being tossed here and there by the constant wind.

He didn't answer right away, so she looked back at the body. "I don't know," he finally answered. Here is the coroner's van now. Maybe the autopsy can tell us more.

"None too soon," said Carrie. She wrinkled her nose at the ripe smell of decaying flesh. The heat was working quickly on the body's decomposition.

The body would be sent to the Watson County Coroner for examination. They weren't in Oklahoma County, unfortunately. Watson County was much more rural and, had little experience with this type of death.

Randy and Carrie walked over to Darren Webb,

young for a police chief. Usually when law enforcement in Kachina had gained sufficient experience, they were off to a larger city, but Darren had plans to stay.

He was a little overweight, about five feet, seven inches tall, with sandy blond hair. Rather than working out, he spent his spare time enjoying his wife's cooking, lounging in front of the TV, or watching his son play little league.

Darren was thankful for the help of the OSBI, not riding high on ego as many in law enforcement did. He had a good, pure heart and just wanted to protect his town. The worry was evident on his face as Randy and Carrie approached.

He didn't ask, just listened.

"I'll be honest with you," stated Randy, "this looks like someone who knew what they were doing. It looks thought out. They considered location and evidence. With the warehouse on the south, the woods to the west and then those vacant lots and rundown shacks to the north, there would not be any likely witnesses."

"The forensics team is about done with their grid search," said Darren. "They found some small bits, but feel certain it was just from years of the wind blowing debris in and the warehouse being vacant for so long. They bagged the cedar branch as well."

Randy thought that maybe they could get some contact DNA or other evidence from that.

"Why in town though? There are acres and acres around

here where they could have done this. They could have easily walked into those woods right there and he wouldn't have been discovered for days or weeks. Coyotes would have gotten to him and that would be an almost guarantee that no evidence would be found," observed Darren.

"You're right," agreed Carrie. "We are just going to have to lay it all out and see where it all points. Could be that they wanted us to find the body just like we did. It may mean something to them. The killer could be making a statement."

"Who owns the warehouse?" asked Randy

"I'll have to look at the records. It has been vacant for at least ten years or more. There aren't a lot of businesses who use these warehouses out here anymore. Most go to the city for that," replied Darren.

"That may tell us something. If you can get us a warrant, we want to look inside," said Carrie.

"Will do," replied Darren.

LATE THAT AFTERNOON Randy and Carrie stood next to the body of Justin Thatcher at the Watson County Morgue. The medical examiner, Janice, was leaning over the body and pointing with her gloved left pinky finger.

"Across here the cut was made from right to left." The cut was deep, so deep it slit his neck almost in two.

"What kind of blade do you think was used?" asked Randy.

"Something sharp, could be a lot of things. There were clean lines with no hesitation. Not something serrated either. A very large sharp knife. But I see no tool marks. The cut is clean, start to finish.

"I sent his blood off to your lab for tests to determine if there were any drugs in his system. I see no evidence he put up a fight. This leads me to believe he was unconscious when his throat was cut," said Janice.

"Did you find any needle marks?" asked Carrie.

"No, none. I have looked in all the places one typically finds needle marks and then I went on to look in his hair, between his toes, and inside his mouth to see if someone was trying to hide the mark. I found nothing suspicious at all."

"What about trace?" asked Randy.

"Very little. Dust and lint. I bagged it all and sent it to your forensics lab."

They stood quietly then. Randy had his face pinched and his eyes were focused like lasers right at Justin's face. It was as if he was trying to mentally communicate with the last moment before Justin died. What had he seen? Who had he trusted that he shouldn't have? "What is your story Justin?" thought Randy aloud.

Carrie shifted from one foot to the other. She wanted to be patient when Randy was like this, but she knew not to disturb his thoughts. He was a deep thinker, and he was thinking now.

Finally, Carrie could not bear it any longer. She wanted to go out and do something, wanted to find this person instead of standing there looking at a body, which to her would tell them nothing more. She cleared her throat and Randy snapped his head back to look at her.

"What?" asked Carrie, feeling a little guilty. "Let's go. I want to get out there and see what we can find. There is nothing else here. Janice will call us when, or if she gets anything else."

Randy nodded, removed his hands from his hips and popped off the plastic gloves. "Okay, let's go," he said. And just like that, he was out the door. Carrie scrambled to catch up, but neither one spoke until they were in the car.

It was like a sauna inside the car and the dark interior didn't help. It was always humid in Oklahoma so when the heat rose it always seemed much hotter than it was. Before she could even get her seatbelt buckled, her hair was hanging in her face and a drop of sweat hit her cheek from a wet curl. She tried to blow it out of her face while battling the buckle.

It clicked, and in an instant, she had also pushed back her hair, grabbing it with both hands and making a pretend ponytail. She held it there off of her neck hoping the AC would kick in quickly.

"So, what did your laser focus tell you back there?" asked Carrie.

"Nothing. Not a damn thing." Randy shoved the car into drive and they headed to the Kachina police station, twenty miles away.

"Is this the start of something? You know, another serial?" asked Carrie. She remembered the first case she'd had in her new job with the OSBI, it had been a serial, and it had been not only physically taxing, but emotionally as well.

Randy looked at her and for a moment said nothing. "We can't know at this point. But the situation seems strange. It was premeditated. They had to do some planning. There were no tracks and no trace that we know of now. No witnesses so far. This person has a cool head about them. If it was spur of the moment, then they did not panic but proceeded with deliberation."

"But they drugged him. They would have had to have planned that, right?"

"We *think* they drugged him," Randy emphasized the word 'think'. "We won't *know* until we get the labs back, and we can't jump to conclusions."

"So if he wasn't drugged, he just laid down and let someone slit his throat?" Carrie's incredulous tone was clear.

Randy looked at her again. He liked his partner. They had been partners for four years and they had worked well together. It was certain, though, that their working styles were different. He felt that the people and places of a crime would speak to him in time. He knew if he could realize the situation and know the people involved, he would see the motive where Carrie was decidedly more about action.

She wanted to be doing something constantly to figure it all out. Dump a big puzzle out on the table and she would immediately start in sorting pieces and turning them all right side up. He would take a minute to look at them. He would look at the colors and patterns to see what made sense together.

"No, Carrie, I don't think he just laid down and let someone slice his throat." His irritation showed. This one was going to be difficult. Yes, he liked a challenge, but he also didn't like feeling so lost without any clues. There were usually clear and evident signs of something, either motive, opportunity, or means. This time, so far, there was nothing. That irritated Randy, and it showed.

"I know you don't," she replied in a softer tone.

They rode in silence for several more miles, both deep in thought. The countryside whizzed by in shades of green. Springtime was here, and there were multiple shades of color. Some trees were yet to bud, but that made the Redbud trees even more vivid in their bright purple glory. They were everywhere.

Passing a small housing addition, Carrie noticed that the Ornamental Pear trees were also in full bloom. Their blossoms looked like tufts of cotton covering the trees.

"What if everything bloomed at once," Carrie said mostly to herself as she looked out the car window.

"What?"

"Oh I was just thinking that I love how the Redbud and Pear trees are blooming, but there are so many trees still dormant and brown. I thought how pretty it would be if everything bloomed and budded at once."

"I've never thought of that," said Randy. He thought for a moment then, "I think dull makes the bright show up more. It might be hard to noticed otherwise."

Randy slowed to make the turn onto Deer Horn Road. It ran east and west and intersected with Central Boulevard which ran through the center of Kachina. After about a mile, a big white fence that looked recently painted, began following along the road. The property beyond had clearly been well tended. Black Angus cattle spotted the grass, and they barely raised their heads to observe the SUV pass.

The spread lasted for the next ten miles. About five miles in was a very elaborate and ostentatious ranch entrance. There were brick pillars with wrought iron scrollwork connecting them. Overhead was a sign bearing the brand of the Big Horn Ranch next to the name.

"Wow!" exclaimed Carrie as she turned back in her seat to watch it as they passed. "That's where the victim worked, right?"

"That's what Darren said. I want to see if there is

anything else they have found and then put a plan together. We can come back out here later and see what they know."

They came to the intersection they needed and turned north on Central Boulevard. After another three miles they crossed a bridge over Deer Creek and they were at the South edge of town. To the left was a large bluff. It seemed to stick straight up from the ground, huge and out of place in the rolling green hills and woods. Around the base of the bluff were thick green woods.

They crossed the train tracks and passed the small train station. They both glanced to their left toward the warehouses. The yellow tape still fluttered in the wind, but there was no sign of personnel.

Seven blocks ahead they pulled into a space on the town square under a shade tree and parked.

"You don't see town squares like this around here much anymore," commented Carrie.

"No, you don't. I don't think that was ever much of a city plan for Oklahoma. Everyone just ran in and staked a claim and didn't care to take time to plot out a town much less a town square."

"It's nice. I like it."

The police office in Kachina consisted of Darren, the police chief, and three other officers. There was Kim the dispatcher and two other support personnel. Because the town was small and rural, they often worked hand in hand with the county Sheriff.

Darren was on the phone with the Sheriff when Randy and Carrie walked in. They waited just outside his door, but Darren waved them in.

He hung up the phone. "Want some coffee? It's pretty good for a police station. The dispatcher used to work for a fancy coffee shop and has made it her mission to make bad station coffee a thing of the past," he said chuckling and shaking his head.

They both commented that they were good and sat down in the two chairs in front of Darren's desk. The office was no nonsense, but he had placed a few photos around. The one on the metal filing cabinet was of a sweet looking young lady and two smaller children, one boy and one girl.

"We just came from the coroner's office. The cut across the neck was clean, done with a sharp blade," began Randy with no preliminary niceties. "No hesitation marks. Just a clean, deep cut. There was no abnormal bruising or other abrasions."

"It's too soon to have gotten the lab results back on whether there were any chemicals or other drugs that might have been in his system," Carrie said. "That usually takes a few days, unfortunately."

Darren sat back in his chair and it creaked and groaned loudly. His right elbow rested on its arm and he was running a finger thoughtlessly across his upper lip. The pinch of his eyes revealed his intent thought.

He dropped the chair forward and put both arms on

the desk. "What do you two think? Tell me any thoughts who might do this and why," he asked. It was evident that he was deferring to their experience. He wanted this crime solved and was more than willing to work as a team.

"Honestly," said Randy, "we don't know at this point. We wanted to meet with you to see if there were any other developments on your end. Our next step is to go to the Big Horn Ranch to find out as much as we can from those that Justin worked with."

Darren shuffled a paper or two on his desk and pulled up the one he was looking for. He began to read, "He was five feet, eight inches tall, and one hundred sixty-five pounds per his driver's license. He has no criminal record, not even a speeding ticket. He's worked at the Big Horn for the last year. Looks like he moved here from a ranch in Texas near Dallas." Darren looked up to see if Randy or Carrie reacted.

"That doesn't give us much," Randy said. "Hopefully we can learn more at the ranch. Do you want to come with?"

"Sure," said Darren. "I know Jack McGivens. Maybe he and the others will warm to you asking questions with me there. My daddy and Jack were friends for years before my daddy passed.

"He's a stern man and quite gruff. But he thinks of me as a second son. I'm hoping that will keep us from all being tossed out on our ears." Darren chuckled and his plump midsection bounced up and down.

"Okay," grinned Randy. He liked this guy and looked forward to working with him. "We'll be back around eight thirty in the morning."

The sun was setting in their rearview mirror as Randy and Carrie headed back to Oklahoma City.

Kachina was a town of about four thousand when the community college was out for the summer and was situated about ten miles northwest of Oklahoma City. To reach the community, one had to exit off the highway south and drive another three miles, so it was rare that anyone just happened upon it.

Randy and Carrie rode back to the office in silence. A murder in a small town was much different than if it had occurred in the city. A small town murder was usually very personal in nature and witnesses would be tight-lipped. As they travelled, they wondered what tomorrow would bring.

CHAPTER 3

On the road to the Big Horn Ranch the next morning, they rode in Darren's patrol car with Randy in front and Carrie in back. It smelled clean, which surprised Carrie. She had been in so many dirty and smelly patrol cars that a clean one was an anomaly. Officers lived in their cars and often had ripe bags of old fast food meals still in there. Even when the bags and trash were gone, she was certain that crumbs and bits of food rolled under the seats to rot.

The ride was the reverse of the one they had just made into town the day before when heading back from the coroner. They followed Central out past the railroad and across the creek. About ten miles later, Darren slowed to turn into the grand entrance.

"This is some place," Carrie declared in awe. The drive

was lined with mature trees on each side, each of which were the same size and equal distance apart. Carrie had no doubt someone had planted them many years ago to achieve this very effect.

The drive was about a quarter mile long and just before the last tree, a large, two-level ranch home filled the view. Carrie gawked at the home's grand size.

It had a lodge feel with a rock face and timbers as trim and supports. There was a large, covered portico to cover vehicles at the front door which was made from those same large timbers and had an open ceiling rising high, showing the structure.

The front entry had beautiful pots with freshly planted flowers and a bench with a colorful cushion. "Definitely signs of a female influence," murmured Carrie.

They rang the bell and waited.

After only a minute or two, the door opened and a woman of about fifty-five stood before them. She was dressed casually, in jeans and a button-up shirt, and had an air of class about her. Her dark, shoulder-length hair was full and slightly wavy.

The lady saw Darren and smiled as she opened the door. "Hi Darren. Lovely to see you but I am certain this is not for a happy occasion. What can I do for you?" she asked as her smile faded.

"This is Randy Jeffries and Carrie Border. They are

with OSBI. Can we come in and talk with you?" asked Darren.

She opened the door wide to welcome them in, motioning toward a large, great room with a huge, stone fireplace. "Have a seat."

They sat in deep brown leather club chairs. As Carrie rubbed her hand along the arm of the chair, she thought about how it would take a month of her salary to buy a chair like that.

"We are here to ask about Justin Thatcher. He was one of your ranch hands, correct?" Randy asked. "I assume you've heard of his murder?"

"Well, yes, but I couldn't tell you anything about him. My husband handles all of that. All the business on the ranch," June McGivens answered. She looked uneasy and stiff.

"Did you know Justin at all?" Carrie asked. She noticed the tendons in June's neck were protruding and taut.

"I've met him. We have ranch gatherings from time to time. We had an all-ranch cookout a week ago last Saturday. I met Justin there, briefly." June's eyes darted to the floor.

"I have it here that he has worked for your ranch for one year," said Randy. "Is that about right?" He was looking at the notes he had written on the small, leather-covered pad he kept in his pocket. It had been a gift from his wife Sandy and she'd had it embossed with his initials, RJ.

As Randy read, Carrie watched June McGivens. She squirmed as she listened to Randy. It was a very subtle shift in the way she was sitting. But her face remained blank.

Randy looked up, waiting for an answer. He knew to wait that eventually the silence would draw it out.

Finally, June responded. "Again, you would have to ask my husband. I do not keep the records, but that seems about right." She concluded with a tight nod of her head.

Randy continued to look her in the eye. He was reading her, looking for signs that showed she was being honest, or hiding something. But he couldn't tell. It was obvious that she was uncomfortable, but he could not pin down why.

"You seem uncomfortable, Mrs. McGivens. Why is that?" Randy asked.

Her eyes grew wide, and she sat up straighter. Her right hand went to her chest just below her collarbone.

"Yes, I am, I suppose. This murder has gotten me on edge. I am confident it had nothing to do with the ranch, but it is all just so unsettling." Her words tumbled out.

Randy watched her for a few brief seconds, then said, "Yes, I am sure it is. May we talk to your husband?"

"Well, he's out at the barns somewhere, I believe. I can

ask our ranch foreman." She picked up her cell phone and sent a text.

There was a whoosh and then a ding. She looked up and said, "Pinky said Jack has gone into the city to get supplies and he is not sure when he will be back."

Carrie jumped in, "Can we talk to... Pinky, was it?"

"Yes, we call him Pinky because when he was a kid he used to drink with his pinky held up. With all the teasing he stopped, but the nickname has lasted. His real name is Andrew, or Andy."

June McGivens looked back at her phone and sent another text. Another reply came quickly. "He said yes he can talk, if you don't mind coming down to the big barn."

"No, we don't mind if you will point us in the right direction," Carrie said as she stood.

Darren had been quiet the entire time allowing the two detectives to conduct the interview. But he never took his eyes off of June.

Randy reached out to shake June's hand. "Please let us know if something—*anything*—should occur to you," said Randy.

"I will. It's a horrible thing. I promise if I think of *anything*, I will call you." She seemed relieved to be done with the conversation.

She walked them to the door and from the porch pointed to a red building that was barely visible through the trees. "That is the big barn you can see there just through the trees. Follow the path or you can just drive down, and Pinky will meet you there."

Carrie smiled and shook her hand. "It was nice to meet you."

June didn't reply, just simply nodded. Her hand was up at her collar again fiddling with the button there.

THEY SHOULD HAVE TAKEN two separate cars. Just as they were leaving, Darren's mike squawked, and a deputy summoned him to another incident. "I'm so sorry, but I have to go," Darren said. "I'll need to take you back to get your car."

"Sure, but we need to let June and Pinky know that we will have to come back," said Carrie.

Darren called June on his cell phone and explained the situation. "June said that would be fine and that she would let Pinky know."

Carrie looked over at Randy as they walked to the car. "Did she act funny to you?" she asked so Darren wouldn't hear.

Randy looked up as he opened the door. The sun was so bright she had to shield her eyes with her hand to see him.

He stopped with the door open and looked at her. "Yes, she did," he said. "She was as nervous as a kitten meeting a new puppy."

"And Darren couldn't take his eyes off of her."

"Yes, I noticed that, too."

Twenty minutes later they were back at their car in town. They got in the hot car and the instant Randy cranked the engine Carrie reached for the AC controls. "You know turning that up will only shoot the hot air straight out to us like a blow dryer. Best to let it cool down a bit."

"I know," said Carrie, "but it's a hard habit to break. It's so hot in here and I just want to fix it and get cool. You would think I would get used to this crazy weather, spring and ninety degrees. Tomorrow it could be fifty."

Once back at the ranch entrance, Randy turned the car onto the drive and this time turned to head toward the barn and other outbuildings rather than take the drive up to the house.

The barn, stable, and other buildings were as well-appointed as the house. Not only void of peeling paint, but beautifully trimmed as well. Underneath the gable of each building they had fashioned a large logo of the ranch.

Anyone looking at this ranch, the home, property, and buildings, could see who the owner was and the statement he was making. He was successful, and he was proud of it, it showed everywhere you looked.

"Jack must have a tight rein on things around here. Look how orderly everything is," Randy pointed out.

They were driving so slow on the gravel drive you

could hear the popping of the gravel under the tires. It sounded just like popcorn in a popper. They were giving themselves time to survey the land and take it all in.

"Hey," said Carrie, "speed up a bit. At least outrun the gravel dust. I can't see a thing. Feels like our car is PigPen on Charlie Brown." Randy gave her one of his looks but sped up.

At the barn that June had directed them to, which was the largest building of them all and the first one on the drive, an old cowboy was just coming out the door. He was slim and short and bowlegged; he looked like he had been born with his legs strapped around the belly of a horse.

His light straw hat was stained with sweat and battle worn. He was taking a red bandana and wiping the sweat and dust from his face. His face was twisted as he wiped, and he squinted at the car coming up to the barn.

As they stopped, he shoved the bandana in his rear pocket and put both hands on his hips to wait.

"Hello, I'm Agent Carrie Border and this is Agent Randy Jeffries from the OSBI," Carrie introduced them as she approached. "Mrs. McGivens said you would talk with us."

Pinky nodded, ducked his head and turned back toward the barn all in one fluid movement. "Come on back to the barn. We'll find a cooler spot to talk than out in this hot sun." He motioned with a swipe of his hand indicating for them to follow.

The barn was an architectural marvel. Carrie couldn't help but stare up at the construction of the thing. The thought crossed her mind that she should watch where she walked since she was in a barn, but someone had swept the concrete floor cleaner than many houses she had seen.

They followed Pinky until he led them into a room within the barn. It appeared to be his office. Who knew cowboys could have offices?

"Have a seat," said Pinky as he moved some tack out of one of the chairs in front of an old beat up, but clean desk. He dumped the tack on an old saddle rack off to the side and fell into the chair behind the desk.

In the window there was a window unit trying to keep the office cool. As he plucked his hat off of his head and dropped it onto his desk with one hand, he reached and cranked up the AC knob with the other.

"Okay, what did you want to talk about?" Pinky asked as he leaned back in the chair not looking enthused.

"Tell us about Justin Thatcher," said Randy.

Pinky took a minute to answer. What did he tell? He pondered what was actually necessary to tell to help solve Justin's murder.

"He was young, but a hard worker," replied Pinky.

"Who did he associate with here at the ranch?" asked Randy.

"Well, everyone associates with everyone. We all have to work together to get things done," replied Pinky.

Randy studied Pinky. Was he trying to be evasive or was he just answering as he felt he should? Pinky's gaze back at him was calculating and deliberate.

"I guess what I am wondering, Pinky, is who did he hang with during his off hours."

"Well, most of the younger ranch hands kept to themselves. They liked to go to town and hang at the bar, play pool, drink, and flirt. You know how it is when you're young."

"Did Justin have a girlfriend, someone in particular?" asked Carrie.

"Not that I know of. Leastwise he never talked about a special someone and he never brought anyone around here." Pinky had a knot in his stomach when he said that. He didn't dare talk about the night he walked around the corner of the back equipment barn and saw Justin and June McGivens in a close embrace.

"Who else could we talk to that might know more about what Justin did in his free time? Was there one particular guy who he hung out with the most?"

"I would say you should talk to Keith. He and Justin were buddies. I'll get him for you," Pinky said as he picked up his phone and sent a text.

"So Keith, you and Justin had gone to the Darkside Tavern earlier that night?" asked Randy.

"Well, just for about an hour. We were worn slick out from working all day. Pinky had us doing a bunch of stuff we don't normally do. We went for a drink, played a game or two of pool and then left." He shuffled his feet trying to find a stance that felt right in order to discuss his best friend's murder, but nothing did.

Keith looked so much like Justin. He was thin and about the same height. His hair was lighter, Carrie thought, but they could almost be twins.

They were standing out in the sun now talking to Keith. They were out in the space between the main barn where they had spoken with Pinky and the bunkhouse. It was hot, the sun bright, and they were all squinting to see each other. Keith kept pushing up his sweaty John Deere cap and wiping the sweat from his forehead. Perhaps it was the heat, or could it be something else?

"Did Justin have a girlfriend?" asked Carrie.

Keith looked away before answering. "Naw, he didn't have a girlfriend."

"Was there anyone that had a beef with him? Someone who had an axe to grind with him?" asked Randy.

"Not that I know of," replied Keith. "This is a small town and here at the ranch we just try to do our work and make it through the day. Justin was a good-natured guy. He was easygoing and everyone liked him."

There was frustration in that statement. Carrie thought to herself that they were friends and his death must have been hard on Keith.

"Look, we know you guys were buds and this must be very hard on you, but the only way we can find out who did this is to ask hard questions. Most of the time we ask questions no one wants to answer when they least like to answer them. Please understand we want to find his killer and the only way is to trace Justin's steps and get to know him and his life better," explained Carrie.

Keith looked at her and she saw the pain in his eyes for the first time. The tough cowboy facade was all gone. When he spoke again, his voice was thick with emotion and it was evident it was difficult for him to talk.

"Yeah it is hard, real hard. We grew up together, went to high school together. We've shared football, hunting, and more days hanging out than I can count. I have no idea who would have done this to Justin."

"Okay. If you think of anything will you please give us a call?" asked Randy as he handed Keith his business card. Keith looked at the card and nodded.

On the drive back to town, neither Carrie nor Randy said a word. They were processing the three interviews they had just conducted.

Finally Carrie said, "Something else is going on that they are not telling us."

"Yes, but what?"

"I don't know. June was fidgety and nervous, and Pinky was picking and choosing each word he said. Keith is grieving and probably not thinking of details that could help us right now."

45

"You would think June would have opened up with Darren there. He's a nice guy, but too willing to step back and let us conduct the interviews. It's evident to me that the local people do not trust us."

Tomorrow we'll go to the Darkside and see what that place reveals.

SENNA'S FAMILY hadn't had a TV while she was growing up. Her father frowned on it and so Senna had never learned to enjoy it herself. She had watched one while at her grandparents', but little time was spent on that activity. Her Gran loved to be spending her time with Senna, doing things like baking or shopping, even just sitting in the backyard in the garden watching Senna play.

So, each day after work Senna came home and read the afternoon paper. She always purchased it from the vending machine just outside the library front door. Because it was so routine, she rarely stopped to look at it until she was home. She would pull it out, tuck it in her bag, and head for home.

It wasn't until she settled on her sofa with a cold glass of tea beside her, that she opened the paper and saw the headlines, 'Body Found in Kachina, Oklahoma', with a subheading of, 'Local Police Say It Is Murder'.

Senna felt shocked. Moving to the edge of her seat, she devoured the article. Apparently, a local resident had been found in a remote part of the town with his throat slashed. There were no witnesses. They had not elaborated on clues. Probably best to keep that out of the paper, she thought.

She read the article again. A strange feeling began in the pit of her stomach. Was it fear? No. Was it anxiety? No. What was this strange feeling? For the first time she could remember, she shut the paper without reading the entire thing.

She jumped up and thought to herself that she needed to get out of the house, *had* to get out of the house.

Walking along the sidewalk, her thoughts jumbled in her mind and distracted her. It occurred to her she must be crazy to be out for a walk with a murderer on the loose. But surely that guy in the paper was killed for a reason. He must have certainly done something or harmed someone. Maybe he was doing something he shouldn't have been doing. If he had been more careful then he wouldn't be dead, right?

Senna viewed people differently as she walked. She wondered if each person she saw might be the one, the one who could take a life. Suddenly, she was bumped out of her thoughts—literally—by a blonde bombshell of fur. She looked down into the happy face of a big, friendly dog. Grabbing the leash, she then stooped to pet the wayward fellow while also looking around for its owner.

A very handsome man about her age ran up to her

and the dog. "I am so sorry he jumped on you!" he said breathlessly, adding a smile.

"No, he's fine. He just wanted a petting I think." What a dope she thought. How dumb did that sound?

"Buddy loves people and loves to be petted. I do my share, but he loves to befriend everyone he sees."

"His happy face makes me want to laugh," Senna said. She felt the urge to laugh and suddenly realized how few things made her want to do that.

The man studied Senna as she petted Buddy. Then she straightened and looked into the man's eyes. She thought he must be about six feet tall. *I'm five feet, ten inches and I can see him nearly eye-to-eye.*

Eye contact made Senna extremely uncomfortable, but they had locked gazes and couldn't look away. It was as if she no longer had control over her own body. Is there such a thing as involuntary eye-lock?

With that thought, a chuckle burst forth from Senna that caused her to break their gaze. She ducked her head and brought her hand to her mouth feeling self-conscious about the laughter.

"What's so funny?" he asked.

"Nothing, it's not you," she said, once again feeling uncomfortable and looking away. She wanted to explain, but couldn't. She couldn't bring herself to have a casual conversation with this guy.

"Okay, well that's good." He took the dog's leash from Senna and said, "I'm Blake, Blake Burton. Nice to meet you." Again, he grinned at her with a half grin and she was able to give him a tentative smile. She wanted to return the half grin with a welcoming smile, but couldn't.

"I like him," she blurted out.

"Oh, you like him, but not me?" he laughed.

"No, that's not at all what I meant," she was feeling like such a fool. This is why she didn't socialize more. "I mean that I *really* like him."

He burst out laughing. "Well, at least then you like me a little even if you like him more."

Her mouth fell open a bit as she looked at him dumbfounded. Realization broke through at how she'd sounded.

She shook her head. "No, that's not what I meant either." She had to laugh then.

"I know. I am just having fun with you." The blonde bombshell jerked against the leash and tried to walk away.

"Maybe I'll let Buddy jump on you again sometime," he said with a wide smile, the kind she wanted to give back to him. And with a small salute he turned and was gone.

He left her watching him jog away. Finally, she slowly turned and walked away, too.

With her mind still on Blake and Buddy she continued walking the two blocks to main street. She thought to herself how she always cooked at home, but felt like eating out just then. She pondered this thought which felt very foreign to her. Growing up, she had been taught that eating out was an unnecessary extravagance. She didn't ponder it for long, however, and walked to the All American Diner, a favorite spot for most residents of Kachina.

It was your typical diner and on any given day it was filled with locals. Senna usually avoided this place because she was uncomfortable socializing and had always felt tense when she found herself in a large group of people.

Finding a booth in the back that was isolated, she sat down. She had never learned to enjoy food, but had to say she liked the taste of meat which seemed odd to her. After reviewing the menu from the rack, she decided on a cheeseburger with bacon. She replaced the menu and waited for the waitress.

To Senna, most women her age seemed so concerned about their weight they would never eat such a thing. Her weight had never been a concern though. She had always been thin, particularly because she was always working at home. Her father had not tolerated laziness. Her mom did not cook elaborate meals either. They were utilitarian and there was never any waste. Father would not have allowed that.

As she sat waiting, Senna noticed that the diner was old. A person could tell that the profit, if there was any, did not go into decor or renovating. As expected in a diner, there were booths along one wall with vinyl tufted red pleather. Some cushions had little rips where a white felt-looking substance peeked through. Others had duct tape repairs.

The diner sat on Kachina's main street between two other businesses. The only source of light was from outside and came in from the wall of windows at the front of the diner. It was spring, and the days were growing longer, so it was still light out. She noticed how the light played off of the walls and floors. Sitting so far back in the diner, she felt like she was almost sitting in the dark, which was okay with her.

The waitress served her burger, and she noticed they had added fries. Senna hadn't ordered them, but guessed they must come with the burgers. She had eaten there so few times she couldn't remember.

The first bite into the burger released juices that sparked her taste buds. The greasy meat and bacon tasted so good that she shut her eyes as she relished the rare guilty pleasure. Once she had eaten just enough to be full, and no more, she asked for a to-go container, paid her bill, and left.

Walking back home, she realized how exhausted she felt. She realized that she had felt very tired, exhausted even, most of the time lately and she didn't understand why. She thought to herself as she walked that she would just rest a bit before doing her nightly chores.

Unlocking the door, only silence greeted her and fatigue overwhelmed her. Thinking she would sit for only a bit then clean, she sat down and pulled the afghan over her.

As she drifted off to sleep she thought to herself, *I have to keep on schedule. That's a rule I made to keep order in my life and I have to have order.*

The sofa was soft and almost instantly her eyes closed and she drifted.

CHAPTER 4

*R*andy and Carrie pulled up to the Darkside Tavern at 10:00 am. They had stopped by to see Darren and share any viable information.

The toxicological panel had come back, and a horse tranquilizer called Ketamine had been found in Justin's system. In a rural area with ranches and horses everywhere that information hadn't narrowed the search.

But it confirmed that Justin had, indeed, been drugged. He had still been alive at the time of death, but had not felt a thing, being deeply tranquilized.

Before exiting the car, they had a good look around at the neighborhood. It was quiet and rundown. The surrounding houses were small, frame houses, only around nine hundred square feet or so.

Almost all the houses had peeling paint and scruffy,

unkempt yards. Many had mini junk yards off to the side where piles of random junk lay abandoned. A few had cars in various stages of decay and/or repair, it was hard to tell which.

It could have been a cute, quaint neighborhood with its lush, mature trees and peaceful quiet, had the residents just maintained the homes and taken some care in their yards.

The Darkside itself was a large, two-story building that had been a grand home at one time. The only large home on this street—or those adjacent to it—caused it to look out of place.

It had been maintained somewhat better. The peeling paint was at a minimum, but there had been no extravagant remodeling or work done to improve the curb appeal that they could see.

What had once been a large front yard was now a parking lot. It had once been covered in gravel, most of which was now pushed deep into the mud and dirt. There were ruts and dips that made driving challenging.

A tall, Cottonwood tree that stood about thirty feet tall, shaded the entire front yard. There were no other cars in the parking lot at ten that morning.

The sound of Randy and Carrie shutting their car doors was the only sound. The entire neighborhood was void of people, pets, and other noises.

Randy surveyed the wide front porch with its old, mismatched rockers and indiscriminate tables as they climbed the wooden steps. The screen door that had once graced the front door was missing with only the hinges left. Carrie turned the doorknob of the old door to enter.

Coming in from the light, even the shaded light, into the darkness of the bar stopped them both. They stood for just a minute to allow their eyes to adjust. As they did, they saw they were in an entryway with stairs on one side. To the left was a wide opening leading to what they assumed had been the parlor at one time.

As they stepped into the bar, former parlor, they saw the typical old bar along the far wall. It was handcrafted from beautiful wood, however it had clear signs of wear through the years from the many customers who had leaned on it while drinking and conversing.

Behind the bar was a wall of mirrors, with shelves holding multiple bottles of liquor. It was the same as thousands of other bars in thousands of other towns.

To their right, in what must have been the dining room at one time, were a couple of pool tables. The wall between the parlor and dining room had been removed to make more open space.

"Hello," Randy called out. "Is anyone here?"

The only response was quiet.

"Hello," Randy repeated as they stepped farther into the bar looking around for any sign of human life.

Finally, a slight noise in a room beyond where the pool tables were, grew louder. It sounded like footsteps coming upstairs. Maybe someone was in the basement.

As the footsteps seemed to emerge from the back room itself, Randy once again called out, "Hello."

"Yep?" came a reply.

Out came Ike, wiping his hands on a towel. "What can I do for ya?"

Holding out their OSBI badges so Ike could see, they explained who they were and asked if they could talk to him.

Ike agreed and motioned to a table in the front room. He had no intention of giving them any more information than necessary, but he also knew not to antagonize them in such a way as to drive them to dig for more. He had danced this dance more than once in his life.

They asked a few preliminary questions to establish basic background info. Then Randy shifted gears, "Did you know Justin Thatcher?"

Neither Ike nor Randy varied their gaze, but stared at each other steadily. After a moment Ike replied, "Justin came in from time to time." His eyes darted over to Carrie, then right back to Randy.

"Was he here in the Darkside three evenings ago on April fifteenth?"

"Not sure I remember who was in here that night. I don't exactly take roll. There were some hands from the Big Horn in here, but I couldn't tell you which ones or what time."

"Do you have surveillance cameras?"

Ike snorted a laugh and shook his head. He crossed

his burly arms over his rotund midsection and leaned back. "No, I don't have cameras—on purpose."

"How many ranch hands were in here on the evening of the fifteenth?" asked Carrie. She held Ike's gaze firmly.

"Two or three, maybe four."

"Are they regulars that frequently come in?" she asked.

"They are all regulars at one time or another." Ike grinned.

"Was there anyone new to the bar that night or in the last week?" Carrie was rapid-firing questions at Ike now. She did not like the waiting game that Randy played. And it seemed to work. Ike was feeling a little unsettled, and it showed.

"The only new one around that I remember was a young lady. She didn't give her name, and she didn't stay long."

"Do you remember her talking to the hands or anyone else?" Randy took up the questioning.

"Yeah she did talk to a few of the hands. They were playing pool, and she played a few games with them." Ike switched his gaze back to Randy and dropped his smile.

"And..." Randy prodded.

"And after a couple of games she left with two ranch hands," Ike said with resignation.

"Do you remember which hands?"

"No, but I don't think one was Justin."

"Why?"

"Well, it seems as I remember, not sure what night is what, but the night she came in Justin and Keith was just here for a couple of beers sittin' here at the bar and then they left."

"Were there any fights or altercations around here lately?" asked Randy.

"Not really. I have a tired clientele. They come to drink and the regulars all know each other and keep to themselves."

"When was the last time you remember seeing Justin?" asked Carrie.

"Probably that night he and Keith came in for just those couple of beers. Don't remember seeing them again after that." Ike seemed sad then, realizing that was the last time he had seen Justin. He had liked him. He was young and good natured and had the entire world before him.

"Can you tell us more about this woman you saw?" asked Randy.

"Well, when she walked in, all the heads in the place turned. She was in her late twenties I'm guessing and walked into the room as if she owned it. She had a kind of brownish hair. It was long. She had on a fire engine red blouse and black leather pants. That I remember.

"She sat at the bar and had a whiskey neat. She drank it like she lived on them. Downed it while she was surveying the room. When she spotted the guys playing pool, she went back to them and worked herself into the game. She didn't have to work hard at it either. They would have done anything she wanted." A wide smile grew across Ike's face.

"Has she been back? Did you see what she was driving? Do you remember what time it was?" Carrie was once again rapid firing. Ike's head slowly swiveled around to look at Carrie.

"Didn't see a car. It was maybe around nine o'clock. I think it was after Justin and Keith had left, but the night was still quite young."

"We just want to find who killed Justin. I can't imagine you wouldn't want the same thing. If you think of anything at all, please call us. Here's my card," said Carrie as she handed her card over to Ike.

He nodded as he took the card. She was right, he thought; he had no reason to not help them find out who did this to Justin.

Ike looked her in the face, "I will. I promise. I like to keep to myself and I certainly don't like getting in others' business, but Justin was a good man and if I hear anything, I'll let you know."

LATELY, the days seemed long to Senna. She enjoyed her job, but she kept remembering the moms at the park and how they laughed. She had misjudged them, assuming them self-absorbed because they were enjoying each other's company, laughing and having a good time.

But she had been wrong. The instant her child was in danger that mother was there. The mother had a loving touch, a soft word, and had been a solid rock to her toddler who needed her.

Senna was also thinking of Blake Burton. She tried not to, but his face would not leave her mind. It would pop into her head unannounced and she would squirm. If all men were like her father, then she wanted nothing to do with them. Her life was safe and orderly and she wanted it to stay that way.

"Senna," called Andrea, breaking her trance, "I'm going out to lunch. I am taking extra time to run an errand."

"Okay, that's fine. I will be here." Another change of routine. Andrea did that a lot so it shouldn't bother her, so why did it bother her, she wondered to herself?

So often, she felt like a huge vat of emotions and unvoiced thoughts that swam around and around, each one surfacing fleetingly and randomly. Feelings she didn't understand, and nothing she did seemed to order them into submission.

Reaching down to pick up a book she had dropped, she noticed an earring on the floor. It lay at the corner of the counter near a table. It was close to the back of the counter and might have been Andrea's or it could have belonged to someone who had sat at the nearest table.

As she bent down and picked it up, she felt dizzy. The

room began to swim, and she literally fell into the nearest chair. She felt like she was going to pass out.

Turning in the chair she put her arms up on the table and laid her head to rest on them. Tears escaped, and she didn't even understand why.

UPON SEEING the beautiful earring Senna's mind went immediately to her grandmother, who loved to wear jewelry.

The first time Senna ever saw her grandparents' home she was five years old. They had come one summer day to get her and wouldn't take no for an answer, promising they would only have her for seven days and then bring her home.

Her father was severe, and they knew they must follow what he said regarding Senna. They also knew that allowing them to have Senna for seven days was a gift from heaven, and they knew not to push it, or they would never get to see her again.

The car ride was nice, Senna recalled. The car smelled peculiar like a new pair of shoes, and the seats were firm and smooth. She remembered running her hand along the seam and remembered how new the stitches had looked.

She could barely see out the window in the back seat and did not know if the treetops looked familiar or not.

Then after about an hour or so the tree tops vanished and there were rooftops.

The drive seemed to take a long time, but to Senna any drive longer than ten minutes was long. That was how long it took to get to the grocery or to church from her home.

When the car pulled up to their house and Senna got out, she remembered thinking that she had never seen a home so grand. It seemed to stand to attention, proud and regal. Even the flowers in the front flowerbed stood firm and tall.

Six steps led up to the wide front porch with two wooden rockers and a wide swing. Imagine, a swing on a porch! The front door was not just one, but two side by side. Whatever did you need with two front doors?

Inside, the rooms were spacious and there was dark wood, mahogany Senna now knew, everywhere. There were wood crossbeams on the ceiling and beautifully colored rugs on the floor.

Senna's eyes could not take it all in. She had never seen anything like it. And she did like it!

Her grandmother was bubbly and happy and loved to tell Senna things. Things about people and places. Senna laughed often with Gran.

The day after her arrival, her grandmother took her to a department store, and they shopped. Up until then, Senna's mother had always made all of her clothing. In fact, she didn't even know clothes came from a store.

If she had thought her grandparents' home was grand, it was nothing compared to the glitter of the department store. Beautiful ladies stood behind glass counters with their hair perfectly done, wearing pretty red lipstick.

They smiled as she passed and she smiled back. There were smells, too. Some were sweet, and some were spicy and she wasn't sure she liked them. There were women with little bottles and sometimes they would spray them on cards and hand them out as people passed by.

Grandmother had tugged her along but not in an impatient or mean way. She was excited and wanted to buy Senna things, beautiful things.

The girls' department had more clothes than she could imagine. They picked out one after another and she got to try them all on. Then they went to the shoe department and Senna got to pick out three pairs of shoes!

Then there were new socks and underwear, headbands, and bows. Once they had finished, they had more packages than they could carry. With the help of a clerk, they loaded the car with their purchases and from there went to eat ice cream.

There was a whole store with only ice cream! She didn't even know what kind to pick. She finally picked the pink one.

The day had been filled with laughter. She remembered laughing now like the little boy in the park had laughed.

Each morning when Gran dressed, Senna stood at her

grandmother's dresser to look at the jewelry laid in beautiful glass trays. They were so sparkly. Little earrings and necklaces. She loved picking them up and holding them up to herself.

She remembered.

~

THE MEMORY, or the dream, faded as Senna felt a hand gently shaking her shoulder. She was still at the table at the library with her head on her arms. She had fallen asleep.

Senna jumped up and tried to shake the fog from her brain.

"Are you okay," the older lady asked.

"Oh, yes ma'am. I'm so sorry! I felt dizzy for a moment and rested my head. But I'm fine now." She tried to regain composure but felt uneasy, unsteady. The fact that she had fallen asleep made her nervous.

As she helped the lady in the library, she tried to push memories of the happy times with her grandparents aside. It was always so painful to have that time with them only to have to go back home and have it all fade away. Her mind felt foggy. She tried to concentrate on navigating the library to help the lady, but just couldn't seem to gain control of her mind and her thoughts. The dream memories wouldn't leave her alone.

That first trip to her grandparents' was so joyful.

They had laughed, shopped, cooked, and they had played. She'd been able to wear new clothes and Gran would let her play with her beautiful jewelry. Senna tried on all of Gran's bracelets, and necklaces even though they were way too big.

She remembered running her little fingers along the pretty stones and along the carved details of the metal, wondering how anything could be so pretty.

On the trip home from her first visit, she was so full of new experiences and couldn't wait to tell Mother. Gran even bought her a new suitcase just to hold all the new clothes and shoes. Senna wore her favorite new dress home and couldn't wait to show it off to Mother.

She had jumped out of the car with her five-year-old joy as soon as they pulled in the drive, but when her Mother came through the front door, her face was pinched with worry. The creases in her forehead were deep and Senna could tell something was wrong.

Seeing her mother's face, Senna couldn't read what the matter was, she thought maybe something bad had happened to Father or something else horrible was wrong.

But when Mother saw her in the new dress and Gran carrying the suitcase with the new clothes, Mother knew exactly what her Father would do.

Father was out in the field working, so Mother hustled them all inside. Mother and Gran had a very heated and nervous discussion. It was about the clothes.

Her Mother wanted Gran to take the clothes and the suitcase back home with her.

Her Gran was upset, and they argued. Finally, Mother said Gran had to take the new things back or Father would punish Senna and she would not get to go back and see Gran again.

When Senna heard that, she ran to her Mother and cried that she *had* to go back, that she loved Gran and Grandpa. She looked at Gran with tears in her eyes and said, "Take them, please. I want to come see you again." Senna was sobbing so hard that she could barely form her words.

Gran nodded with resignation. Her face steeped in sadness. She had gotten down on her knees and looked Senna right in the face and said, "Senna I will take the clothes because I want you to come see me again. I do not want to do anything that will cause you or your mother pain. Gran loves you so much."

They hugged. Senna laid her little head on Gran's shoulder and cried hard. She remembered her Gran's smell, the perfume she wore mixed with other things that were uniquely hers. She remembered feeling the texture of her jacket on her cheek, and the feel as it grew wet from her tears. It was rough just like that moment.

Senna did not want to let her go, and she now remembered the pain of that moment. Gran was holding her tight and, with one last squeeze she let go. She had tears, too. Senna could see them rimming her eyes.

"Okay, Senna. Be strong for Gran now. It will all be okay. Gran will write you letters and you will come again."

They agreed that she could keep the one dress she was wearing, but Gran took the suitcase full of all the other beautiful things.

She couldn't help crying as Gran drove away. Mother waved goodbye to Gran "You can't cry over this. Father will be home soon and you can't let him see you crying. He will ask why. If he thinks you are crying after Gran or the pretty things, he will never let you go back."

Senna had choked back her tears and wiped her little cheeks with the back of her hand. She had been determined to see Gran again. It wasn't because of the nice house or beautiful things. It was because she loved Gran more than she knew she could love anyone and she knew Gran loved her.

No other person had ever made Senna feel loved that way before or since. She had smiled with her and they laughed. She felt free with Gran to be herself and she resolved herself to do whatever she had to do to see her again.

The memories flooded through Senna as she worked. Andrea would talk and Senna would respond woodenly, her mind was trapped in those memories. She felt so sick inside.

Suddenly, she remembered the earring which had started the avalanche of emotional memories and rushed over to where she had last seen it. It had been knocked just under the edge of the counter. It was crushed a bit and bent.

The earring was like so many of her Gran's things, forbidden things. Things that she did not need and should not want. She pulled resolve from somewhere deep inside and hardened herself to the beauty of the earring and the memory it revived within her.

Andrea came over to see what she was doing, and she handed her the earring explaining about finding it on the floor. They put it aside on the counter to wait for its owner.

CHAPTER 5

*S*enna sat at her usual park bench for lunch. The park was almost empty today. It was windy and hot, but she didn't care. She liked the park, and it was her routine to sit on the bench for lunch.

Suddenly there was a movement from her left and as she looked up, Blake Burton was standing there with that smile of his again.

"Could I join you?" he asked.

"Sure, I guess." Senna immediately felt uneasy.

Blake sat down next to her on the bench and leaned forward with his elbows on his knees. Senna noticed he had long legs and sitting like that seemed casual and natural to him.

"Kind of windy and hot out here today," said Blake.

"Yes, it is, but I try to sit out here as much as possible to eat lunch. I like the park."

"I know. I've seen you. My office is just over there on the second floor. When I turn my chair around and look out the window, I have a great view of the park and this bench," he said. He was grinning at her.

Senna squirmed. She hadn't known she was being watched.

"Don't feel uncomfortable. I don't just sit and watch you. I've just noticed that, at lunchtime, you are out here eating your lunch."

Senna looked down and nodded. "I guess I never thought about anyone watching me."

"Oh, everyone watches everyone else from time to time, don't you think?" He turned his head to look at Senna.

She remembered watching the mothers with their children and realized he was right. "Yes, I guess we do." She looked at him and gave him a brief, shy smile.

"I'm assuming you work around here close since you eat here so often," said Blake. He wanted to ask outright where she worked but didn't want to be so bold.

"I-I work at the library."

"The library," he mused out loud.

"I'm a lawyer. I've done my fair share of reading in my life."

Nervous and fidgety, Senna wanted to have a genuine conversation with Blake, but anxiety in these types of situations always blocked the words she sought. She felt a tug to at least give it a try rather than shut herself off as she usually did.

"Do you read for fun or just for work?" she asked.

"I read for fun when I can. I like Clive Cussler and John Grisham novels."

"What does someone who works in the library like to read? With all the books in the world at your disposal, what do you choose?" Blake leaned back on the bench and crossed his ankle over his knee. He placed the arm nearest Senna on the back of the bench turning to face her fully.

"I like love stories," she said as she dipped her head and blushed. She couldn't believe that she had admitted that. It would mortify her father. He had been so strict on Senna, never letting her date or attend school functions where there would be opportunities to socialize with boys. But, secretly, Senna longed for a relationship. Reading about them seemed the closest she would ever get.

"Most girls do, I think," Blake replied. His casual demeanor helped to put Senna at ease.

"Where does your dog stay while you work?" Again, Senna attempted conversation.

"Oh, he hangs out in the backyard. I have a doggie door from the backyard into the garage where I keep his water and food, so he can go back and forth."

Senna smiled. There was something about animals

that was soothing to her. She had never had a dog as a pet, but she would spend hours on the farm with the animals. They had been her only friends.

"You have a pretty smile, you know. You should do it more often."

Senna turned her head to look at him. She rolled Blake's words over in her mind and pondered them, a pretty smile. Her look was inquiring, searching his face for truth or jest.

"I think you have had far too few people in your life tell you how beautiful you really are."

Hot fire flushed up through Senna. Was it shame or fear or something else? She looked at the ground in front of her.

No, it was embarrassment and disbelief. Her parents had taught her that beauty was vain and so her parents never told her she was beautiful. Her Gran had, but those times were so few and any belief she could have had in her words was suffocated once she was back home.

"I didn't intend to make you uncomfortable. I think the fact that you don't realize just how beautiful you are is one of the most attractive things about you," said Blake. "I get so tired of women whose whole focus is on their beauty. Yes, I understand the desire to dress pretty and look nice, but it seems women today have become obsessed with it. It is nauseating." Blake looked out into the park.

Blake's words had surprised Senna. She thought all

men wanted beauty, artificial or not. As she looked at him she studied his profile and felt something warm inside her.

She remembered this kind of feeling when she would visit Gran. It felt good and soft and inviting. It scared her a little, too.

"Hey, I have to get back to work, but I would like to see you again. Could I take you to dinner?" Blake asked.

"Din-dinner?" Senna stuttered. Blake had caught her off guard.

"Sure, I would like to get to know you better." When Senna didn't answer he continued, "We can meet at the restaurant if that would make you feel more comfortable. Or maybe we can just get a coffee or something."

In every romance novel she had ever read the women had to take a chance. She could take a chance or never experience what she longed for.

"Yes. Yes, I would like that," she said and smiled.

"Wonderful!" Blake grinned from ear to ear.

They both stood then and Senna squeezed and released the top of her paper lunch bag, not sure what to do next.

Then Blake reached up and slid a strand of hair from across her face and rested his hand on her shoulder.

Was time standing still for Senna? She thought so.

"I'll pick you up tonight?" Blake asked with the suggestion hanging in the air.

"Okay. I can do that," Senna said, knowing her

response sounded awkward. She gave him her address, and he confirmed the time. As he turned to walk across the park and back to his office, Senna watched. He had an easygoing air about him. He seemed so carefree. She wondered what that could be like, to feel so free.

~

"I HAVE A DATE," Senna said to Andrea as soon as she walked back into the library.

Andrea's eyes grew as big as saucers. "What...Who... When?" she blurted out, stunned.

Senna blushed from head to toe, now nervous to tell Andrea what she had just blurted out so boldly. "Tonight at six thirty. He's picking me up and we're going into the city to eat. I think he said a place named Savannah's."

"Oh wow, that is nice," crooned Andrea.

"Nice? How nice?" asked Senna. "I don't know what to wear!" Of course she knew what to wear. The same plain dresses she always wore.

"Oh girl, you need something new! Who is the lucky guy, anyway?"

"Blake Burton. He's a lawyer and works in the building on the other side of the park."

Andrea was shocked and stood with her mouth half hanging open. She knew Blake. They had grown up together. He was the most eligible bachelor in town, and he had asked Senna out?

Andrea had always thought of Senna as plain-Jane. She never wore make-up and only kept her hair pulled back tightly in a bun. She supposed that she could be beautiful if she would let her hair down and smile. It was because of this that it confused her that Blake had asked her out. She just didn't seem the type for someone like Blake.

"Well...that...is...wonderful," Andrea pushed out. She didn't want her excitement for Senna to fade but she was beyond bewildered.

"Okay, we, we have to go get you a new outfit," said Andrea recovering from her shock.

"Are you sure? I am not sure I would feel comfortable in something flashy. My father always wanted us to wear clothes that didn't draw attention to ourselves, particularly from men," Senna said, a worried look on her face.

"Okay, well, we can get you something nice, something new that won't be flashy. Something understated that will show off how beautiful you are." Andrea wanted Senna to feel beautiful even though it was hard for Andrea to see.

There it was again, someone saying she was beautiful. Senna felt undeniable turmoil when she heard herself referred to in that way. Her entire life she had been forced into a box of rigid self-denial and yet she was feeling such a need to break free.

"When Joyce comes to do the after-school program. We can go then and shop. The part-time students will be here then as well to watch for customers. Not much here in Kachina, but there is one little shop that has great stuff."

As the afternoon wore on, Senna vacillated between feeling excited and mortified. This was the first date she had ever been on. If sitting on the park bench with Blake was hard, how much more difficult would it be to go on a date with him?

Joyce showed up precisely at three, then Renee and Alex shortly after. Andrea and Senna walked to the only dress shop in town. It was a cute little boutique with clothing meant to attract the college crowd.

The colors drew Senna in. Memories of shopping with Gran came flooding back. Each year when she visited Gran, they would shop and shop, but only buy one dress which she would wear home. To have bought more would have been a waste as Father would insist they be returned. But it was practical for him to allow her one new dress.

"Over here, Senna," called Andrea. "This is great! Not too much, but very pretty." She held up the dress and Senna looked at it.

The dress was a pale pink color with a white wave print running through it. It had capped sleeves and was sewn to fit with tapering seams growing fuller at the skirt. It was wonderful!

"I like it," Senna said, smiling. "Where can I try it on?"

Andrea led her to the dressing room and Senna undressed and slid the new dress over her head. It fit perfectly. It wasn't tight though it fit through the waist. She twirled in front of the mirror like she had with Gran as a little girl.

"Come out here and let me see," demanded Andrea, excited.

As Senna walked out from behind the curtain Andrea gasped. "Senna, you look amazing!"

She did too, Andrea thought. As she was putting the dress on, the bun she wore had come loose and her hair fell down her back in loose waves from having worn it twisted so tightly.

Most women had to wear a whole regime of makeup to look this nice. Senna had full dark lashes, so even though she didn't wear makeup she looked as though she had added an entire tube of mascara, complete with fiber extensions.

Those lashes with her big, blue eyes were stunning. Why had Andrea never noticed before just how lovely Senna was?

"Shoes. You have to have new shoes," instructed Andrea. She walked over to the shoe section of the store.

She picked up two different shoes holding them up, one in each hand for Senna to see.

Senna wrinkled her nose, so Andrea turned to look again. Then Senna noticed a shoe that caught her eye. It was exquisite. It was pink just like her dress. Leather that was soft and supple. There was a thin strap across the instep with an adornment where it attached on the side, made of crystal beads. There weren't too many beads in a big and garish way, but just enough.

"These," Senna exclaimed as she shoved the shoe in Andrea's direction. Her free hand flew to her mouth as she laughed. Oh how she had longed for a life like this, freedom to have fun and to laugh with friends.

"Perfect! They are perfect," agreed Andrea.

ANDREA CAME to Senna's home after stopping by her house to pick up an arsenal of beauty supplies. She agreed to help her with her hair, and makeup if Senna felt comfortable with that.

They gave Senna's hair a gentle spiral curl which was so popular at the time. Andrea took her curling iron and wrapped large sections of Senna's hair.

The result was full looking hair with soft curls that did not look forced. Andrea did not want Senna to feel uncomfortable but suggested just a bit of blush and colored lip gloss. Senna agreed.

Once done, Andrea turned Senna's chair around to face the mirror. They both stared at the reflection coming back. Senna was beautiful. She didn't really need makeup, but the subtle pink blush and lip gloss stressed her already present natural beauty.

"My goodness girl!" exclaimed Andrea; "what I wouldn't give to do so little to look so good."

Senna sat and looked at herself in the mirror. She did not know this person who was looking back at her. She was foreign, yet familiar. Senna thought she liked her. She wanted to like her.

"Well, what do you think?" asked Andrea.

"I like it. I do. I'm just in shock," said Senna. She wanted to ask Andrea if she was sure she looked okay, but she knew she did. Was that confidence, or maybe pride? Father always warned about being prideful. No, she thought, it was just the knowledge that the woman looking back at her in the mirror was beautiful, but it felt like she was looking at someone else.

Andrea scurried around gathering her stuff. "Blake will be here soon and I want to get all my things and be gone by then. Oh, but how I would like to be a little mouse in the corner to see his face when he takes a gander at you for the first time tonight!" Andrea giggled.

Once Andrea left, Senna paced the floor. She rubbed the palms of her hands together, a thousand thoughts running through her mind.

She had suffered rejection from her father and only knew acceptance from her Grandpa. But with that, she rarely saw him. When she would visit, it was Gran who spent time with her. Grandpa always had smiles and hugs, but they hadn't spent a lot of time together.

She also knew the only way her father ever accepted her was when she complied to the rules and rigidity of their religion. But was that true acceptance? Was that really him accepting her?

What if Blake was like Father and he liked her because he saw her plainness? What if tonight he saw her differently and rejected her? No, that made little sense, she thought as she continued to pace back and forth.

She was working herself into a frenzy, pacing back and forth and wringing her hands. Just about the time she had convinced herself to change into another dress and shoes, and wipe the makeup from her face, the doorbell rang.

As she stared at the door from the middle of the room, she wiped her sweaty hands on the afghan laying on the sofa, took a deep breath, stood up tall, and went to open the door. No turning back now.

The look on Blake's face as the door swung open told her all she needed to know. Slowly, that smile she loved grew broad across his face.

"Senna," he breathed, "you look absolutely stunning!"

She ducked her head feeling her cheeks grow hot. Blake reached out and lifted her chin so they were face to face, and again he smiled.

THE RIDE to the city began with Senna feeling nervous and unsure of what to say or do. Blake talked about his work and his family. He sensed Senna was uncomfortable, so he didn't want her to feel the need to talk until she felt more relaxed.

He asked about where she grew up, and giving few details, Senna explained that she had grown up on a farm in the far western side of Oklahoma. Both her parents had passed away.

Senna had moved to Kachina to go to the small community college. She chose it because it was a small town and she had thought she would feel more comfortable there.

The restaurant was lovely. The lighting was designed so families and friends would feel cozy and intimate. The hostess seated them in a booth across from each other near the back of the restaurant.

They ordered and Blake suggested a bottle of wine. Senna gave a slight shake of her head indicating no. She wasn't ready to cross that line yet and wasn't sure she ever would be.

By the end of the meal, Blake had Senna laughing, and she was feeling things she had never felt, but it also felt a little uncomfortable to her.

Once back at Senna's house, Blake walked her to the door. He was very aware that he must be a complete gentleman at all times with her, so after she had unlocked her door, he simply reached down resting both his hands on each side of her face, and kissed her on the lips.

One kiss and he moved back a step for her to take it in. And then he watched her face. What he saw was a smile.

"Thank you Blake." It was a sincere thank-you from her heart.

"Honestly, it was my pleasure. I want to see you again if that's okay with you."

"Yes, please." Senna felt waves of elation and fear fight for attention inside her.

He got her phone number, a land line as she had not indulged in a cell phone, and he left with his characteristic two-finger salute.

Once inside, Senna sat in the same chair in front of her bedroom mirror where Andrea had helped to transform her earlier. As the stress of the evening drained from her, she suddenly felt exhausted. She leaned over onto the vanity and rested her head on her arms.

SHE SAT in her car and watched the apartment complex close to the community college where so many students lived.

It was Friday night and, after a week of studying, they all stayed out late partying. She sat and watched as they came home, two by two and one by one.

She slid back into the driver's seat and let the soft leather envelope her. She loved the smell of the rich leather and the power of the engine. It was amazing what money could buy.

This car stood out in a town like this though, so she only came late at night when there was less likelihood of calling attention to herself. With all that she had bought for herself with her trust fund, the one thing she could not buy, however, was peace and wholeness.

She had freedom, excessive freedom, and she took advantage of it. She went where she wanted, bought what she wanted, and did what she wanted, whenever she wanted to. She indulged herself in whatever way suited her fancy, no matter how sinful or decadent.

But money could not push away that deep dark hole down inside her, and it made her angry, violently angry. The only thing that brought her any relief, any sense of washing away the pain and despair, was seeing the rich red warm blood flow from a human body.

The act of taking a life itself was unnerving to her. That gave her no pleasure at all. But it was necessary to have the relief that only the fresh, dark red blood would give.

It was fleeting to be sure, but the way an addict could not go without a fix, neither could she. At first she could not appease that gnawing inside. That is when she went on a shopping spree unparalleled in history.

The best house, car, clothes, jewelry, whiskey, and sex,

none of it touched that need inside her. The only thing that could temporarily cover it was the blood. It couldn't really wipe it out completely, but it did cover it for a while.

In the beginning, she planned the murders for days on end so that she would not get caught. She was smart, and she knew it, so she used her brain strategically to get what she needed. It had worked, too. To her knowledge, none of the other bodies had yet been found.

But just like any other addict, she was getting sloppy, and she didn't care. She needed what she needed and that was all that mattered. So she hunted and found men she could manipulate and off they would go with her without a second thought.

Ketamine was easy to get and after they were well into an evening of drinking, they never knew what hit them. It made it easier to kill with them passed out. In fact, she could not have done it if she'd had to see them as human beings. This was the most humane way to get what she needed.

She left the parking lot and drove until she was at Crown Rock Park and sat looking at the stars. *The night is beautiful*, she thought, as she listened to her cell phone ringing from the call she had just made.

"Yeah?" asked Keith. He was very groggy, having been asleep for hours.

"Hey, it's me," she said. Her voice was soft, sexy, and enticing.

"Oh wow, what time is it?" Keith sat up in bed and rubbed a hand over his face to help clear his head.

"It's late. I'm sorry, but I was alone and just couldn't sleep. I need you tonight. Can you come to me?"

He could not resist her. "Yeah. Where to?"

"I am at the top of Crown Rock Park."

CHAPTER 6

"There's been another murder," said Randy the next morning when he was picking Carrie up at her house.

"Another one," she responded. It wasn't a question but a statement of incredulity at the thought of yet another murder in Kachina.

"Yep."

"Where?"

"On the Big Horn Ranch."

The Crown Rock Mesa stood tall and red at the far northeast corner of the Big Horn Ranch. It separated the ranch from town. Being a bit of a draw for the locals, a park had been fashioned on top. If you can call one picnic table, a trash can, and a welded charcoal grill on a stand, a park.

The view from the top was splendid though! You could see for miles in any direction. But Randy and Carrie were not seeing the view right then; they were at the base of the mesa on the ranch looking at the latest body.

It was Keith Thompson. The body was battered, but not from a beating while alive. His throat had been slit like Justin's while up on the mesa. Then it had been dumped over the edge. The tumble down the cliff had battered the body.

As before, the forensic team had been called in and was almost finished with their search. The coroner, as well, was standing by to claim the body.

"What can you tell us about his death?" Randy asked the coroner.

"At first glance I am going to venture out and say that the COD is exsanguination from the cut in the throat. It hit the jugular and he would have bled out quickly.

"We can also determine that he must have been killed from the mesa above because of the lack of blood here and also from the post-mortem cuts and abrasions characteristic with hitting brush and rocks on the side of the mesa," said the coroner.

Randy and Carrie looked at each other and nodded, "Let's go," they said in unison.

To get to the top of the mesa from where they were, they had to exit across the ranch in a southwesterly direction until they reached Old Bones Road, and then turn north on Central Avenue which went through the center of town. About six miles north from there, they came to Crown Rock Road. It was on the southern edge of Kachina and the next to the last street on that side of town.

They wound to the west until they emerged on to the top of the mesa at the park. The trees were all scrub cedar trees that were wind worn from the constant Oklahoma wind. Here and there were a few tall dry tufts of various dead wild grasses.

The mesa was genuine red sand rock. Most of the natural dirt in Oklahoma was brick red. This mesa was formed out of that same red sand rock.

From where they stood they could see no footprints or other unusual signs of a struggle or disturbance. Standing on the edge of the mesa, Randy could see a path where the body had tumbled down the side of the cliff as well as the body below.

"Hey Randy, come here," called Carrie. "Here are some hoof prints." Carrie pointed with her gloved finger.

"Let's get forensics up here. Hopefully, they can match the prints to a horse should we find one that could have been here," said Randy.

"Even if they find a match, it doesn't necessarily mean they're from the killer or tied to the murder."

"No, but we have so little to go on, we need everything we can get. Maybe we'll get a break," Randy said as he texted the lead tech, who was working below, and instructed him what they had found and the location.

Senna bolted upright from sleep, her heart racing. The nightmare. It was the nightmare that had jolted her out of sleep.

Trying to regain her composure, she began to breathe steadily again. She swung her legs over the edge of her bed and sat looking at the floor. Her hands gripped the bedclothes at her sides, arms rigid and elbows locked.

Even though the nightmare was fading, fierce physical trauma remained. There were images she could not reconcile. There were feelings and emotions foreign to her, taunting her and toying with her.

Then a racking, breathtaking sob wrenched from her body. She missed her Gran so. She needed that love and that acceptance. How could emotion run this deep? How could that need for her, cause such physical pain?

Senna laid back down and pulled the covers close to her chin as she curled up in a ball. Tears streamed down her cheeks. Damn the rules. Damn the laws. Damn it all if she had to feel so unloved and so broken. The only thing that had ever made her feel loved was Gran and rules had nothing to do with it.

Yet the turmoil would not leave her. This driving force to comply and to be accepted, void of love, fought against her dire need to feel freely loved.

Senna wailed from the pain of it all, sobbing herself back to sleep.

She awoke again mid-morning. It was time to start her day, but the fatigue of the emotional meltdown, and what felt like a lack of sleep caused her to operate in slow motion.

It was Saturday, and she did not have to work at the library that day. Usually on her days off, she had a long list of productive things she would get done, but today she had no desire or motivation to do so.

She pulled herself up from her bed and made her way to the sofa. Laying back down, she pulled the afghan over herself, feeling numb. She dozed, but never really rested. At around 11:00 a.m. Andrea called.

The sound of the phone ringing woke her, and she got up to answer it.

"Hey there!" greeted Andrea.

"Hi," replied Senna.

"Oh my. Was the date last night that good or that bad?"

"What do you mean?" Senna asked as she took the cordless phone back to the sofa.

"Well, you sound awful. I mean…I don't mean that in a bad way, but you sound so down. Did things not go well?" Andrea was really concerned. She couldn't remember Senna ever sounding this way.

Senna's mind tried to connect with what Andrea was asking. The date. The date with Blake. She had pushed that to the back of her mind after the ordeal of the nightmare and her crying spell that morning.

"Oh, the date with Blake. It was nice. It was very nice." Senna smiled as she remembered. It was a nice memory. It was something to hang on to rather than dwell on the darkness that had tried to overtake her early that morning.

"Whew! That's awesome. For a minute, I thought it had been a disaster. Are you okay?" asked Andrea with genuine concern.

"I'm okay. I had a horrible nightmare early this morning, and it wrecked me. It carried so many emotions with it, that I honestly don't know how to deal with them, or even where they came from."

Listening to Senna, Andrea suddenly had an idea, "Hey, what do you say I come over and bring some comfort food and we can hang out today. We can eat, watch movies, and talk."

Senna felt immediate resistance to that suggestion. She felt an urge to push Andrea away and to guard herself as if she had secrets to hide.

"Oh that's okay. I'll be fine," she said, even though she craved the connection.

"Nonsense. I'm coming over whether you like it or

not. That's what friends do. Plus, I want to hear all about the date!"

Friends. Andrea considered her a friend. "Okay, I'll be here," Senna finally agreed.

She hung up the phone. Her mind was fraught with conflict as if she had no sense of what was real. She knew she was not normal. She knew she was not right. No matter how many rules she followed, she knew she was broken and she couldn't pretend anymore.

But tragically, she had no idea what to do about it. At this point, she didn't even have the energy to really care. Everything her parents had ever taught her felt like a coat of tight armor that was constricting her and suffocating her. Yet her mind screamed that she must obey all that Father had told her through the years.

"HEY THERE," greeted Andrea, her arms loaded down with grocery sacks full of goodies.

"What on earth have you got there?" asked Senna. She was dumbfounded that Andrea thought they could eat all that food.

"Well, you never know in the moment what you will want to eat, so you have to be prepared," Andrea said. The look on her face confirmed she was quite serious.

"Oh." This was a whole new realm for Senna. She had never had girlfriends like other girls did. She had never experienced the closeness of what a friend truly was, but she had longed for it for a very long time.

"So, first, we're going to start with these breakfast burritos. They are so good. Packed to the gills with sausage, eggs, peppers, onions and cheese. Mmmmm good! That will give us protein to start and then we can just eat whatever after that," Andrea said unloading the large paper sack, her head nearly buried inside.

The burritos were thick, gooey, and yummy. Andrea and Senna dove in and enjoyed every bite. There was something freeing about being with Andrea. Senna felt permission to relax.

When Senna laid her burrito down after only a few bites Andrea looked at her with wide eyes. "What's wrong with it?"

"Nothing. I just don't want to overeat."

"Oh darlin', that is what this day is all about! We're going to eat until we are so stuffed we can't move! Pick that burrito up and dive back in," said Andrea as she herself took another huge bite.

Senna picked up the burrito and looked at it. Andrea wanted her to overeat? She took another bite and tasted the robust flavor of the expertly done burrito. It *was* good, and she wanted to taste it again and again, so she did.

Finally, near the end of the burrito Senna laid it down. "Okay, I cannot eat another bite!" She held her hand on her stomach.

"Now that is what I want to hear. Wasn't that good?" Andrea had a huge smile on her face. She herself had relished every single bite. "So, lets waddle into the living room and let this digest."

They picked up the remnants of the burrito debris, tossed it into the trash and headed for the living room. Senna curled up in an extra-wide upholstered chair and Andrea took the sofa. They were both enjoying the after-glow of eating.

"Senna, we have known each other for some time now. I hope you know I am truly your friend."

There was only silence in the room after Andrea's statement. Andrea was genuine in her concern for Senna. Through the years she had seen a young woman, a kind woman, who was in pain. Senna had always treated Andrea with respect, never once did she seem annoyed or at odds with her no matter the situation.

Silence filled the air for a few more moments. "I know," Senna responded.

"Please know I want you to feel close enough to me so you can talk to me. Every single person needs someone to talk to and to share things with. Someone to encourage them and help them through. Someone to laugh and to cry with.

"I know that you've had a tough childhood. I know, not because you have talked about it, but from the pain I have seen in your eyes. Please tell me about it. I am convinced that if you do, if you share it, you will feel better," Andrea concluded.

Senna tried to gather her thoughts so she could explain. There was such a jumble in her mind. There were threads of thought running through that even she did not understand, so how could she tell Andrea when she herself couldn't make sense of it all?

"My father was very strict," she finally began. "I grew up on a farm and he worked hard every day to take care of us. Mom worked at home cleaning and taking care of us in her way as well.

"When something is all you know, you assume that is all there is to know. But growing up and watching other kids at school, I carried a feeling that my life was different.

"At home there seemed to be only work. When we were together, there was no laughter. My mother always seemed sad and Father was always quiet and even seemed a little angry."

Senna took a deep breath and continued. "I enjoyed school, but the other kids didn't really want to play with me. I know I was quiet, I had learned to be quiet at home, and didn't know how to interact with the others at school because of that."

Andrea listened as Senna continued to tell her how isolated she had felt at home and at school. She talked about the new little girl who came to their school in the third grade and how she and Senna had become friends. But when the little girl had asked her to come over and play one day, her father had put his foot down and said no.

They had continued to be friends at school, but they grew apart as other girls in the class could go and do things and have fun when Senna couldn't. Soon other friendships developed and grew stronger for her friend.

She explained about their church and how strict it was and how she felt it was the driving factor in her father's behavior.

"Gosh, Senna," Andrea quietly commented. "I am so sorry you had to go through that. What about your mom? Was she like that, too?"

"Mother was sweet. She was always good to me, but she was continually conscious of Father and what he would say or do. I can see now just how afraid of him she really was."

"Are your parents still alive?"

"No, they were older when they had me and my mother passed away when I was eighteen. I had just left home to go to college and, soon after that, Mother became ill and passed away. The doctors said it was some type of infection. They tried to treat it, but they didn't catch it in time and none of the medicines worked.

"I was away from home and couldn't make myself move back to take care of Father even though that was what he wanted. My Gran encouraged me to stay away and keep going to college, and so I did. In less than a year, there was an accident with the tractor and it killed my father."

"Wow! I am so sorry!" Andrea sat up and swung her feet around to the floor. She watched Senna. She was not sure when she had felt such compassion for someone.

"Don't be. I don't feel it like I think I should. In my life he was just a man even though he was my father. I always knew I should love him, feel something for him the way I did my mother, but there was nothing there."

Senna had also sat up and was resting her forearms on her legs. She looked at a thread she had picked up and was toying with. She was thinking of Gran.

"What are you thinking about?" asked Andrea after seeing how quiet Senna had gotten.

"Gran. My sweet Gran," said Senna, a gentle smile emerged.

"Tell me about her. She must have been really special."

Senna explained about Gran and how much she had loved Senna, and how Senna had loved her. She told her about the first time she had gone to stay with Gran and how it was when she had come home.

Senna told how each year she was allowed two weeks in the summer to go to Gran's and how each year she had hated going home more and more.

She and Gran would write letters and Gran would send cards. As she had gotten older Gran would send her money to buy things she needed, things she could hide from her father.

Gran was always encouraging. She couldn't call Gran on the phone because to call her was long distance and there were charges; but Gran would call her when she thought her father would not be around to listen in.

She explained to Andrea how Father always taught her that the things that Gran and Grandpa had were sinful. That people were to live simply and work hard, wanting nothing beyond the absolute necessities. "He said the Bible taught they were to live a sober life which he believed meant a *somber* life," Senna said emphasizing somber.

"I have always felt so torn," she looked at Andrea full on. "I wanted so to please Father and Mother, and God, too, but it was so much work and so hard to do. I would never have known there was another way of life if I had not had Gran and been able to go stay with her from time to time."

"Where is your Gran now?" Andrea asked.

A lump rose in Senna's throat and with husky words she said, "She passed away a year ago."

Senna paused and looked back at her hands working the little thread. She was trying to swallow the lump to continue, but it just seemed lodged there.

Andrea got up from the sofa and came over to where Senna was. She sat beside her, and put her arm around her friend, pulling her close. "I am so very sorry you had to go through all of that."

Senna allowed her friend to comfort her. Maybe she

was so drawn to Andrea because she was so much like Gran. Having her head on Andrea's shoulder reminded her of all the times she'd had her head on Gran's shoulder.

Finally, Senna raised her head and wiped her tears. "Thank you."

"Senna, your father was wrong and your Gran was right. Life is meant to be lived and enjoyed. There is nothing sinful about enjoying all the wonderful things provided for us in this life."

Senna nodded. "After I left home, I was free to see Gran more. She paid for my college and bought me a car. She would buy me some clothes and shoes and things, but I was never comfortable in living that lifestyle, no matter how hard I tried.

"For some reason, I have never been able to walk away from what father taught me. No matter how much love I felt from Gran and how much I enjoyed all the wonderful things she bought and did for me, I have always felt down deep inside that to be accepted, I had to live the way Father and Mother did."

Senna then looked at Andrea and smiled. "But I am trying to. I want to change. It all just feels so embedded into my DNA."

After a few moments Andrea breathed deep and let it out as she stood up. "Ice cream. We need ice cream," she declared as she disappeared into the kitchen.

Two bowls and spoons clattered onto the counter as

the freezer door opened. "I cannot believe you," said Senna. "It's the middle of the day and I am still stuffed from that breakfast you made me eat."

As Senna entered the kitchen, Andrea said, "Ice cream is not food when it is used for comfort. Then it is medicine and is necessary. It will melt in your mouth and just fill all the little cracks and crannies around the burrito," she said. The certainty of her words made Senna chuckle.

While eating the ice cream, they left weightier topics behind and laughed at stories Andrea told of growing up with her two brothers. In time, Senna thought, she might be able to leave all the pain behind, too, and live life, really live it.

CHAPTER 7

Even though it was Sunday, Carrie was in her office at the OSBI headquarters in Oklahoma City. Calling it an office was a stretch. It was really just a glorified cubicle.

The lines on the legal pad in front of her called to her to pour out her thoughts on them. It had always helped her to write out threads of thoughts on paper. There was something about writing a thought down that spurred one after another and usually when done, there was an entire page or more of avenues to explore further.

There was the white board they used, which contained both Justin's and Keith's pictures with facts of the case written on it, but Carrie liked to jot down 'what ifs' on a sheet of paper where she could scribble and mark through things, to see if ideas would take form or had substance.

But today her page was blank. The Kachina murders had provided so little evidence and the theories were endless. Having so little to go on at this stage gave Carrie pause over her paper.

Motive was foremost on her mind. Why on earth would someone want to kill these two young men? Had they seen something they shouldn't have? Were they into something like drugs or some other nefarious business on the side? A love triangle or something to do with jealousy didn't seem to fit, there was no passion in the killings the way jealousy emerges.

She drew a line down the center of a new page. At the top of one side she wrote, 'saw something' and at the top of the other she wrote, 'did something'.

Then she just wrote down thoughts as quickly as they came to her, under the topic where they fit. When she did, she didn't over-think each thought. She would just be quick about it before she could discard it with reason or doubt.

When she had nothing left to write, she sat back and looked at the two columns. Now it was time to use logic to eliminate the impossible.

Under column one, SAW SOMETHING, she had written:

1) saw a theft

2) saw an affair

3) saw a drug deal

4) saw a crime

Under the second column, DID SOMETHING, she had written the following:

1) were taking drugs

2) were stealing

3) were partners in a crime

4) were loose ends

The list was pretty slim and wimpy, Carrie decided as she sat back and studied it. These were boys who had both grown up on adjoining ranches in Texas. They had no history of crime. There were speeding tickets, but anyone around here who had a pickup truck had a speeding ticket.

The only drugs in their system was ketamine. There weren't even prescription drugs. These boys were healthy. *But they could sell and not use,* she mused.

Who would they be selling to? Other ranch hands? She shook her head and leaned back in her desk chair. No, the drug angle wasn't coming together. It just didn't seem to fit. They often worked long hours, particularly in the spring and summer. They got up with the sun and often worked until the sun went down.

The old desk chair creaked as she got up to go fill her coffee cup. She chuckled to herself wondering how long coffee had been an addictive lifeline to civilization. The Folgers Columbian that the agency provided wasn't bad if a heavy hand wasn't measuring out the grounds. And if it was refreshed at least twice a day.

Carrie breathed in the aroma of her coffee as she stirred in her creamer. What if they saw something they shouldn't have seen? Leaving the bodies like that could be a clear message to others. If they saw someone commit a crime, then they would certainly be loose ends that needed to be eliminated.

Carrie thought about the day they spoke with Keith as the fresh rush of coffee flooded her system. He was hurting over losing his friend. Her mind systematically went over each moment of their conversation. Had she missed any indication he was hiding something? She didn't think so.

Walking to the window she shut her eyes to enjoy the warmth of the sun. It was a beautiful day and here she was inside yet again. Thinking about Pinky, she thought how she had left their interrogation with him feeling lacking, very lacking. She decided it was a perfect day to go back to the Big Horn and have another visit with him.

Carrie scooped up her papers and the files of the investigation then stopped to send Randy a text about where she was going and what she was doing. Then she stopped herself. Sunday was family day for Randy unless there was a critical emergency, so she shoved her phone in her pocket deciding not to bother him.

Her decision to leave the building was a good one, she decided, as the cool breeze and warm sun greeted her exit from the building. The remaining trees were leafing out and there were smudges of bright green everywhere.

The thought crossed her mind to see if Darren would go to the ranch with her, but he had a family too, so she tossed that idea as well.

At the ranch, she didn't stop at the main house but drove on back to the barns where they had first met with Pinky. Getting out of the car, she noticed it was quiet. It was about ten in the morning and this place should be busy, but looked abandoned.

She walked to the barn where Pinky's office had been and opened the door. The cool of the barn met her as did the smell of large farm animals. It was a mixture of hay and manure.

She noticed that the stalls hadn't been mucked yet. *Maybe they do that later in the day*, she thought. She walked on down to Pinky's office and knocked on the closed door. There was no answer.

She stood for a minute looking around the barn. There were eight horse stalls, three with horses. There were two other rooms besides the office, the one with its door open appeared to hold saddles and other various tack. The closed door of the other one hid its contents.

She stepped over to the closed door and knocked. Again, no answer. She was curious, so she turned the doorknob and pushed the door open and flipped on the light.

The walls were lined with shelves and cabinets. The

upper cabinets on her left had glass inserts so you could see the contents. Carrie stepped up to the first glass and read the labels on the bottles and jars. Pharmaceuticals.

There were many types of pills and medicines. Most of them she had no idea how to pronounce. One dark brown jar held pills of some sort and it made Carrie realize that the term 'horse pills' was true. They were huge.

There were creams and salves as well. She walked along the length of the wall reading all the labels that she could see without opening a cabinet. Only the last one had a lock on it.

In that last cabinet she saw a familiar word, ketamine. But then as they had suspected this was not unusual. Ketamine was a large animal tranquilizer.

Carrie jumped as a strong voice interrupted her thoughts with a fury. "Hey! What are you doing?"

In an instant Carrie swung around and had her hand on her hip where her gun lay. It was Pinky at the door and he had caught her snooping. She didn't have a warrant and no legal excuse to be in here.

She took a deep breath to calm herself and removed her hand. "Pinky, there you are. I was looking for you."

Creases crossed his face emphasizing the scowl he wore. "In here? You got no business in here! What are you snooping for? You got a warrant?"

"No, I came in the barn looking for you and when you

didn't answer your office door, I thought you might be in here," she responded hoping it sounded plausible.

"Did you knock on this door to see if I would answer?" He almost spat out.

"Yes. I'm sorry," she replied feeling contrite. "I truly am." And she was, well, sorry she had gotten caught, anyway.

"Is there somewhere we can go and talk?"

"Sure," he turned and led to his office.

"Where is everyone? It seems like a ghost town around here this morning." She tried to naturally put him at ease.

"It's Sunday morning," he stated.

Carrie tried to reconcile that statement with what she had asked. When she didn't comment in return, Pinky clarified.

"They go to church on Sunday morning. Well, most of them do."

"Oh, I see," replied Carrie. She hadn't gone to church since she, well she couldn't remember.

"You don't go to church?" she asked.

"I used to go every Sunday, but lately I have gotten a little lazy about going. At my age I am fighting aches and pains. Sunday is my only day to take it easy and so I have gotten into a bad habit of sleeping late on Sundays."

"I see," Carrie paused. "Well, I came by because I wanted to talk to you again about Justin and Keith."

"Go on." There was unmistakable pain on Pinky's face. Pain and sadness.

"From all I can determine, those were good boys. There was no record of previous or current criminal activity. Can you please help me? You knew them as well as anyone. Give me a picture of their life from your vantage point."

"You're right. They were good boys. Ever since they came here they worked hard, were always on time. Hell, they livened up the place. They sparked some life into these old codgers out here.

"They're always cuttin' up and playin' around. But it was just plain old fun. There wasn't a criminal bone in their bodies."

"My partner Randy and I went by the Darkside and spoke with Ike," explained Carrie. "He gave us the same impression. When they went there, he said there was never trouble, just two boys having a drink and some fun.

"We can't find any information showing that either of the boys dated or had girlfriends. Do you know if they had girlfriends, or," Carrie hesitated, "were they in a relationship together?"

Pinky squirmed. "No, they weren't in a relationship together!" The old guy was indignant at that suggestion.

"Help me Pinky. Why do you think someone murdered them?" Carrie looked at Pinky with pleading eyes.

He sat forward in his chair and placed both forearms

THE BLOOD

on his desk and looked her squarely in the face. "Honestly, I do not know."

"Someone had drugged them with ketamine," she stated and let it lie there.

Pinky's mind raced as he assimilated this new information. "Ketamine? Why, we use that around here. You don't suspect someone from the ranch here, do you?" Pinky was genuinely worried about that. Was he working side by side with someone cruel enough to murder those good boys?

"I need a motive. Then I will be much closer to determining who did it."

"What if there was no motive?"

"You mean just random?" Carrie pondered that. The killings were controlled and planned. The phrase *randomly controlled* played in her mind.

"I can't give you a motive. In my wildest imagination I can't begin to guess who would want those boys dead. And as for the ketamine, it is everywhere on every ranch in this part of the country. It could have come from anywhere."

Carrie nodded in resignation and agreement. "You are right. Thank you for your time. You have my card. Please, if something occurs to you that you hadn't thought of before, call us."

As she was walking out she turned back. "Randy and I will need to conduct formal interviews with each of the hands. We don't want to disrupt their work here or put a hardship on the ranch. Could you send them all in to Darren's office tomorrow two at a time in thirty-minute intervals so you aren't completely short-handed?"

Pinky nodded his agreement, apparently lost in thought.

She thanked Pinky again and turned to leave. She thought about motive. There was a motive even if the motive was some unimaginable, twisted desire living deep inside the killer.

IT WAS a quiet Sunday afternoon for Senna. She felt a sense of peace and happiness she had not felt in a very long time.

She was curled up in her favorite chair reading, but had stopped to contemplate the day before with Andrea. The dust motes danced in the sunlight beaming in from the window and Senna stared at them transfixed as she thought.

It had been difficult to share such painful things with her, yet on the other hand, it felt like with that confession, a cleansing had come to her soul.

She realized now how much shame she had been carrying for a past which had been totally out of her control. Why should she feel shame for events surrounding her life, which she had not chosen or caused? She pondered how shame was unique in that way. Realization was dawning on her that shame would attach itself whenever and however it could. It made no difference if you were the guilty party or not.

Even amidst this newfound peace, there still seemed deep inside her an unsettled layer of emotion that tempered everything with deep sadness. She wanted to be completely free from it all. She just did not know how. But she knew now it might be possible. She hoped it was possible.

This attempt to break free felt to her like a new baby deer trying to stand on wobbly legs. Each step, each new attempt to break free was met with uncertainty and, for her, fear.

She found herself questioning each and every word that had been drilled into her when she was growing up. What was true? Was any of it true? How could she know what to keep and what to throw out?

It had been a long time since she had prayed, a small child maybe, but she whispered one now. "I need to know the truth. Please help me."

The room remained filled with silence and so she picked up her book and continued to read.

An hour later her phone rang. "Hey girl!" Came chattering through the line.

Senna smiled. It was Andrea. "Hi yourself."

"So, I thought we needed to go to the city and go shopping this afternoon. It is a beautiful day and I want to get out."

Shopping. Senna thought about shopping with Gran and also her and Andrea's trip on Friday when they had shopped for the new dress.

"Yes, let's go shopping," Senna said smiling. There was a knot in her stomach, but she was determined to push past it.

"I'll be there in ten minutes."

Senna went into her bedroom to change out of her sweatpants. Looking in her closet she saw it as if for the first time. She shoved hangers aside looking for something she could wear that would not embarrass Andrea.

Ten minutes later when Andrea arrived, Senna was still in her sweats.

"What on earth went on in here," Andrea exclaimed, rather than asked. Before her was disarray everywhere in the bedroom.

Senna sat on the edge of her bed in a pile of clothes she had flung out of her closet. "I think I am seeing myself and my life differently for the first time. I look at you and you have cute things, then I hear my father's voice in my head. But I can't reconcile the things he said when I look at you.

"I need to find a way to be me and not some staid figure that my father forced me to become. But trying to break out of all of this feels like I am trying to be you. The truth is I don't know who I am."

"Well, let's find who you are!" Andrea said. She hunted

through the ravaged pile on the bed and what was left in the closet.

"Here, put this on."

"That?" Senna asked quite surprised. It was yet another skirt and button up blouse.

"Yes, but here put this t-shirt on, tuck it in and put the blouse on over it and leave it unbuttoned."

Senna did as she was told and then Andrea rolled up the blouse sleeves. She stood back and looked to see what to do next. Looking around and digging in drawers she found a belt.

Shoving that at Senna she commanded her to put that on too. She also found a necklace and earrings in a little box way at the back of a drawer.

"Okay, let me see," Andrea said as she looked at Senna. "Cute. You look cute! Leave your hair down, no tight little bun in the back today. Look. Turn around and look." Andrea took Senna's shoulders and turned her around to look in the mirror.

"Oh!" Senna said. "Wow, it is cute. Okay. Okay. I like it!" A big smile spread across Senna's face.

Soon afterwards, they were headed to the city with the pile still on the bed.

"Girl we will fix you up today. This is so much fun. What is your budget?"

"Budget?" Senna looked at Andrea as if she had not understood.

"Sure, I know you don't make much at the library but

having seen the contents of your closet I am assuming you never, ever spend money on clothes. So, how much do you have pigeonholed away to spend?"

Senna blinked and thought to herself. Gran had left her some money. The thought to be conservative, pressed in on her, to be wise, pressed in even harder.

By force of sheer will she said, "I have money. Gran left me some."

"Awesome," Andrea smiled. Shopping was fun, but shopping with other people's money was even more fun!

EVEN THOUGH IT was Sunday afternoon, Blake had a ton of work to do. He would rather have been out playing golf or fishing or a thousand other things, but he had a trial coming up and he needed to make sure he was prepared.

The windows were open to his upstairs office. Spring in Oklahoma was unpredictable, but the weather was still holding out cool enough so he could leave the windows open. Silly as it seemed, it gave him a connection with the beautiful day outside, even if only a small one.

To be honest, he wasn't a hundred percent focused on his work. He had been reading the same page for thirty minutes. He would find himself halfway down the page only to realize he hadn't processed a single solitary word he had read.

It was Senna. She kept floating through his mind. She was a mystery to him. She was beautiful, no doubt. But there was something else so attractive about her.

Giving in to his wondering thoughts he leaned back in his chair and locked his fingers behind his head.

The thought of the first day he had met her and how he thought her very strange. She even seemed to dress a little odd. But she was sweet and awkwardly funny. The fact that she was not trying to impress him, in and of itself, was attractive.

She seemed, he thought, groping for a word, *a little lost.*

A breeze gusted through his open window and he stood to gaze out. The town square was empty, but his eyes only saw the empty bench where Senna usually sat to eat lunch. He realized his heart ached to see her.

Their first date had been nice. She seemed genuinely interested in what he'd had to say, absorbing everything including the dinner and her surroundings. Blake pondered her innocence that was so charming. She was very gracious, too. But she had no clue about all these things. In fact, she seemed to be under the impression that she was completely unimpressive.

The quiet in the office pressed in on him, urging him to get done what he came to do. So taking a deep breath he sat back down, determined to finish.

Blake leaned forward and once again tried to concentrate on the documents he was reading. After another hour he gave up, picked up the phone and dialed Senna's number. No answer.

Her machine left instructions to leave a message.

"Hi. This is Blake. I was just thinking about you and thought I'd call…. Well, okay, call me back when you get this message." Then just before hanging up he left his cell number.

He hadn't expected to get the answering machine and was caught off guard. He wished he'd left a more enticing message.

He smiled as he thought about this curiosity. Who in this day and age still had an answering machine and no cell phone? What did that say about a person who felt no need to be in constant contact with their phone and Facebook and all things social? It was unheard of to find a girl who was not taking constant selfies trying to capture the exact perfect one.

With that thought, he turned to his computer and did a Google search on Senna. Nothing came up. Nothing at all. No Facebook page, that was no surprise. No, nothing. Well, not everyone has their whole life plastered all across the internet.

Old-fashioned came to mind. Old-fashioned, but in a sweet and charming way. He couldn't stop thinking of her and he knew he wanted to see her again.

AFTER FIVE LONG, hours Andrea and Senna stumbled into Senna's house with loads of shopping bags. They had gone to countless stores.

The bags pulled on Senna's arms begging to be dropped to the floor, but their weight only brought joy. She felt she was getting her footing. She knew she thought longer and harder about what to buy than most people did. Most people already knew who they were and what they liked. With each item she picked up, she had to stop and contemplate.

"What do you feel?" Andrea drawled out time and time again. "Does it make you happy?"

"I don't know," Senna would reply each time, deep in thought.

The dressing room had been an adventure. Even though Senna had a body and stature to die for, they often picked things that were just hilarious in the way they fit or looked once they were on. They had frequently doubled over in laughter.

By the end of it all, Senna had bought a ton of great things. Andrea talked to her about practical things for every day that would still be cute but comfortable. She showed her how to match things together and how to accessorize, also how to mix and match what she had bought.

And six pair of shoes! Senna had always loved shoes. Then there were purses and other accessories. It had started off slowly, but by the end, the gates had busted open and they were shopping with a vengeance.

Senna plopped into her chair. "I'm too tired to put it all away, but I can't wait to look at it all again. It makes me want to go in there and just grab everything I own and shove it into trash bags."

"Well, you just need to learn to put things together. The clothes you have on now are great clothes and just putting them together differently was all they needed. Don't throw anything out yet. I'll come over one day this week or next weekend and we can see how to work in what you have, with what you just bought."

They both sat for a bit, totally exhausted. "Okay, as soon as I can pry myself up from this sofa I'm going to go home and crash," said Andrea.

They laughed and talked recounting the day. Then, finally, Andrea picked herself up, but as she turned towards the kitchen, she saw the flashing light on the answering machine. "Hey girl, you have a message."

They both stood there as Senna played Blake's message. "Oh, my! He called you. He is hoooooked," Andrea said as she drew out the o's in a singsong way. Her eyes were big and her smile was wide. She was genuinely happy for Senna.

Senna felt a combination of sick and excited. She had no idea how to be in a relationship. She knew all men were not like Father, but how would she know?

"I'll leave so you can call him back."

"Call him back?" Senna replied. It surprised her that Andrea expected her to call him back.

"Yes, call him back! He asked you to please call him back."

"Okay. I will." Senna felt a knot grow in her stomach as Andrea walked out the door.

CHAPTER 8

"*D*id you call Blake?" Andrea asked first thing as Senna walked through the door the next morning.

"Good morning to you, too," said Senna.

"Well?"

"No, of course not!" exclaimed Senna.

Andrea stood there a minute watching Senna to see if she was telling the truth or not. "You really didn't, did you?"

"No. That wouldn't be appropriate." Senna was serious.

"But he *asked* you to call him," Andrea drew it out as if slowing the words down would help Senna understand them.

"I know. I don't feel comfortable doing that." Senna

120

busied herself with the books that had come in through the slot overnight. She was uncomfortable with their conversation and the topic of her calling Blake.

Andrea let it drop, for now. They both had plenty of work to do that day since they were getting a new shipment of books. They also had to pack up books which were to be removed from inventory and shipped back to the central storage facility.

At noon, Andrea suggested they place a lunch order at the All American and she would go pick it up. Senna agreed after only a moment's hesitation. It would be good to do something different for lunch rather than just sit alone with her typical sack lunch.

The smell of the fresh, hot burgers hit Senna's nose the moment Andrea came through the door and her stomach responded with an intense growl.

As they were sitting toward the back of the library eating their lunch, the front door chimed. Senna had finished her burger and offered to get the door. It was Blake.

"Hi there," he smiled as he saw her come around the corner.

"Hi," replied Senna. Tension shot through her body and she felt herself start to wring her hands.

"I left a message on your answering machine yesterday. I was hoping you would call me back last night."

"I know. I didn't feel comfortable calling," Senna's hands were sweating again, and she felt awkward.

Blake thought he understood. It fell right in line with her conservative behavior. "Well, I'm on my way to a meeting, but since I had to pass by here on my way, I wanted to just stop in and see if you were okay." It was good to just see her if only for a brief moment and he smiled.

"Oh, yes I am," Senna tried to dig deep to come up with something to say, but she was at a loss. She just choked up around Blake.

"Would you like to go out again?" Blake volunteered.

"Yes," Senna replied and gave Blake a smile before dipping her gaze.

"Great! I'll call you this evening around seven."

Senna nodded and watched as he walked out the door.

"Cat got your tongue," said Andrea as she emerged from around the bookshelf. She wore a teasing smile.

"I have no idea why I can't seem to find words to say to him. My mind just goes absolutely blank."

"You talked the other night on the date, right?" confirmed Andrea.

"Eventually. But when he got there, it was just like this. He did most of the talking but after a while I did relax quite a bit."

"It will be okay," Andrea patted Senna's shoulder. "He likes you. I can tell."

"Andrea, this is the first guy I have ever been friends with, gone on a date with, or even thought about having a relationship with. I am terrified!" Senna was serious. It was just that age old fear that she had known forever plaguing her now in a different way.

Andrea looked at Senna thoughtfully. "I never really thought about that. I can see why you have such anxiety about it." It all seemed so strange to Andrea. Even though Senna had told her about her childhood and home life, it was still hard for Andrea to comprehend how all that had formed Senna. Even though Senna was in her twenties, this experience was the same as Andrea had experienced in junior high school.

"Senna, everyone goes through this. Some are older than others when it happens, but everyone feels this way when they start dating. I can tell that Blake likes you. There is something about you, not the way you dress or fix your hair, but you. So, don't worry about it. Just be you. Eventually you will feel more and more comfortable."

Senna nodded as she picked up a stack of books to pack. Once again she felt the turmoil rage within her. She really did like Blake, too. How could she shut down the voices that tried to pull her back? No matter how encouraging Andrea was, she kept feeling waves of doubt and fear dragging her backwards.

Reading romance novels had given her such a vast array of relationship knowledge. Senna was smart enough to know that there was very little reality in those books. But then that left her even more doubtful about what to do.

Working on packing the books, she allowed her mind to remember Blake and their date. Thinking of that warmed her heart. He was so good looking, mannerly, and considerate. She could see that maybe, just maybe, he could be her forever love.

"Good morning," greeted Carrie as Randy walked in.

"Good morning to you, too," Randy replied.

"How was your weekend?" Carrie asked.

"Well, it was okay," he said with hesitation. "Just crap going on at home. Not really in the mood to talk about it."

Carrie looked at Randy getting a sense that she should not inquire further. "Sure. Well, yesterday I went back to the Big Horn and had a long talk with Pinky."

"Oh?" Randy gave Carrie a sideways glance. "You went by yourself?"

"Yes. I didn't want to bother you and I didn't feel I was in any danger. I thought about asking Darren to go with me but both of you have families and I didn't want to pull either of you away from that."

"Did you find anything?"

"Talked to Pinky again. He caught me in the room in the barn where they keep all the meds for the animals.

They have Ketamine, but that's no surprise. We talked for quite a while, but I didn't get anything new."

Randy stood at his desk, shuffling papers distractedly. Carrie wasn't even sure he had heard her, so she waited, watching him.

Finally, he realized she had finished talking and turned to respond. "Hmm?"

"You didn't hear a word I said? You asked me a question and then didn't even listen when I answered it." It irritated Carrie.

"Sorry." Randy was definitely distracted. Things weren't going well at home. It was cliché, but this job put distance between him and Sandy.

"Today all the hands are coming in for interviews. We have to be at Darren's office in about an hour. I told Pinky to send them to us in thirty-minute intervals so that would not leave them short-staffed at the ranch. They are coming in pairs, so I thought we could do the interviews individually and cover more ground."

A stuffy silence filled the air on the ride to Kachina. They arrived at the precinct only three minutes before the first two hands showed up. Thankfully, Darren had the interrogation rooms set up and ready to go.

The day was a repetitive grind. By midday, not one hand had anything new to contribute. They all loved Justin and Keith. And they had all appeared sad that they were gone.

About mid-afternoon one of the hands, Tad, let it slip

he had seen June McGivens and Justin a few times. He thought they were having an affair. He was the only one who had mentioned that so far.

Carrie didn't know if that was because no one else knew or because no one else wanted to divulge that nasty little secret. She wondered if that was what Pinky had been so tight-lipped about.

"Well, that was a big waste of time," said Randy. It was the end of the day and He was feeling disappointed they had found nothing.

"Maybe not," replied Carrie. "Tad told me he had seen Justin and June McGivens back behind the big equipment barn a few times, so I switched gears in my interviews. I found one other hand who admitted to having seen them. Motive?" she asked.

"Well, if Jack McGivens saw them, then yes. But what about Keith?"

"What if Keith saw Jack kill Justin? He would be a loose end." Adrenaline was starting to pump through Carrie and she was renewed with energy.

They both sat and thought the scenario through in their heads for a bit. It was plausible. The nervousness of June in that first interview could be directly related to their affair.

They both knew the very next person they needed to talk to was Jack McGivens.

~

RANDY MADE arrangements for Jack McGivens to come into the Kachina police station for their visit. Jack had not been at all happy about the request, but conceded anyway.

At approximately three that afternoon, Jack arrived, thoroughly disgruntled. Randy and Carrie chose to speak with Jack in Darren's office rather than an interrogation room. They hoped that the office would put Jack at ease where the interrogation room might create more tension.

"Thank you, Jack, for coming in to meet us today," Randy began while motioning towards a chair for Jack to sit.

"I don't know why you couldn't come out to the ranch. I am a busy man and I don't need to be coming in here wasting my day." His face was red, but from the sun or from irritation, they didn't know.

"We understand, but felt this would be more private," said Randy.

Jack met Randy with a scowl. "So what do you want?"

"We know that both Justin and Keith worked for you. What can you tell us about them?" Carrie asked.

"They were ranch hands. Pinky handled all of that. I met them when they hired on and worked with them from time to time."

"Did you have any complaints about them?" Carrie asked, she was itching to get to the real question she wanted to ask.

Jack considered Carrie for a moment before answering. "None at all," he said.

"How much interaction did your wife June have with the hands?" asked Randy.

Jack huffed out a laugh and said, "Next to none! I doubt she even knows most of our hands' names."

"So if I told you that there were witnesses to June and Justin in an intimate embrace back behind one of the barns, what would you say?" asked Randy

Jack sat stone cold as the question was being asked. Both Randy and Carrie were looking for the slightest tell of his true emotion. Jack's eyes told of confusion, but he quickly recovered. He was used to keeping a poker face.

"You're lying!" Jack replied. His neck was tense and his jaw was rigid.

"No, we aren't. We have two eyewitnesses who have individually stated that they saw June and Justin locked in an intimate embrace."

"Who the hell are they? They're fired," Jack was furious. It appeared the fury was more from an employee betraying a confidence rather than from the possibility that June and Justin had had an affair.

"So you don't think it is possible that what they said was true?" asked Carrie.

"Hell no!" Jack yelled then stood up. "I am done with this slanderous crap." As he headed for the door, Randy stopped him.

"Sit back down. We aren't done here yet."

"I'm done!" said Jack.

"No, you're not," said Randy. His look was stern, and it was evident that he was not going to let Jack get past him.

Jack reluctantly moved back to his chair and sat down, clenching and unclenching his jaw. His hard eyes bored into Randy.

"You may be telling us the truth, but with two eye witnesses we have to wonder if you knew they were having an affair and confronted Justin about it," said Randy, watching Jack closely.

"You son-of-a-...," the words hung heavy in the air, threatening. "My wife has never had an affair. I would know!"

Carrie shifted gears, "So who do you believe killed Justin and Keith?"

Jack shifted his stare from Randy to Carrie. "I told you I have no idea. I don't follow those hands around like a babysitter to see what they are doing. They are grown men. All I care about is that they are getting their work done."

Randy followed up with a few more questions attempting to re-circle back to the affair, but Jack was impenetrable. Randy finally conceded and ended the interview.

Once Jack had left, Carrie said, "I don't think he did it. I don't like him, but there was a moment of confusion when you asked about a possible affair."

"Yeah, I saw it," said Randy as he scrolled through his email on his phone. It deflated him. He knew they were back to square one and so did Carrie.

"Hey," he said with new hope. "Justin and Keith's cell phone records just came in. Looks like they each had a call not long before they died. Tech is tracing it now."

"Is it from the same number?" asked Carrie.

"Looks like it. This could be what we've needed."

"You know we need to talk to June McGivens again, right?" asked Carrie. "Even though we don't think Jack knew, there could still be something there."

"Yes, let's give her a call to come in. Jack would hit the ceiling if we went out there to see June while making him come in," Randy snorted.

WHEN JUNE MCGIVENS received the call to come into the station for an interview, her stomach knotted up tight and she thought she would be ill.

All the way to the station her mind flooded with worry. If Jack were to find out about her and Justin, she didn't know what he would do. His frequent rages over the smallest things were iconic. What on earth would this information cause him to do?

Soon, she was pulling into the parking spot and then walking into the station. They directed her to interroga-

THE BLOOD

tion room one, offered something to drink, and then left her to wait.

Randy and Carrie watched her behind the one-way glass for five minutes or so to determine her demeanor before going in to conduct the interview.

"No doubt she is nervous, even more so than the other day," said Carrie.

"I wonder if she has talked to Jack?" said Randy. He pondered that for a few minutes. *How would that affect their interview? If she had talked to Jack, then she would know we know about her and Justin. But if she hadn't talked to him, then she may still lie to us.*

"Okay, let's go see what she has to say," said Randy.

Both Randy and Carrie walked into the interrogation room and sat across the table from June. Randy laid the folder he carried down on the table. It was as much a prop as anything.

"Before we begin, we want you to know two things," began Randy. "First, that we know that you and Justin Thatcher were having an affair. Second, that Jack now knows as well."

June felt the color drain from her face. She felt deathly ill and light-headed. Jack would kill her, she thought.

"We have two witnesses who saw you and Justin behind the equipment barn on the backside of the property," said Randy.

"So now, you need to just be honest and tell us every-

131

thing. If you did not kill Justin, then you have no reason to lie or to hold anything back," said Carrie. She was looking straight at June and watching for even the slightest sign of emotion. The cool calm, but slightly nervous June from their first interview, was now replaced with a fearful June. Her face was pale and beads of sweat dotted her forehead.

June tried to wet her dry lips with her tongue. She felt as though her throat was so dry she couldn't force out a word. "Could I have a glass of water?" June asked. Her voice was small and quiet.

Carrie jumped up and went to the door. She cracked the door slightly and leaned out. "Sam can you get Mrs. McGivens a bottle of water? Thanks." She waited at the door and was soon presented with a cold bottle of water.

Once June drank at least a third of the bottle, she sat it down and began. "Yes, we were having an affair. It's not something I'm proud of. I'm not sure one just wakes up one day and decides that they will have an affair. It's just something that happens."

"So set the stage for us. How did it all start and why?" asked Randy.

"Jack was a good husband the first ten or so years we were married. But as each year came and went, he grew increasingly hungry for money and power. As that hunger grew, so did his anger.

"It was common when something did not go as planned for him to take it out on me, even though I had nothing at all to do with it. He likes control, absolute control. As the ranch grew, the need to depend on others and relinquish control to them also grew.

"He knew he couldn't do it all himself, so he stepped back. The problem is though, that to Jack, no one can do anything as well as he would have done it. He flies into fits of rage at whatever human target is in front of him.

"He trusts Pinky. That's the one and only person he trusts to this day. But even Pinky has to delegate as large as the ranching operation has gotten. Jack drank from time to time when he was younger, but as the stress of running the ranch and trying to maintain control grew, he drank more.

"His drinking has gotten to where he passes out right after dinner. When he is awake, he wants nothing to do with me except use me as someone to vent to and use as a punching bag.

"It's a lonely life." June looked down at the table before continuing. Both Carrie and Randy gave her a moment to compose her thoughts.

"After dinner, I often go for walks around the ranch. It's beautiful as the sun is setting. The hands are often outside the bunkhouse playing horseshoes or a game of cards on the bunkhouse porch.

"Pinky and I would sit and talk for a long time. He's loyal to Jack, but he knew what I was going through.

"Then one evening a few weeks ago, I honestly don't know the exact date, as I was sitting out there watching them, Justin came over with two bridled horses and asked me if I wanted to go for a ride. I hadn't been on a ride in a long time, so I agreed.

"When I was young, I rode all the time. I actually competed at Barrel Racing until I married Jack. When the kids were smaller, I would often go riding with them. But they are grown and gone now." June reached for the water and took another drink. Honestly, it felt good to confess all this to someone else.

"It began as a regular thing, Justin and me riding. He made me laugh, and I felt young again. It grew into more. One day we had ridden to the far northeast pasture, and we were walking our horses. As we were talking, he held me and then we kissed." A tear slid down June's cheek and she wiped it away.

"Jack was so caught up in his own world of running the ranch and drinking, I never thought he would find out. We were careful, but there were a few times when we would wind up behind the big equipment barn." June was riddled with guilt and shame. *How had her life come to this,* she thought? *How had she sunk so low?*

"If you are wondering if I killed Justin, the answer is a definite no. I cared deeply for him. I am so ashamed of what we did, but knowing him and being with him was a life raft thrown to a drowning woman." June was now looking at her hands resting in her lap, her mind far away.

Carrie asked, "If Jack is as angry and controlling as

you say, could he have found out about the affair and killed Justin?"

Before Carrie finished her question, June was shaking her head, "No, he didn't know, not until today, that is."

"How can you be so sure?" Carrie asked.

June looked up at Carrie. "If he had found out, Justin wouldn't be the one dead, I would be."

The remainder of the interview revealed nothing of substance that could help their investigation. Other than possibly Jack, they had no idea who would have killed Justin.

CHAPTER 9

*R*andy's phone rang as he headed into the office the next morning. "Hello," he answered.

It was Carrie already at the office. "Got a call this morning. A developer north of the city broke ground today on a new development. The land was dense with woods and as they began to bulldoze trees and brush, they found something that looked like a body, so they stopped and called the police.

"There were five bodies in all, and at first glance it appears that all five died from having their throats cut," Carrie waited for Randy to process what she had just said.

"Are you saying that these bodies could be tied to

Justin and Keith's murders?" asked Randy as he continued to process what she had just told him.

"It looks like it very well could be," replied Carrie.

"That means we have to rethink everything we've done so far. If those deaths are tied to the same killer, then this likely has nothing at all to do with the Big Horn Ranch. The killer could have just chosen their victims at random based on convenience." Randy wiped his hand across his face in frustration. "I'll be there in a bit and we can start from square one. He hung up the phone and hit the steering wheel with his fist.

In ten more minutes, he had arrived at the office and was making his way to his desk when Carrie met him in the hallway and said, "Let's go. The bodies are all at the Oklahoma County Morgue. We need to see if they can shed some light on whether we are dealing with the same killer."

Since they were at their OSBI headquarters in Oklahoma City, it was only a fifteen minute drive to the County Morgue. Two detectives from the OKC Police Department and the medical examiner were waiting on them to arrive before starting the review.

Detectives Morris and Brown greeted Randy and Carrie. They had worked a case together a year prior with a successful outcome. Carrie looked at Detective Morris' balding head and thought that, in the year since they had worked together, there was even less hair there than there had been. *Was it the job or hereditary,* she wondered, *or both?*

But Detective Brown was the one who had Carrie's real attention. She had been attracted to him since the day they had met. He was everything the magazines say you should like, tall, dark, and handsome; and he was single which was always a plus.

Henry Bloom, the medical examiner, hated to break up the sweet little reunion, but he had things to do. Five bodies lay on five separate tables in the room. They were in varying degrees of decay.

"As you can see we have five bodies all disposed of at various intervals. They are all male and have marks indicating that their throats were cut. There was no blunt trauma otherwise that I can see. We are running a full toxicology screen to determine what drugs, if any, were in their systems.

"I saw no signs of ligature marks on the hands and legs. The rate of decomposition is varied. The heat we have experienced this spring would have sped up the decay once they thawed from the cold, winter months. Of course, the bodies were dumped at random times so some were only out there during the spring. As I get more into my examination, I will be better able to tell dates and times of death.

"For now, I have the bodies laid out in the order I believe they died." Henry moved around the tables to stand at the first table on the left. "The oldest I believe died between ten and eleven months ago. The newest one I believe died between two and three months ago," he said as he pointed to the table on his far right.

Detective Morris explained to both Carrie and Randy as well as to Henry, "The bodies were dumped, not buried. The woods were thick and almost impossible to walk through. The trees were growing very close together and the sharp bramble vines were thick. They were growing all along the floor of the woods and up the tree trunks and in the branches of the trees."

Rick continued, "I can't see anyone carrying a body through that mess. We searched the perimeter of the dump and we could barely get through. The dozers, though, tore up the path we think the killer used to access the area. The foreman of the site said it didn't look to him like there had been any tracks or activity before they dozed, but he couldn't be sure."

"Could they have used a small ATV?" Randy asked.

"Possibly, but they would have still had to cut a path to go in very deep unless the trees were less dense where they dozed. The trees we saw were so thick that Chubby there had to go in sideways," Mike winked at Rick.

"Ha Ha. Very funny," said Rick. "But he is right, that was one heck of a dense area. The bodies were just thrown down and fell where they could. Some weren't even flat on the ground but leaning up against the trees."

"And there were scavengers. Apparently coyotes and birds don't mind the sharp brambles," Mike concluded.

"We have been working the two bodies we've had in Kachina. Until now we were under the impression that the killings could have been personal. This changes everything," said Randy.

"We will give you all we have," said Mike. "I think we should see about forming a joint task force to try to get to the bottom of this."

They all thanked Henry and left with his promise to expedite any medical or forensic findings.

They made plans while walking out, to coordinate information and plan for a task force, if their supervisors approved. They couldn't imagine that they wouldn't, given the gravity of the situation.

On the drive back to their office, Randy and Carrie were processing all they had learned and were attempting to readjust previous theories.

"Well, the dead end we thought we had with Jack McGivens seems to be just that. What on earth have we stumbled into?" asked Carrie.

Randy slowly shook his head, thinking. "I have no idea. When we get back, let's talk to Bracket about a task force. We need to call Darren in Kachina to let him know as well."

Carrie sat, quietly remembering the first day they had started this investigation and how she had wondered if this would turn out to be another serial murder. She felt sick. She had to muster up the stamina and fortitude that solving a serial case would take. Then, she felt a new determination to find this killer, before they could do any more damage.

BACK AT THE OFFICE, Randy and Carrie quickly met with their Supervisory Special Agent in Charge John Bracket, and succinctly gave him all the information they had just received.

Bracket readily agreed that a task force was necessary and agreed to assist in forming it. He led them down to a seldom-used room, large enough to hold the large conference table already in place, and as many white boards, computers, and chairs as they needed.

Carrie went straight to retrieving the files from the Kachina killings that she and Randy had been compiling. So far, there were two cardboard banker's boxes. While she was walking back, carrying the boxes, she could feel her phone buzz in her pocket, but with her hands loaded she refrained from answering.

"Here are the two boxes we have so far," Carrie said to Randy back in the war room, which it would now be referred to until no longer needed by the task force.

"Okay," Randy said. He was rearranging the room for a more efficient setup.

Carrie pulled her phone out of her pocket and looked at the missed call. It had been Mike Brown. Her stomach did a flip before she realized he was probably only calling about their case.

Mike answered the phone with a quick hello and dove in, "Our Lieutenant is in agreement on the task force. I am assuming you and Randy are already setting up a place. We will gather what we have and come on over."

"We have. Randy is arranging things now. I saw a few emails in my in-box I need to check. I think one was from the techs who are tracing the calls on Justin's and Keith's phones. Both Justin and Keith received a call from the same number right before each of their deaths. I know it is too much to hope for that it isn't a burner phone, but you never know."

"Well, we are headed that way. See you in a few."

Carrie went back to her desk and pulled up the email from the tech department. The phone was a burner phone and was now off and untraceable. "Of course," Carrie mumbled out loud.

She continued to answer emails and finish up paperwork while she waited on the two detectives to arrive. She disliked paperwork more than any other part of this job, but she knew it was important to get every detail recorded. You never knew what tiny item might jump out at you later when more evidence had been gathered.

"Hey there, gorgeous!" A voice came thundering through her thoughts as she typed. She looked up to see Mike's smiling face.

"Hey there yourself," Carrie grinned. She couldn't

help be a little flirtatious with Mike. She stood up and found herself standing very close to Mike, but he didn't move.

"I am going to like working with you again," he said. A dark curl accentuated his comment by dropping onto his forehead at that very moment.

"Maybe you will and maybe you won't," she replied, letting the double meaning hang in the air. She wanted to readjust that curl back where it had come from, but knew there were multiple sets of eyes on her, so she didn't.

"I was going to call after that last case, but you know how it is, I got busy," said Mike backing away from Carrie as she pushed him away with the tips of her fingers.

Carrie just looked up at him with a coy grin and led the way to the war room. "Here you go. Randy has set up all we have. Where's Rick?"

"He got a call in the car. He'll be right up."

Mike and Randy worked to lay out the victims on the white boards. For now they used gray silhouettes with a question mark overlaid for the five unknown victims. Just above their pictures, they had written the names of Justin and Keith while leaving the other five blank. Below each picture, they wrote the date and time of death, leaving room for the remaining five.

Rick bounced into the room out of breath. "Sorry about that. It was our Lieutenant with last-minute info. They had Sylvia run these victims against possible missing persons. She is sending us a few possible matches. You guys got a computer I can use?"

Randy got him set up with one they intended to use in the war room and Rick was soon logging on. Sylvia had sent twelve possibilities. They printed out a detail page for each, including a picture. They placed them on a separate white board until they determined who, if any, of these were their victims.

They spent the next hour going over details of the Kachina cases with Mike and Rick. They asked some great questions, but none that Randy and Carrie had not already asked themselves and either answered or tabled, hoping for more info.

The forensic team had taken molds of all the horse's hooves on the Big Horn Ranch but none had matched the prints found at Crown Rock Park. Without a direction to go, they set that aside. There were hundreds of horses in Oklahoma, everywhere you looked, so it would be like looking for a needle in a haystack, and may not even be connected. If they did come up with a suspect though, and they had a horse, then they could compare their horses' hooves to the molds.

Speculation on how the killer was able to leave no footprints or other forensic clues, was foremost in their conversation. They all agreed that bull-dozing the woods where the last bodies were found was a decided setback. The suggestions came up, though, that they interview the equipment operators and surveyors for the development to see if they could remember any details about the area prior to dozing.

The next detailed focus was to dig into the backgrounds of the twelve missing men. They wanted to have as much info as possible when the coroner came back with their report. The more info they had to compare it to, the easier it would be to make a match.

"I'll work on getting dental records from the missing," said Carrie. "We also need medical info such as surgeries, implants, or other similar physical characteristics for comparison."

They agreed on one thing as they parted: They wanted to find this killer before there was another body.

LAST NIGHT'S conversation with Blake kept playing over and over in Senna's mind as she worked. She thought she was getting more comfortable with Blake and that it was becoming easier to talk with him. Usually by the end of their conversations she had relaxed enough to enjoy it.

The stories Blake told of his life growing up and going to college fascinated Senna. He was a natural storyteller and as he told of his life; it was as if she were reading a really good book, only better because it was Blake. She smiled as she thought how he would become animated as he told tales of he and his brother going fishing and rafting down the river.

Senna thought of the crinkles next to his eyes when he laughed at his own tales, and how his hands would motion to demonstrate some unseen episode. She remembered just how sore she had been from laughing so hard; it was a new experience she couldn't wait to have again.

Little by little, day by day, she felt herself coming alive. The feeling of fear still crouched nearby, but she was driven by a determination to overcome it. No longer would the shackles she had been bound by hold her back. The more of life she experienced, the less the fear from her father's dictatorship held over her, but she felt anger creeping in and taking its place.

The urge to throw the stacks of books surprised her. But she stopped, shut her eyes and attempted to stuff this new feeling of anger down.

How could he have done this to me? Was a constant thought ringing through her now. How could he have stolen my life from me? She felt anger rise up again within her and flush through her body. When this would happen she would tamp it back down as the old fear would rise up to challenge and overtake the anger. Fear of dishonoring her father. Fear of the consequences of not obeying all the strong dictates that had been constantly pounded into her for her entire life.

Senna was working alone since Andrea had called in sick that day and had not come into work. For a moment she was wondering how her friend was. She thought she would call her on her lunch break, which she would take there in the library, but then reconsidered. If Andrea was sick, she would not want to be disturbed.

Senna knew her life was changing, for the better she thought. But if that were true, then why did she not feel more at peace? She was pushing forward to break free of invisible emotional and mental restraints, but there seemed to be even more turmoil than before. She constantly felt the fear and anger seesawing inside of her, replacing the previous complacent fear, which had only left her feeling dull and flat.

Which was worse? She breathed deep and knew this was better. She also believed that this was a process and that it would get better each day. It had to get better, right?

The front door chime rang and pulled Senna from her thoughts. The rest of the day was filled with work, library browsers, and the after school reading group. By closing time, Senna felt exhausted. She turned the key in the lock and welcomed the warm sunshine on her body.

Walking home, Senna was once again lost in her thoughts. So when two young boys on skateboards nearly ran her over on the sidewalk, it totally caught her off guard. Stumbling, she regained her balance. Then she felt anger rush up through her that was difficult to push down.

She remained standing against the lamppost that had

stopped her tumble. It was hot from its day in the sun and burned against her skin.

Senna noticed for the first time she was grinding her teeth and then tears welled up in her eyes causing her view to be distorted. She would have never felt such anger at two kids like this before. I am not strong enough to battle this struggle; she thought to herself.

Instead of noticing the beautiful day around her, as she continued home, she dwelled on the intense emotions which she had no idea how to control.

AFTER A HARD WORKDAY like the day she had just had, Carrie liked to unwind. The curiosity of the Darkside in Kachina had piqued her interest long before the day they did the interview with Ike. She liked the quiet, laid-back atmosphere, and more specifically, the *don't ask, don't tell* philosophy. She had her share of skeletons that she would prefer stayed locked away. The Darkside seemed the perfect place to relax, knowing those skeletons were safe.

Since that interview with Ike, Carrie had come on her own two more times, but not for work. She liked to drink, and she liked to flirt, and so she did at the Darkside without worry that a colleague would happen in.

Walking in at eight o'clock that night, she noticed that there were only about six people in the bar. The jukebox was playing an old 70s rock tune, and the room was only partially smoke-filled. She walked in and pulled out a barstool. Ike walked over and asked what she wanted to drink by only raising an eyebrow.

"Whiskey," Carrie said. There was no sense in beating around the bush if a person was going to drink, get drunk really. No need to play around right? Just do it. Isn't that what Nike always said, *just do it?*

In the first ten minute's Carrie had downed two whiskeys and was working on her third. She could feel the stress of the day was well on its way out of Dodge, replacing it was a slow fade into oblivion.

Movement to her right put Carrie on semi-alert. The cop in her could never completely rest. She didn't look, but shifted her eyes slightly to see who had walked up. It was a biker that Carrie had seen before but had never spoken to.

To Ike he said, "The usual." To Carrie, "Hey there. How're you t'night?" His ruddy face had seen too many days in the sun and had given his face a permanent deep red color. Craggy lines ran through his cheeks from his eyes to his mouth. His eyes were a faded blue and fine red lines disturbed the whites.

The do-rag he wore on his head, was black with a pattern of white skulls. His black leather vest was void of gang patches. It made Carrie wonder if he was a wanna-be or the real thing.

Carrie didn't respond immediately, but took her time wondering what he was about and why he had sat next to her when there were a dozen other stools he could have chosen. The obvious reason was that he wanted to *get to know* her. So her dilemma was what did she want to do about it? All of these thoughts sprinted through her inebriated mind before forming the response that would bring the outcome she wanted.

"Just gettin' a drink," she replied without turning to look at the biker.

"You want to play a game of pool?" *For all the elements of age that defined his face, his smile was genuine and nice,* thought Carrie.

After a few drawn out seconds, Carrie slowly sat her drink on the bar, then turned her stool to look full face at him. She looked him up and down without hiding the fact that she was. "You any good?" she asked.

He snorted and grinned, turning his head away, embarrassed. "Yeah, good enough," he said as he turned to look back at her, square in the eyes.

"Okay, let's play." Her double meaning hung in the air as she slid from the stool and worked to walk a steady line to the table. She picked up a cue and chalked it up, then used the stick to lean on. She needed it.

"Name's Gene," said the biker.

"Good to know," Carrie replied. She was not in a hurry to get familiar and if at all possible, she avoided giving her name.

Gene racked the balls and broke. He was stripes and

continued a couple of shots until his run ran out. He then stepped back to make room for her.

Surveying the table, she casually walked around until she spotted the best move. She leaned over the table, always seductively whether she intended to or not, and lined up her shot. Her tight pants stretched over her fit frame and her low top slipped down even farther as she stretched to make the shot.

She missed. The booze would have to wear off a bit for her to be steadier. She didn't care. She'd rather have the booze than win at pool.

As Gene ran a few more shots, Carrie began to see he was probably only a few years older than she was. He was attractive enough, stocky, but not too heavy. He would do.

It was her turn again, and she lined up her shot, pocketed that one and moved to find another. She knew Gene was watching every move she made and not on the pool felt. She liked the control over men that she had with her firm body and seductive moves.

Moving to take his next turn, rather than walk the short way around the table, Gene purposely crossed behind Carrie brushing up against her, placing his free hand on her waist.

This dance continued for the next several hours as they played and drank. Carrie kept her drinks spaced to reach that equilibrium where she did not lose complete control, but was still lost in the haze. When it was time, a look passed between them, they racked the balls and cues and left.

Carrie was not sure where they were going, but she didn't really care. It was another evening she would not have to be alone.

CHAPTER 10

*D*espite drinking and staying up late the night before, Carrie was at work early the next morning. The slight headache did not slow her down from reviewing each of the potential missing persons in order to add additional details to their profile. Dental records as well as medical records had begun to arrive in her in-box. She worked her way through to build solid profiles on each one.

The files were growing thicker. Uniforms in the OKC police department had canvassed the area around where the bodies had been found. A few possible leads had emerged that needed to be followed up, but it was slow going for the officers. Everyone wanted to glean information for gossip rather than focus on helping the officers.

The woods where the bodies were found was approximately a quarter section, one hundred-sixty acres, give or take. Across the road to the north was a housing addition behind a nice, tidy brick wall. To the east the same, with only more woods to the south and west.

It was not uncommon to have a housing addition, then acres of dense woods or farmland right next to it. This was only a partially developed area. Nice housing additions sprang up randomly in what had once been farmland or woods. There were still many undeveloped areas separating most.

The area around where the bodies had been found was a nice suburb where families came to shelter their children from cruel people and events. Carrie was sure they were all mortified that bodies had been found so close to them. She was also sure that Realtors' phones were ringing this morning and for sale signs were quickly appearing within a mile radius of the dumpsite.

Reading through the reports, she noticed that one officer reported that someone had heard, then seen, what appeared to be a small utility vehicle in the woods. This type of thing was often used on ranches to haul things short distances or to traverse rough terrain.

Carrie's father had used one on their farm to haul salt blocks out to the cow pasture. They were four-wheelers, but not like the traditional recreational ones. These often had actual seating and a bed to haul things in. Attachments were also available to accomplish tasks such as digging, moving, and mowing.

Carrie's mind began to race as she envisioned what could have taken place. Her rise in blood pressure pushed that slight headache aside and her mind began firing on all cylinders.

If this was true, then that would explain how someone could get the bodies into the woods. If the woods had been less dense on the side where they had dozed, just removing a few of the smaller trees would have allowed this type of vehicle to get in there and back out again. She knew those ATVs could navigate over very rough terrain.

There were two witnesses stating they had seen this vehicle, but had no recollection of the person driving it. They had witnessed from over a half mile away on a moonlit night. They did however, remember the vehicle appeared to be camouflage, most likely green in color.

She sat to attention as her fingers began flying across her keyboard in order to research four wheeled ATVs that came camouflaged. She had been lost in the world of ATVs for about twenty minutes when Randy came through the door to the room. By the look on his face, it had been another hard night. Carrie thought it best to give him some space until he settled in.

Randy flopped into his chair and turned on his computer, still not speaking to Carrie. The fronts of their desks faced each other with only a short cubicle wall between them so they sat face to face, eye to eye.

Her gaze flittered from her computer screen, which sat at an angle on her desk, to Randy and back again. When she couldn't stand it anymore, she commented, "Rough night, again?"

He looked straight at her over the top of the divider. "I am sick and tired of getting the third degree every single morning when I walk through that door."

"Woah! Just askin'," replied Carrie. Looking back to the research on her computer screen, she was boiling inside. *How dare he talk to her that way? She had only been concerned about him,* she thought to herself.

The inability to focus while attempting to push down her anger at Randy, almost caused her to miss the ATV she realized might be the one that had been seen at the body dump.

Excited, she printed out pictures and details of the ATV so she could pin it to the whiteboard in the war room. "What's that?" asked Randy.

"If you hadn't been such a crap this morning, I would have told you," said Carrie.

"OKC officers found two witnesses to an ATV coming and going in the middle of the night around the body dump. The only thing they could say was that they thought it was camouflaged. This is the only one I have found that could be it. I am going to post it on the white-board, then we need to get verification from the witnesses if this might be the one they saw."

When he didn't comment, she continued, "I sent the

pic to Rick and Mike. They are going to go re-interview those two witnesses and ask about the pic. Maybe they can get more info from them."

Randy still hadn't commented. He had his head down at his phone reading something on the screen. He had been in a bad mood almost every single morning for a week. When anyone asked about what was wrong, he would bite their head off. She wasn't even sure he had heard a word she'd said.

Carrie went back to her computer screen and looked through her in-box, finding another email from the forensics department. They had categorized and labeled all the trace bits of fiber, lint, and other debris found at both crime scenes. Reading through the list Carrie found nothing unusual or out of the ordinary, except for one thing.

At the second scene they had found a tiny bit of blue vinyl. The report read, *Poly tarp fragment. Poly is short for polyethylene. Polyethylene is a synthetic polymer: a plastic polymer of ethylene. Most poly material is used for the manufacture of containers, packaging, and electrical insulation or in this case poly tarps. Polyethylene tarps a.k.a. Poly tarps are made with polyethylene, nylon tarp threading inside the material with a rope reinforcement around the perimeter of the poly tarp material...* Carrie glazed over at the next bit which was filled with the chemical components of a poly tarp.

A blue, poly tarp. That made sense to her. If the killer had placed the victim on the tarp to cut his throat that would catch the blood. Then they could use the tarp to roll the body down the hill by pulling the tarp up and towards them, thus rolling the body forward.

Carrie continued to read. *Low-density polyethylene (LDPE) is the most widely used of all plastics, because it is inexpensive, flexible, extremely tough, and chemical-resistant. LDPE is molded into bottles, garment bags, frozen food packages, and plastic toys or in this case polyethylene tarps a.k.a poly tarps.*

Extremely tough and chemical-resistant. Carrie rolled this around in her head and she began to visualize what the killer might have thought or seen. It was tough enough that a heavy body would not tear it and it could be cleaned with strong chemicals that would not harm it.

The killer could have placed the victim unconscious, on the tarp. Then cut his throat, containing the blood on the tarp, at which time they could have rolled the body up and loaded it onto the ATV using its wench system, then drive to the dump sites. Once there, they would unfurl the tarp, depositing the body on the ground.

Sounds good in theory, but a body is heavy, thought Carrie. Then she thought about the first body in Kachina. It had been on the ground and the blood had pooled beside it. No tarp had been used.

"Randy I really need to run some things by you," said Carrie. She didn't care if she sounded short or irritated with his lack of communication and interest. "If you can't have your head in the game when you come to work, maybe you need to take some time off."

"At least I don't come to work with a hangover several times a week," Randy's eyes bore into Carrie. She stood with her mouth half-hanging open, speechless.

SAC Bracket's voice boomed through the room, "Jeffries and Border. In my office now!"

Both Randy and Carrie walked towards the SAC's office like two children summoned to the principal's office.

"Sit down!" Bracket's voice roared. When Randy and Carrie had each taken a seat, he continued, "What on earth is up with you two? Fightin' like you're married or something. Get over it!" His voice bellowed even louder.

Carrie flinched from the vocal onslaught. She was still reeling from Randy's comment about being hung over. She sat with her legs crossed and her elbow on her her chair in such a way that her back was half turned to where Randy sat.

"Spill it, now." SAC Bracket stood behind his desk with his hands on his hips. His face was red and his eyes were like laser targets at the two of them. Carrie fully intended to let Randy begin the conversation. "Well?" he insisted.

Carrie glanced sideways at Randy who just sat stone-faced. His jaw was clenching and releasing, but he was silent. Finally Bracket took a breath and sat down attempting to provide a calmer atmosphere to the room.

He hoped it would diffuse the tension and encourage them to talk.

"I don't know what is going on with the two of you. For the last week, well almost since you started this murder investigation, you have both been increasingly piqued toward each other. I want to know what it is about, and now."

Finally Randy looked down for a second before looking back at Bracket. "Sandy wants a divorce."

Carrie's head jerked around to look at Randy. She'd had no idea. He'd never said a word. "Why didn't you tell me? I'm your partner."

"Exactly. You are my partner, not my therapist," Randy spat at her.

His words stung and Carrie was hurt to the core, so she sat back in her chair and just looked at the edge of Bracket's desk in silence.

"Hey, Jeffries, I am so sorry to hear that," Bracket's voice was much softer now. He knew what divorce was like, he'd been through two. "Do you need some time off?"

"No," Randy replied. "Not right now anyway." Randy squirmed in his chair. The discussion made him very uncomfortable. The last thing he wanted was a divorce.

Bracket looked over at Carrie. "What about you?"

Carrie looked up in surprise. "What do you mean, what about me?"

"I mean, what has been up your craw lately?" Bracket asked.

Carrie's mind raced, attempting to search for clues to what he was specifically referring. Neither he nor Randy were *her* therapists and Carrie wasn't about to start divulging details of her private life to either of them.

"Okay, okay. I can see that this isn't going anywhere productive so I'll just say that the two of you had better get your heads straight and work this case like your own lives depended on it. You got that?"

Both Randy and Carrie nodded their heads and mumbled in agreement. As they were leaving SAC Bracket's office, Carrie looked at Randy and said, "I really am sorry."

Randy nodded in an attempt to say thank you. Then Carrie continued, "I really do need to go over some case stuff with you. I think we finally have some new clues to go on, and I need your opinion about some things," the hint of excitement in Carrie's voice made Randy smile.

He blew out the personal smoke from his mind so he could focus on the case. As they walked to the war room, Carrie filled him in on all she had learned so far that morning.

Just before they entered the war room that booming voice came rumbling back through the room, "That's more like it!"

ANDREA WAS FEELING COMPLETELY WELL and was back at work the next day, chipper and excited for whatever the day held.

"You're in a good mood today," noted Senna. "I thought since you were sick yesterday you would still be feeling bad."

"I think it was just a quick stomach bug. I woke up feeling great this morning," replied Andrea. "How was it here at the library yesterday?"

Senna looked at Andrea in a way that conveyed, *really, you had to ask, same as every other single day.* They both broke out in laughter.

Senna watched Andrea as she went through paperwork checking to make sure it was all complete and correct. She pondered about Andrea and the continual and deep joy she saw radiating from her. She wondered where it came from and how did you make it your own.

Happiness was one thing. She had been experiencing that more and more lately with Blake and Andrea. But what she saw in Andrea was something else, something deeper.

Senna still internally roiled with turmoil. It seemed that, yes, she had experienced more happiness, but fear and anger had come out from somewhere deep inside her to challenge it. The result was a horrific toxin of emotions.

It also seemed that she was less in control of her emotions than ever before. A good example was the anger she felt rise up in her over the boys on the street. Before she even realized what was happening, it had overtaken her. She did not like feeling out of control.

"Andrea, can I ask you something?" asked Senna. She paused momentarily as she tried to form the right question. The knot in her stomach was growing the more she hesitated.

"Sure, what?" asked Andrea while still scanning through her paperwork.

She took a deep breath and began, "I'm not even sure where to begin. I have felt much happier lately. Both you and Blake have brought friendship into my life that I've never had before. It's changed me so much and it's nice to feel that happiness." Senna paused collecting her thoughts.

"But...," Andrea had looked up from the paperwork to give Senna her full attention.

"Before, I felt I had a firm lid on my emotions. It is true I never felt much of anything, maybe sadness. But learning to laugh and cry with you seems to have opened a Pandora's box of emotions, not just the good ones." Now that she had started, words began to tumble out from within her.

"Yesterday when I was walking home, I nearly got run over by two boys on skateboards. I literally had to grab the light post to keep from falling. They were just playing and really didn't mean anything by it. But I suddenly got so angry. Then I thought of my father and got even angrier, so much so that I started grinding my teeth. I have never felt that way before." Senna's face was pinched with deep lines of concern.

Andrea listened to her friend. Internally she was quietly contemplating, praying what to say to her. She knew her friend was fragile and she wanted to say the right thing.

Senna continued. "I feel happy one minute, then fearful the next, and then angry. There is such a cauldron of emotion inside of me like I've never experienced. They don't just rise up and quietly say 'hi', they violently fight for attention." Senna mimicked incredulity as she ended her sentence.

A customer walked up to the counter just then, so the conversation had to be tabled. Andrea walked back to the office to file her paperwork. The bright light of the computer screen glowed before her and it took her a moment to realize she needed to login. She was so lost in thought over what to say to Senna. Slowly she continued to the library system to file her monthly reports.

Her thoughts were on Senna though. It seemed the beginning of an outward change had caused a drastic internal conflict. She was not a psychologist and really had no idea what to say to Senna. For someone who had gone through the abuse and torment that Senna had, it would probably be best if she went to see a counselor or therapist who could give her the right support, the support specific to her needs.

Her monthly report didn't match what it should, so she shifted her concentration and became lost in figuring out where the error was. It was lunchtime before she thought again about Senna and her problem.

Leaning back in her chair the thought that she should see if she could find a good counselor to recommend to Senna came back to her. Andrea knew just presenting the suggestion to go to a counselor without presenting an actual person to call, would not be a solution.

Sitting at her desk staring across the room, she thought of someone she knew that she could email and ask for recommendations. She quickly sent that email right before she stopped for lunch. Hopefully, Senna would not feel she was intruding in her life. *It may have never occurred to her to seek professional help with what she is going through*, Andrea thought.

With the email sent Andrea went out to see how things were in the library. She doubted that Senna had been overrun with customers while she had been attending to paperwork. Wednesday mornings were typically very slow.

"I finally got all that paperwork done for the month," Andrea said. She was relieved to have that monthly part of her job out of the way for now.

"Everything is fine out here. We only had one lady come in to see what was new in the novel section." Senna was dusting bookcases and furniture.

"What did you have planned for lunch?" asked Andrea.

"Well, I brought my lunch, but honestly I am kind of tired of bringing my lunch every day. I've been doing that for so long that I can't bear to eat the same thing day after day any longer."

Andrea chuckled, thinking she would have grown tired of it long before now. *This was a welcome change in Senna's life*, thought Andrea.

"How about a pizza?" asked Andrea. "I heard the Razorback Corner bought a pizza oven and is making pizzas now. I thought it couldn't hurt to try one. How does that sound to you?"

It didn't take much thought from Senna, "Sure, sounds good. You pick, I'm willing to try whatever you think looks good. Here, I'll get you some money for the whole thing if you will go pick it up."

"Sure!" exclaimed Andrea.

With lunch plotted and planned Andrea left and Senna continued with her cleaning. This job provided an enormous amount of time to think, *sometimes too much*, thought Senna as she made sure she didn't get sloppy in her dusting routine.

Today she was thinking about the changes in her life, and how nice they were. She was also thinking how she wished the person she was on the inside would match up to what she was becoming on the outside. She knew

Andrea was seeing a new Senna, and it was true, much had changed.

But inside, she almost felt more broken. It seemed as though new emotions, thoughts, and considerations were invading her internal workings and messing with all the things she had thought to be certain. It was as if these new intruders were sticking up the gears of her mind causing them to disengage and falter.

She snorted to herself, thinking how stupid it all sounded. But this was new territory for her and she honestly had no idea how to navigate it. Maybe she should talk to Andrea about it. Would her friend be disappointed in her? She didn't know, but knew she had to do something. The new inside was tearing the new outside to shreds and she couldn't keep going on like this.

Just then the bell on the front door rang and in walked Andrea with the pizza. "I got Spinach Alfredo with chicken. Sound good?"

"Oooh yes," Senna's mouth was watering from the smell of hot pizza.

Andrea took the pizza back into the office and sat it on the little table she had in the corner of the room as Senna followed her. When Andrea walked into the room, she noticed that she had a new email in her in-box. She thought about the request she had sent to a friend asking about a recommendation for a counselor.

As they ate, Andrea was distracted by how to best

approach Senna with suggesting she talk to a counselor. She knew her friend had been through so much and didn't want to hurt her further, but she really felt she needed someone else who could really help her through this.

"It seems like something's on your mind. Do you want to talk about it?" asked Senna. Maybe she could help her friend by listening to her for a change.

That was an open door, thought Andrea. She looked at Senna for a minute longer attempting to form the perfect sentence. "Yes, there has been something on my mind. First, let me say how proud of you I am that you have been courageous enough to try new things and are trying to break free from your difficult past. I admire what you have been able to overcome. I don't know that I would have been able to do it."

"But..." Senna felt like a brick wall was about to fall on her.

"But, I think maybe you are only partially there. I feel you have come so very far, but that there is still a way to go and I don't know how to help you get there." *There, it was out*, thought Andrea. Good or bad, it was out there. She half-held her breath waiting for Senna's response.

There was no change on Senna's face as she thought about what Andrea had just said. It seemed ironic that she herself had just been thinking about managing her feelings and where to go from here.

"You know how I hate talking about myself," replied Senna.

"Yes, I know," she used a soft voice when she replied to her friend. Senna looked sideways and down at the floor, thinking. Andrea sat waiting, she didn't want to push.

Senna thought to herself about needing to take yet another step forward that seemed so very difficult. She knew if she didn't keep pushing through this emotional quagmire, though, she would never come through it completely. But she didn't know if she had the strength to let one more person into her pain, her past, her heart.

Andrea reached across the table and rested her hand gently on her friend's wrist. "Senna, I only make the suggestion because I care about you deeply. If I had the ability to help you through this I would, but I don't. I will stand beside you and be here for you to confide in. But there are things from your past that you need an experienced professional to guide you. Someone who has experience in helping people put these kinds of things to rest; hopefully, once and for all." Andrea's eyes were sympathetic but pleading.

Senna smiled at her friend and a tear slid from the corner of her eye. She nodded quietly. That quiet agreement spurred more tears to flow softly down Senna's cheeks.

Andrea reached out and hugged her friend. "I know it will be hard at first, but you will see that each time you talk about it, the better you will feel. Someone who knows how to handle this, can help you learn how to release your past so you can truly move forward."

Wiping her eyes with her fingers, Senna said, "But I have no idea where to start. Where to find the right someone."

"If you would like, I can get a recommendation from someone I trust." She didn't want to tell her friend that the recommendation was probably already sitting in her in-box. She was concerned that Senna would feel hurt that Andrea had gone ahead without asking her first.

"Yes, I trust you to help me. If you trust the recommendation, then that is good enough for me." Senna took a ragged breath and wiped the remaining tears from her face. She was no longer hungry and just sat staring at her plate.

Finally Senna smiled and took another bite. They continued to eat their lunch until the front door chimed. Andrea got up to see who had entered as Senna sat reflecting on yet another bend in the road ahead.

THE COURTROOM in downtown Oklahoma City was cold when Blake first arrived. The throng of bodies that would soon challenge the AC system had not yet arrived. Today was the final day of trial when he would give the closing argument for his client.

He knew he had done all he could do, or he thought

so. No matter how much effort, research, and planning he put into these cases, or how clear his client's innocence seemed to be, he could never shake the overwhelming doubt about how twelve jurors would decide.

Lawyers were professionals at portraying confidence on the exterior while hiding the insecurity which raged within them. Blake knew most of them would never admit that they were just trying to play the best hand presented to them, hoping that their hand was the winning one. Blake thought, *everyone tries to appear to the world like we know we have the winning hand and are so skilled at acting genuinely surprised when we don't.*

On the first and last day of a trial, the days he would give his opening and closing arguments, he always arrived early. He liked to sit in the quiet and feel the courtroom. He would often slowly pace in front of the jury box mentally rehearsing his argument.

At his first trial, he had not done this. He had planned to arrive about ten minutes before court was set to start. He did just that, but the traffic had been a beast, and he'd had to juggle his briefcase, coffee, and extra files—unsuccessfully; so when he finally sat down in his seat, he felt as tight as a piano string with no time to calm himself and focus.

Ever since that day, he made it a point to arrive extremely early so he could have the courtroom to himself. The drive would usually be quiet because the normal commuters were not yet out. He would enjoy the easy drive, listening to music that helped him feel stronger and ready to take on the day.

Criminal defense was not the glamorous life that it was portrayed on TV. He firmly believed in the US Constitution and the concept that all people deserved a fair and speedy trial and, above all, to have their side heard in a court of law. As noble and glamorous as that sounded, it was often messy and uncomfortable.

In law school, he naively held the firm resolve that he would only defend innocent people. His righteous and moral indignation initially pushed the guilty into a category he did not want to pull clients from. But somewhere along the way, his heart had changed.

First of all, it was incredibly difficult to tell whether someone was guilty or innocent. But more than that, as he sat and listened to guilty people, everyday people like himself who had done the wrong thing, he'd found compassion.

True, there were hardened criminals who just didn't care about right or wrong, or who they hurt. But so many that came to him for legal help had just lost their way. And most were repentant and already paying an emotional penalty far more painful than what a state or federal incarceration would enforce.

In time, he grew to believe this was a calling. Blake was in a place to extend love and acceptance to these people at their lowest place in life. He gave them the very best legal defense he could in the courts, but he also extended to them an ear to listen, somehow letting them know they were not alone. He wanted each client to know he cared because he did care.

Today, his client was a young woman who had been abused as a child. When she was a teenager she had found solace in relationships with men. She had felt what she thought was love when boys desired sex from her. There had been no one in her life to teach her about her worth as a woman, or that love was the exact opposite of what she was undertaking.

Now, at twenty-three she had been discarded by more men than she could count. The deepening black hole in her soul had led her to drugs in an attempt to make the pain go away. She was broken and used, and when Blake looked at her, his heart broke.

She was guilty of selling narcotics to the undercover officer, but it was Blake's hope he could get the judge to recommend a minimum security treatment facility. He hoped to one day see her healthy and whole.

The Assistant District Attorney the case had been assigned to hated to deal. When he knew the jury would see obvious guilt, he always pushed for the maximum he could get. Blake was sure he had an actual scoreboard set up somewhere that he added hash tags to with each win.

So they went to court. Blake would have loved to spare his client the ordeal, but then maybe this particular hard time would help her in some way. He had bought her a few changes of clothes for court out of his own pocket. She had cried when he gave them to her and she sat fingering the soft new fabric of each piece. He wondered how long it had been since she'd had something new, or since someone had shown her a true act of kindness.

His assistant Mandy had met him there each morning and helped his client with her hair and a tad bit of makeup. Each day he had seen a chipping away of the hardness which she had used to block out the world.

Blake had seen hope in her eyes. His only hope today was that he would not see that hope shattered if he could not get her the help she needed. It was a lot of pressure, but he didn't carry the weight alone. It was his faith in God that had brought him this far and it would be that faith which would give him the power to do the best job he could do for her.

The sounds of people entering the courthouse increased and Blake looked at his watch. It was time for his client to have arrived in the holding room. He gathered his things and headed that way.

Mandy was just beginning to start with his client's hair. He could tell that she realized the reality of what this day held. She gave it her best attempt to smile, but it was faltering. As she watched Blake pull out a chair and sit down, she was trying not to cry.

"Mr. Burton, I want to thank you so much for all that you have done for me. I know that they may decide that I have to go to prison instead of treatment, but either way I won't do those drugs any more. I am truly scared about prison, but I feel stronger having had you here with me."

"You just remember that you are not the bad experiences and wrong choices you've made. You are a woman of worth and you have a hope and a future. No person or prison can take that away from you," Blake held her gaze to make sure she heard what he was saying to her. He truly wanted her to know there was hope beyond this moment.

Back in the courtroom when they were all in their places, the judge brought the court to order. Through the course of the morning, Blake gave his closing argument. He could deliver it with sincerity about his desire to rehabilitate his young client. He spoke of the unfortunate evils of prison life and how low the stats were for positive rehabilitation. After an hour, he sat down and gave the floor over to the judge.

The prosecution came out with guns blazing. This was his last opportunity to get the jury angry and indignant at the young lady at the defense table. He spat vehemence out when describing her and that she was just one more of society's ills and how we needed to protect our youth from such as she.

Blake could tell the ADA's words were having a hard effect on his client. He quietly patted the hand she had resting on the table. He was careful to draw firm lines between himself and his clients when it came to physical contact, but there were times compassion dictated it was necessary.

Finally, the day was done and after the judge had given jury instructions and they had exited for deliberation, Blake spent a few moments expressing hope and encouragement to his client. She would be taken back to jail until the jury had reached a verdict and he would not see her again until then.

By 7:00 p.m. that evening, he had received word that the jury had reached a verdict. They would reconvene the next morning at 9:00 a.m. for the reading of the verdict and sentencing.

CHAPTER 11

The tension was high in the court as the jury filed in to read their verdict. Blake's hands were sweating, and he was exercising extreme discipline to remain externally calm.

His client sat rigidly still beside him while his assistant Mandy sat on the row directly behind him. She usually left after helping prep for court, but today she wanted to be there for moral and emotional support should the verdict return unfavorable.

"All rise," the bailiff boomed.

The judge took his seat at the bench and rapped his gavel. He asked the defendant to rise and then requested the jury foreman to read the verdict. Blake felt his client slip her small thin hand into his. He did not pull away but gave it a gentle squeeze.

She was found guilty as they knew she would be; however, by the end of court, the judge had ruled that she be admitted to the facility that Blake had recommended, but added specific stipulations and specifications which the judge hoped would ensure the greatest success for her rehabilitation.

The relief that Blake, his client, and Mandy felt was undeniably overwhelming. The judge had stated that she be checked into the treatment facility by five p.m. that day. In the meantime, she had been relinquished to Blake's custody. Should she not arrive by said time, a warrant for her arrest would be issued and she would be incarcerated in the state prison.

For the first time, Blake saw a broad smile spread across his client's face. It was just about lunchtime, so he suggested that they all three go to lunch.

During lunch, they all felt free to laugh and enjoy the relief of the sentencing. Near the end of the meal, Blake looked seriously at his client and talked with her about the severity of the bullet she had just dodged, but more importantly the new opportunity that had been provided to her. As compassionately as he possibly could, he wanted to be stern about the seriousness of what was at stake here.

She nodded and listened intently. He believed she had every intention of giving this her full effort. But Blake knew there were so many factors that would determine her long-term success. No matter how much resolve his client had, if certain lifestyle changes weren't made, then success would be short lived.

He spoke to his client of an organization that helped women just like her transition from the treatment facility back into a better life. They offered an education, housing, and opportunities to volunteer in various other charities across the city. They'd had great success, and he was hopeful for his client.

After lunch, they made sure she had everything she would need at the treatment facility. The clothes he had bought her for court were not the kind of clothes that would be casual and comfortable for everyday. He knew of a charitable closet where they could take her and allow her to pick out several things she needed. They took her by her old apartment as well.

Mandy went inside with her and helped her collect the most important items. She got toiletries, a few additional clothing items, and photos and mementos. They had agreed she would not return to this apartment after treatment. A new life truly meant a new life. The more difficulty the old crew had finding her, the better.

A letter would be written tomorrow by Blake to the apartment complex, once his client was safely in the treatment facility, stating the situation and that they could re-lease the apartment.

The rest of the day flew by and before they knew it, it was time to say goodbye. Blake and Mandy stood and waved goodbye to their client as she entered the facility, exiting her old life and entering what they hoped was a fresh new beginning.

As they turned to walk to the car, Mandy said, "This one turned out well."

"Yes, it did," said Blake.

"They don't always," she said.

"No, so many rarely do."

ON THE WAY back from the treatment facility, Blake felt happy and realized that the one person he wanted to share it with was Senna. He dialed her home phone, and she answered on the second ring.

Senna happily listened as Blake shared his day with her. He was so excited about the outcome of the trial that he had been working on for the past week. She loved it that he cared so much for his clients and loved helping them change their lives for the better.

Blake and Senna had gone on three dates total. The last week, Blake had been absorbed in this last case and it had limited their time together. Senna's concerns that Blake would be like her father faded a little more every day. Blake was nothing like her father.

Being kind to her was one thing, but Blake was kind to everyone. She saw genuine concern for each client he had. He didn't just want to win the case; he wanted to achieve an outcome that would benefit his clients in a profound and lasting way. This alone endeared her heart to Blake.

"I want to take you out to dinner tonight," said Blake.

"Well, I don't know how much I'll eat. Andrea and I ate until we were stuffed on that new pizza from Razorback Corner. We've had it twice this week. It's great for a glorified convenience store."

"I ate a pretty hefty lunch, too. Mandy and I took our client out for a victory lunch. How about I pick us up a couple of salads and we take them to the park and eat?" asked Blake.

That sounded good to Senna, so they hung up after planning on Blake picking up Senna at her house at seven o'clock.

Senna went to her closet full of new clothes and picked out a pair of white pants and a pink top. Then, thinking the white pants would not be good for a picnic, she put them back. Remembering the navy capris, she found and pulled them out. *Yes,* she thought. *Those will look very nice together.*

Andrea had helped her a few times try to find a good balance between her natural good looks and makeup, but Senna still felt somewhat uncomfortable when putting it on. Because of this she usually stuck to a slight bit of pink blush and lip gloss.

She had found, though, that she had a love for shoes. Who knew that had been hiding in her all along? She laughed to herself as she slipped on the sandals she had bought just for that pink top. They were the same soft pink with floppy leather flowers all across the front strap.

A few strokes with the brush through her hair and she thought she was ready. She was excited to see Blake. Smiling, she remembered the night of their first date when she had paced a path on her living room carpet waiting for him. Butterflies were still a given, but not the anxious knot that she'd had then.

Blake soon came and they found a great shaded spot by the fountain at the park. He'd even thought to bring a big quilt to lay down. As they ate, Blake continued to remember and tell her things about the trial and his client. He expressed his hope she could stay on a positive path.

Blake's face reflected the excitement he felt and Senna quickly became caught up in that excitement. His hair was flying in the wind but he didn't even notice as he spoke with passion. Nothing as exciting as that ever happened at the library.

Soon the salads were gone, and the wind in Blake's sails seemed to have settled. They were sitting facing each other on the quilt and Blake had Senna's hands in his, playfully toying with her soft fingers. He could smell her soft scent and he took her in, lingering on her eyes.

"You've changed so much since the first day I met you," said Blake as he studied her vivid blue eyes.

Small dollops of sunlight danced through the leaves and onto the quilt. Rather than look at Blake, Senna looked down and watched them dance. She had tensed slightly at his words.

Looking back up at Blake, his smile soothed her. "I know I've changed. Andrea has been so wonderful to me, such an amazing friend. And you, you've helped me to feel comfortable with me," she chuckled as she thought how funny that sounded.

Then her brow creased. "There is something I want to talk to you about," she said.

"Sure. You know you can talk to me about anything."

Senna looked down at their intertwined fingers. "Andrea has suggested that I talk to a professional counselor." She looked up to see what Blake's reaction would be.

"Why does she think you should do that?" asked Blake with concern on his face.

Senna looked away and her face pinched in thought as she tried to organize her thoughts. "Things have definitely changed for the better with me. But some things seem to be worse," she said. She was trying to explain to Blake what she had a hard time sorting out on her own.

"I used to just accept what my father and mother had said and done as gospel, something that was correct and right and necessary. Something that had been in my best interest for me and that they had done for me out of their love for me.

"The more I see how much more there is to life and I see what was kept from me growing up, I have begun to feel angry. I am not talking about the material things that were kept from me, even though there was a lot of that, but emotional things. Love, happiness, joy..." her voice trailed off.

"I lived my life—afraid all the time I was not going to measure up by Father's standards. I tamped down personal desires, hopes, and dreams in an effort to conform to his standards. I think I became so successful at pushing down emotions that I only felt numb.

"Now it is as if stepping out and beginning to feel again has unleashed not only great emotions like happiness but also anger. It catches me off guard and I don't know how to respond.

"The other day I was opening a jar, and it slipped and splattered everywhere. I felt outraged! Not just frustrated, or a little upset, but outraged. Blake, it scares me."

She had finally said all she could think to say. Blake sat and lovingly looked at her for several moments before speaking. "I think what you are going through is a natural reaction to what you have had to deal with. You've never learned how to handle various emotions. I think Andrea may be right, I think you need someone trained to help you navigate through this.

"You have already changed so much for the better. I can only imagine that with just a little help you can change and grow even more." Blake smiled and leaned in to kiss her.

It was at that moment he realized he had fallen in love

with her. All at once, a surging need to comfort, protect, and give himself to her in whatever way she need overtook him. He was careful to not let her see it though. He could see she was in no emotional place to reciprocate those feelings. And with the wounds she carried and the healing that must take place, it would be awhile before she was whole enough for that.

Senna searched Blake's face and knew she wanted to love him. She felt so safe and comforted when she was with him. But until she could reconcile the tide of emotions within her, she knew it was not possible. It wasn't fair to him either. He deserved to be loved fully, without reserve.

"I feel so broken," she said. Her words were soft and frail. "I feel ashamed that I am this way, that I am not stronger."

"But you are stronger than you think. You have courageously made great strides to change and break free and you have done so amazingly. It is not your fault you must break free of all this. It was something done to you, not something you chose.

"And just remember when you start to feel angry at your parents, they were human, too. I heard someone say once that hurting people hurt people. I don't know what your father experienced, but you have to know that he had been hurt and damaged himself at some point. He must have been far more broken than you for him to have treated you and your mother the way he did."

Blake took a breath and continued, "You have to forgive him Senna. Un-forgiveness is poison. It will eat your insides out, but never touch its target. For your own sake Senna, forgive." His eyes were soft, yet pleading.

"I-I want to. I just don't know how to," said Senna.

Blake had a thought he'd had several times, but had held off asking her. He didn't know when it would be the right time, but maybe now was.

"Senna would you consider going to church with me on Sunday?" He held his breath. Would this push her away from him?

After a brief moment she started shaking her head. "No, no I can't do that. I've had enough church to last a lifetime!"

"I understand," said Blake visibly disappointed.

Senna realized what she had done. She'd pushed him away without meaning to at all. "Well, I will think about it."

Blake smiled and leaned in to kiss her once more. He wanted to lay her down on that quilt right then and there and make love to her, but the immense amount of respect he had for her quickly pushed that urge aside. Someday she will be my wife, he thought. I know she will. I hope she will.

CHAPTER 12

*C*arrie had another hangover. The sun coming in from her bedroom window felt like stabbing daggers through her head. She groaned and rolled over.

She'd gone back to the Darkside again. Something kept drawing her there. But each time she found herself less and less able to gather her wits about her to pull herself together the next day for work.

I need a vacation, she thought. I need a full week of nothing I have to do and nowhere I have to be.

Her mouth was dry, and she wished she had the energy to get up and brush her teeth. But she didn't and soon drifted back off to sleep.

Ninety minutes later, an annoying buzzing sound penetrated her hazy sleep. At first, it was faint and only a slight intrusion into her dream. It increased to the point she couldn't avoid it and she found herself fully awake.

She reached for her cell phone and looked at the screen. It was Randy. Oh, my goodness! What time was it? Nine in the morning. Oh crap! She scrambled out of bed and threw on some wrinkled clothes she found on the floor. Snapped on her badge and gun, which she had failed to lock away in the safe, and headed out the door.

As soon as she started her car and was pulling out of her driveway, she called Randy.

"Where in the hell are you?" he asked.

"I'm on my way. I overslept. I don't feel too well this morning." She immediately wished she hadn't said that. He was always on her about her drinking. She knew saying 'not feeling well' would be translated as 'hangover' by Randy. She had brushed her teeth, gargled with mouthwash, and was now cramming gum in her mouth. Would it be enough?

"I'll be there in twenty," she was able to add before Randy could start his lecture on the evils of the lifestyle that she was living. In her opinion, though, he didn't have much room to talk. After all, if Sandy wanted a divorce, how good of a husband could he be?

Soon, she was pulling into her parking spot and locking her car door. Her reflection peering back at her from her car door window looked a little rough. She did a quick finger comb of her unruly curls and thought, good enough.

Randy was waiting on her just inside the door. "You stink," he said. "You didn't shower did you?"

"Are you going to start with me again?" She hadn't showered since she was so late but the stink she knew Randy was referring to wasn't body odor, but ketoacidosis from having drank so much in such a short period of time. She had smelled it on her uncle many times, it was unmistakable. If Randy smelled that, then she'd crossed a line last night that she tried very hard never to cross.

"I'm sorry. I'll go to the locker room and shower," she said. She kept a change of clothes and toiletries in her locker. With this job you never knew how long you would be out.

In less than thirty minutes, Carrie was showered and dressed. She felt better and wished she had taken the time to have done that at home. She avoided eye contract with Randy as she came to get him to leave.

"I'm ready. Where are we going?"

"The coroner has matched four of the five bodies with dental records of the missing persons. In other words, we know for sure four of the five unknown victims. We need to go visit the next of kin," said Randy.

Carrie felt ashamed that she had almost showed up in the shape she had been in to victims' homes. How disrespectful. She had to get herself together.

Randy and Carrie rode in silence to the first victim's home. Randy stopped a block away in a convenience store parking lot and put the car in park. "Since we didn't have a chance to go over details of the victims this morning, I'll brief you on this one.

"Ken Burns, male, five feet nine inches tall. Dark hair, green eyes, worked as a bank teller. Lived at home with his mother. She is the next of kin that we need to notify."

A lump rose in Carrie's throat. She did not feel up to this today. "We'd better go," she said.

No one answered the knock on the door. In reading the file they read a note that Ken's mother worked as a teacher. She wouldn't be home until after three. Randy put that file on the bottom of the stack and they looked to find one that might be available during the day.

When they reviewed David Brasher's file, they saw he was married with two small children. Wife Cindy and he were in the final stages of a divorce.

"Oh boy," sighed Randy. "I hate doing these."

As expected, Cindy did not take the news well. Even though she and David were getting a divorce, she still loved him, and he was the father of her children.

Randy and Carrie gave Cindy time to take a breath and let the news soak in. "Mrs. Brasher, we have to ask you some questions in order to find out who did this to David. Are you up for that right now?" asked Randy.

Cindy nodded her head in agreement. She sat dabbing her tears with a twisted up tissue. She was quite attractive but her yoga pants were not as flattering as something else might have been.

"Is it fair to assume that since you and David were getting a divorce that you were no longer living together?"

"That's correct. He had an apartment. The address was 2417 NW Blanchard St., Apt. B9."

Randy jotted the address down in his notebook. For the next hour, they asked as many questions as they felt Cindy could stand. Truthfully at this point, knowing so little, there were few questions to ask. It felt as though they were starting all over again with the discovery of the new bodies.

By three thirty, they were back at Ken Burns' mother's house. It was almost more than Carrie could take, seeing his mother collapse from distress. This was too many notifications to have to do in one day. Her heart was breaking for this poor woman.

They helped her to a soft chair and brought her a glass of water. They inquired about someone to call and made that call to her daughter, Ken's sister.

By the time the daughter arrived, they had completed their series of questions and left the two ladies to grieve alone.

"How are things with you and Sandy?" asked Carrie on the ride back to the office.

"She has filed for divorce, but I'm trying to get her to consider counseling," said Randy.

"Isn't that like shutting the barn door after the horse gets out?" asked Carrie. She knew it sounded insensitive, but couldn't work up the wherewithal to care.

Randy knew exactly what she meant. It was like that, and he was furious at himself that he had neglected the signs, neglected his family, and neglected Sandy. "Yep, it is."

"SENNA, here is the name I was able to get for you, if you are still willing to go see her," said Andrea not long after Senna arrived for work that morning. She handed Senna a piece of notepaper where she had written the information she had received in the email.

"Thank you," Senna said, somewhat uncomfortably. She knew she had agreed and Blake had confirmed that counseling was the best thing for her, but now that she was faced with taking that step, she wasn't sure she could.

Senna stood and looked at the note that Andrea had handed her. The card read: Dr. Marion Specter, MD, 18759 North Radial Avenue, Oklahoma City, OK. And the phone number 405-555-3344

"She's a medical doctor?" Senna asked Andrea.

"She's a psychiatrist. A medical doctor with a specialty in psychiatric medicine."

"I thought you were going to get a name for a counselor, not a shrink." Senna was caught off guard when she felt anger rush through her.

Andrea saw Senna's face get red and her body tense. "It doesn't mean anything. She's just really good. Please don't read more into it than is there," Andrea pleaded with her friend.

When Senna saw the worried look on Andrea's face, she tried to stuff her anger back down. Her friend was only trying to help, but still... a psychiatrist.

"I guess I am crazy," said Senna.

"Please don't say that! A psychiatrist is not just for what people consider crazy. They are there to counsel and help. Please Senna, I don't think you are crazy!" exclaimed Andrea. She cared about her friend deeply and she was concerned that she had crossed the line with her. Andrea knew when she read the email, and saw that the recommendation was a psychiatrist, that Senna might be offended.

Senna remembered the night before with Blake. She could tell he cared for her and he agreed that it would be good for her to talk to someone. If there really was a chance for her and Blake to make it, she had to keep moving forward. Finding someone on her own was not an option. She had no idea who to call or where to start.

"You're right. I overreacted. I'll call her," Senna said and smiled at her friend. "I'll call right now." Hesitation showed in her slight smile and her quiet voice.

Senna did call and stammered through the preliminary questions the receptionist asked when making the appointment. She wasn't sure when she had felt more vulnerable and uncomfortable.

"Actually we've had a cancellation. If you can come this afternoon at three, Dr. Specter can see you then."

Senna's mind raced. She was not expecting such a quick appointment. Closing her eyes and taking a deep breath, she agreed.

"Okay," she told Andrea, "I have an appointment at three this afternoon if you will be okay to work here alone until the volunteers get here.

"That's awesome," Andrea said as she reached out and gave Senna a side hug. "It really is. You can always talk to me, but what your father did was abusive. I don't have the right words to say to help you heal. I am sure Dr. Specter does."

The remainder of the day at the library was pretty ordinary. They'd planned a book drive at the local school that would be coming up next week, so both Senna and Andrea worked to make sure everything was done for that.

They had put out flyers and sent out email invitations to their email list. The school had called and asked for more cards to send out in the students' weekly folders, so Andrea took the cards to the school.

Finally, a little before two o'clock, it seemed as though the rush had stopped and Andrea and Senna could sit for a bit before Senna had to leave for her appointment.

Senna had been thinking about something Blake had said the night before and kept trying to put it aside, but she finally thought she would bring it up to Andrea to see what she thought.

"Blake asked me to go to church with him this Sunday."

"Oh, cool! You know we go to the same church, right?" Andrea was immediately excited. She'd never asked Senna to come with her to church because she knew she'd had a bad experience with church and wasn't sure what she would say.

"I told him I wouldn't go," said Senna.

Andrea deflated. "Oh." Andrea started to ask why, but she knew.

"The thing is, I can't get it out of my mind. I think I should go because he asked me to. I don't want to disappoint him."

"Why don't you just try it one time? Tell Blake that you will try it for him and just see how it goes. I can promise you it will not be like what you experienced as a child."

Senna looked at her friend with skepticism. She felt bombarded with new things. New everything. She needed her life to slow down. "I'll think about it."

"Oh," Andrea squealed, hugging her friend. "I am so excited. I have wanted to ask you for the longest time." Senna thought Andrea was literally bobbing up and down.

Not in Senna's wildest dreams could she ever imagine why anyone could be that happy about going to a religious meeting to get yelled at for all the wrong things you were doing or might do. But she was growing to trust her friends, so she thought she might try it.

Senna hurried to leave. She was not familiar with where the doctor's office was located, so she wanted enough time to find it. Andrea had helped her look on the computer on a map, but Senna didn't have a smart phone or any type of GPS. She wrote the directions down on the note paper Andrea had given her with the name and address.

On the way to the appointment, Senna's mind was flying out in a thousand different directions. The anxiety she felt was palpable. Several times, the thought crossed her mind to just cancel and go back home, but she kept seeing Blake's face. That handsome, compassionate face with love in his eyes kept urging her forward.

The office was empty when Senna arrived and a receptionist helped her with paperwork to fill out and asked her to be seated to wait. Very soon, she was shown into the room where she would meet Dr. Specter.

It was a nice, comfortable room, Senna observed. It felt more like a little living room than a doctor's office. She was sitting on a nice blue sofa that was soft to the touch.

Dr. Specter entered the room from a door on the other side of the room. Senna stood to greet her and was met with a kind face. The doctor was about forty-five and attractive. She was dressed casually in a blue skirt and white blouse.

The interview began subtly as if it were just two friends chatting. Senna knew this was to help her to relax and become more comfortable with the doctor, and it helped, to a degree.

Dr. Specter explained that the sessions were a process and for Senna not to feel she had to dump everything out at once. They would take their time and explore things one at a time, hopefully gaining healing step by step.

For this session, Dr. Specter had Senna just talk about why she had made the choice to come to her at this time in her life.

Senna couldn't tell if the room had grown hot or if it was her anxiety causing her to feel as though her skin had caught fire. There seemed to be an impenetrable barrier between her tongue and those first words.

Finally Senna began to explain how she and Andrea had become friends, and the changes that Andrea had helped her make. Then she stopped to gather her thoughts wondering what to say next.

Dr. Specter calmly and patiently sat and waited for Senna. It was not uncommon for patients to work their way through what they wanted to say in their minds before they could actually say it.

Senna looked at the rug under feet. It was shades of blue that matched the sofa. There were swirls of other colors and Senna's eyes followed their path. The chaotic pattern created a thing of beauty. She felt the chaos on the rug resembled the chaos in her mind. She wondered if her chaotic life could ever become a thing of beauty as well.

Finally, Senna told Dr. Specter about her childhood just the way she had told Andrea. It seemed a bit easier this time. The more she talked, the more comfortable she felt with Dr. Specter and, all too soon, their time was up.

Dr. Specter brought the session to a close giving Senna encouraging words that she was on the right track and that they would continue until she was able to reconcile her past with her present. She encouraged Senna to set weekly appointments, to which Senna agreed.

"You know, I was offended when Andrea gave me your information and I saw that you were a psychiatrist. I had agreed to talk to a counselor and was stunned when she gave me the name of a psychiatrist." She stopped for a moment then added, "I'm not crazy, you know."

SENNA AND BLAKE were going to go to a movie and eat out that evening, but she felt so drained from the day she wasn't sure she had anything to give to Blake.

It felt comfortable telling the doctor what she had told Andrea and Blake, but now she just felt drained and agitated and had no idea why. The thought crossed her mind to call Blake and cancel their date, but Blake always had a way of calming her and helping her feel better about things.

She thought again about going to church with Blake on Sunday. The coincidence was interesting to Senna that both he and Andrea went to the same church. The thought made her feel sick inside when she remembered going to church growing up. How could she go back to an archaic institution that had helped to damage her when she was just now starting to heal? She just didn't think she could do it.

Blake and Andrea had become the two closest people in her life. When she looked at them, at their lives, she could not reconcile the condemning and judgmental church she had known with what she saw in them. How could they thrive in that kind of environment? What made them want to?

The more she thought about it, the more curious she became. Finally she decided that she would go out of sheer curiosity and for no other reason. She could sit through it one more time, just as she had done countless times in her youth. She wanted to watch Andrea and Blake as they sat there and were told just how bad they were. She wanted to watch their faces and see their reactions.

Once home, she lingered in the shower. She had grown to enjoy the act of selecting outfits and getting ready for work and dates with Blake. For most of her life, choosing clothing and getting dressed was just another chore to be done. If it had not been for Gran, she would have never realized that there could be enjoyment in it.

The shower felt warm and soothing against her skin. The driving droplets helped calm her anxiety and she could feel the tension flow from her body. Outside she could hear the kids in the neighborhood laugh and play and she smiled. She made the decision right then and there to no longer grieve for what she had lost, but to live for what was ahead.

Soon Blake arrived, and they agreed that they were both very hungry and that dinner should come before the movie. Blake's choice was low-key and quiet. He enjoyed Senna's company so much that the typical noisy places caused too much distraction and certainly hindered conversation.

During dinner, Senna felt the courage she needed to talk with Blake about church.

"I've given it a lot of thought and I have decided to come to church with you," she said.

Blake was shocked, but tried to not let it show. He'd been hoping that she'd change her mind, but didn't think it would happen so soon.

"I would love that," he said.

"Just once. I'll come just this one time," she was adamant. She didn't want to set up expectations that this was the start of her routinely going back to church. It was important to her that he knew and understood that this was a onetime thing.

He smiled at Senna. Once was enough because he knew if she took the chance to do it once, she might take the chance to do it again. "I'm thrilled and I do understand that this is a onetime deal. I do not want you to ever feel pressure from me to go to church."

She could sense his sincerity and felt much better about her decision. It set a comfortable tone to the remainder of the evening. Dinner was great, and the movie was fun. The evening seemed to end way too soon for both Senna and Blake.

Standing on her doorstep yet one more time, Blake was exercising self-control. He had never felt such passion and desire for a woman before. His physical desire was almost overwhelming. But he had chosen to be celibate until marriage, a point of view pretty much unheard of in this day and age. But the respect he felt for Senna helped hold him to that commitment.

Blake wondered what Senna thought and felt about sexual intimacy. He assumed that with her strict upbringing it was ingrained in her the evils of sexual relationships before marriage. But he also knew that some old teachings taught that it was never to be enjoyed even by a husband and wife. He had a feeling that was just what she had been taught. Someday he wanted to talk with her about all of that, but tonight was not the time.

They stood close together. Blake had his arms around her pulling her close to him. Senna's arms were folded in and resting on Blake's chest, with her head resting on his shoulder. She was soaking in the comfort that is arms gave her and never wanted that feeling to end.

Blake could smell that beautiful scent that was uniquely hers, a combination of shampoos, lotions, and other things she chose just for herself. Her head laid on his shoulder and her hair which was done in a loose braid, had fallen to the side. Her neck was bare and beckoned for him to kiss it, and he did, gently at first and then more passionately.

Senna felt a surge of desire rush inside her. She both loved and hated it. It was yet another new emotion in her life to reconcile. But she felt herself surrender to the feeling. She looked up at Blake and his lips found hers, first simply then passionately.

Soon Blake pulled away so he could regain his composure, looking her lovingly in the eyes the entire time. He did not want her to think he was pulling away from rejection, but out of respect. She'd had way too much rejection in her life.

He rested his forehead on Senna's. "You drive me crazy," he said. His voice was low and soft.

Senna once again didn't know what to say. She didn't know what was appropriate to say, so she stood quietly in Blake's arms.

"I think I should go now even though it is the last thing I want to do," said Blake.

"Sunday evening my family is having a cookout. I want you to go with me. I want them to meet you." Blake's voice was excited.

Hope dominated the gaze he gave Senna, but with everything else going on in her life she just wasn't ready. The look on her face told Blake what he knew was true. It wasn't time yet.

"I want to, but I don't know if I'm ready. It's only been two weeks since my world started to change so drastically. Two weeks. I'm overwhelmed, Blake," her eyes were pleading with him to understand. "I need to catch my breath."

Blake was disappointed, but he understood. The last thing he wanted was to rush her. She was healing, he could tell, but that could all change if he pushed for too much too soon. She would be going to church with him on Sunday and that was a huge hurdle.

The awkward moment passed quickly when Blake gave her one of those huge smiles and kissed her. He took her back into his arms and held her. "I don't want to rush you. I am so thankful for all the changes you've been willing to make. Take your time. There's no hurry."

Senna felt relieved. She felt like she was navigating new territory every single moment, with each word having the capacity to topple this wonderful new life she was experiencing. So each time she spoke what she felt, she didn't know if she would be accepted or rejected.

Blake finally pulled away, kissing her one last time and saying goodnight. He waited until Senna was safely inside before he walked to his car and drove away.

THE ROUGH MORNING had not been enough to deter Carrie from another night out. She once again found herself at the Darkside.

The place was unusually full. She found an empty stool at the bar and ordered her usual whiskey neat and motioned for another before the other was all the way down. The warmth of the amber liquid was familiar and welcoming.

After the second drink, she turned to survey the crowd. It seemed all the usual people were there and many more just like them. She watched the pool room as several cowboys laughed and played pool. *Nice looking men*, she thought.

Over at a table in the back were the regular bikers, but a few new, younger faces, as well. *Hmmm, that's intriguing*, she thought. Then scanning the room, she noticed a man about her age sitting alone at a table near the back. A very nice looking man.

She wondered what his story was. Could he be drowning his sorrows after a breakup? A good-looking guy like that couldn't be desperate for female companionship. It looked to Carrie that he was oblivious to the rest of the room. She thought he needed company, her company.

Just before sliding off of her stool, she ordered yet another drink to take with her. She didn't want to show up at his table empty-handed. He never saw her approach and only looked up from his drink when she was standing right next to his table.

"May I sit down?" Carrie asked.

He looked up at her, disinterested. She'd broken his dark concentration. Before he could decide what to say, she'd sat down across from him, drink in hand. "Suit yourself," he said, then looked back down at his drink.

Carrie felt a weird tingling in her 'cop senses' which usually put her on high alert. The alcohol, however, had dulled them considerably.

She sat watching him for a while as she slowly nursed her drink, not saying a word. He was very interesting to her. He seemed out of place here, but yet somehow still at home.

"I'm a good listener," she said.

He looked up. "What makes you think I need a good listener?" he asked. His voice was neutral. He did not appear irritated at her question, but he also didn't appear as though he wanted to continue the conversation.

Maybe Carrie should just leave him alone and find someone else to entertain her. No, she thought, he would be a challenge. She decided he would be her fun for the night.

She sat her drink down on the table and resting her arms there, leaning forward. Her blouse slipped low showing voluptuous cleavage that had never been turned down. She had used it often to get what she wanted.

"I think you're deep in thought. By the look on your face, the thought you are deep in, is pulling you under," Carrie said.

He looked at her. Her face and her body. Nice, he thought, very nice. But what did she want, he wondered? He had his own problems and didn't need another needy female adding to them.

Almost as though reading his mind, Carrie said, "Hey, I don't want anything but a good time. I want to enjoy tonight and not think about tomorrow."

He thought about her words while watching her face. Did she mean it, he wondered? Why not? What did he have to lose?

He picked up his glass to indicate they should toast. Carrie smiled and picked up her glass.

They talked very little. Carrie had as little interest in getting to know him as he seemed to have in her. Finally, when she felt she'd put her time in with small talk she asked, "Do you want to get out of here?"

He did. He was sufficiently drunk and ready to do anything at that point.

They walked out to the parking lot with Carrie

leading the way. About two feet from the car door, he stopped with a start.

He couldn't believe the car he was about to get into. He'd never ridden in something like this, but had always wanted to. He looked from the car to the lady standing on the other side. What was up with her? A beautiful woman in a small town seedy bar driving a Porche. It didn't fit, but oh well!

They were soon tucked inside the soft leather feeling the roar of the engine underneath them. With sweet intoxication still lingering, they rode in silence for several miles.

Finally he asked, "Where are we going?"

"I have a spot," she said and looked over at him once again giving him a seductive look.

They were driving on a small highway, going north away from town. With each mile there were fewer and fewer businesses, houses, and traffic. The man didn't care and eventually closed his eyes, drifting off.

Then the crunch of gravel beneath the tires jarred him awake. He had no idea where they were. He'd sobered up somewhat, but still didn't have his full senses about him.

"Where are we?" He asked looking around. They were in a very wooded area and had been traveling down a long gravel road.

"I said I had a spot," replied Carrie. "I don't like people in my business. This is an old family cabin that I use sometimes. It's quiet here and no one will see us or bother us."

She parked the car around back in a detached shed she used as a garage. She opened a small compartment in the car and pulled out a separate set of keys that were just for the cabin.

When they entered the backdoor of the cabin, the man saw that it was clean and cozy. There was no electricity, but it had been fitted nicely with gas lanterns, one of which Carrie lighted immediately upon entering. The lanterns filled the room with enough light to see, and the low light was quite enticing.

The cabin had a living room, one bedroom, a kitchen and a bathroom. All rooms looked as though someone lived here from time to time. "You live here?" he asked her.

"No, it is just a private little getaway when I can't take the stress of the city anymore," Carrie said as she finished lighting that last lantern.

She walked over to a cabinet where she kept a liquor stash. She uncorked a bottle and poured them each a glass. The man took his glass and drank it down as did Carrie. They each felt a refreshed surge of heat and intoxication.

He sat his glass down and walked over to her, putting his arms around her. The embrace led to passionate kissing and fondling. Very quickly, the man became very aggressive. Carrie pushed him away.

She gritted her teeth and glared at him. She was the aggressor, not him. They were to play her game and follow her lead, not the other way around.

But no one had told the man the rules of her game. Carrie's rejection had only fueled the anger he had been trying to overcome earlier in the evening. He would not be denied. She wasn't going to set this whole thing up and then stop him cold.

He grabbed her and pulled her so tightly to him she had no room to fight back. Then his mouth found hers and the mutual aggression soon led to rough passion.

Carrie was so drunk by then she didn't care.

CHAPTER 13

*I*t was late afternoon before Carrie came to consciousness. Blinding pain shot through her entire body. It wasn't the normal pain of a hangover. She couldn't even open her eyes. The light seemed so bright it blinded her and she felt an incredible pain throughout the rest of her body.

She laid there with her eyes closed. She tried to remember where she was and what she had been doing the night before, but nothing came to her.

Void of memory, she attempted to determine where she was. Beneath her hand she felt a rough wooden floor. She smelled sweat and vomit. It was repugnant but she couldn't move to avoid it.

She felt like she would be sick and when her body violently convulsed to reject what was no longer in her stomach; she felt something snap. She gasped as what must have been a cracked rib, actually snapped in two.

The pain was so severe that she could hardly breathe. Each slight movement, even her lungs taking in air, shot her with unbelievable pain.

It was then she also realized her left eye was swollen completely shut and her right eye, almost. As she lay there on the cabin floor, tears dripped one by one out of that eye and puddled in the dust.

She wished she was dead. The grief of her life flooded through her. It had all led to this. Why wasn't she dead? Why hadn't he just killed her?

It must have been at least another hour that she laid there. She had no desire to move or to live. A warm sensation between her legs caused her to realize that she had just wet her pants. She didn't care.

She drifted back to sleep. Maybe this time she wouldn't wake up.

WHEN CARRIE once again opened her eyes, the light was fading. She was stiff and sore, and still alive. She wasn't sure if she felt disappointment or relief.

Choices had to be made. She could continue to lay here and hope she finally died or she could get up.

Being so constricted by pain, she laid there a little

longer. Her body was in no shape to move, but her mind was finally fully alert.

It forced her to think. Think about her life and how she had gotten to this horrifically low point. This horrifically, shamefully, low point. Tears once again began to drip from the corner of her eye.

She had to decide to live. And if she did live, she had to come to terms with where her life was and where it was going. It was evident that all she had to do to die was to keep living the way she was. It would lead her straight to the grave if that was what she wanted.

If she wanted to live, she had to stop all this. Then sobs wracked her broken body; as painful as it was physically, the pain inside was greater. Waves of shame and remorse flooded her, hitting her hard, wave after wave. She felt as though she were drowning and had to move. She sucked back the sobs and tried to stuff down the pain.

From somewhere deep inside, the faint will to live, picked up its head ever so slightly. It was afraid to come out. Living would mean there would have to be major life changes, changes that would be hard, very hard.

But she *was* alive. Why, she didn't know, but she had to commit fully one way or the other, so she would live.

Clearing her head, she continued to lay there attempting to assess her situation. She knew physically she was in bad shape. She knew at least one rib was broken and probably more. She had been beaten, but had there been more?

As she took a mental inventory of her body beginning from her feet, she came to realize with surprise that she had not been violated, only beaten. She was still fully clothed, even though her clothes were ripped and torn.

She felt relief and gratitude, a genuine gratitude for the first time in many years. She was going to live, and she wanted, really wanted, to live differently. With gratitude came hope, and she breathed a small prayer, "Help me. Help me, please."

Calm blanketed her. She felt peace for the first time since she had been a young child. She could do this. She wanted to do this.

Instinct kicked in. She hurt, but the only critical physical place she needed to protect was her ribs. She held her left arm across her mid-section. She was lying on her right side and that arm was numb clear to and including her hand.

She tried to roll to her back very gently, then to her left side. Needles immediately assaulted her right arm as the blood rushed back through. She could feel the ribs grinding and the pain was so intense she thought she might lose consciousness. Once on her left side she stopped to take a breath and allow the feeling to come back fully in her arm. She would need it to help pull herself up.

Rolling over had put her smack up against the bed.

She was in the bedroom and lying on the floor next to the bed. She decided she would reach up and use the bed to pull herself up.

Using her right arm, she reached up and grabbed the covers on the bed, pulling hard. Her left arm continued to hold her mid-section. Just as she thought she was making progress upward, the covers slipped, and she fell back hard to the floor.

The pain took her breath away yet again. But she had resolve now to live, so after only a brief moment, she thought she could pull then press on the bed frame to leverage herself up.

It worked! She was up on her knees beside the bed. "Thank you," she said to no one. Her voice was barely audible even in the silent room.

She still needed to muster the strength to get all the way up and then out to the car. There was no landline in the cabin and her cell phone was in the car.

As she sat kneeling beside the bed, she thought that this time when she would sink her body into those precious leather seats, she would be filling them with her dirty body covered in stale urine and vomit. She didn't care. She wanted out of here and out of this life.

The pain finally subsided enough that she could use her right hand to push herself up enough to get her wobbly legs underneath her. Standing upright relieved some pain that she had felt while lying prone on the floor.

She slowly shuffled to the bedroom door. The eye less swollen had opened more in the last few hours. It allowed her enough vision to see the door and the way out.

Keys. She needed keys. *Had she brought them in with her or left them in the car?* She couldn't remember.

In the living room, she glanced around to see if she could see any sign of them. The room was in disarray. A faint memory of a struggle teased her mind. All but one lantern had burned out completely and with the night coming on, it was dim in the room.

Standing in the doorway she could not see any sign of the keys. She didn't feel like she could walk the room looking for them in this much pain and in this much mess.

They had come in from the back through the kitchen. Maybe she had left them in there. She used the wall to steady herself as she made her way to the kitchen, her left arm still across her midsection protecting her ribs.

By now it was almost completely dark, and her swollen eyes made it even more difficult to see. She drug her hand across the countertop to see if she could feel for them.

Suddenly a sharp blinding pain sped through her hand. Broken glass. In the struggle they had broken at least one glass and maybe the bottle. A chunk now protruded out of her hand.

Carrie took a deep breath releasing her other hand

from her side and moved to pull out the glass. When she did, blood rushed out. She had to find something to wrap around it. There would be a towel hanging by the bath-room sink.

The towel was hanging right where she remembered, which was good since it was dark in the bathroom. Carrie wrapped it the best she could around her cut hand. She stood bracing herself against the sink to gain enough strength to continue.

She tried to think hard about the keys. The car. She thought she remembered leaving them in the car. She hated to walk all the way out there only to have to come back. But if she could get to the car, her cell phone would be there even if the keys weren't.

The loudness of the woods was almost deafening when she left the quietness of the cabin. The woods were filled with insects welcoming the night with their mating ritual sounds. Carrie had never stopped to realize just how loud it was this time of evening in the woods.

The light was dim outside and fading fast. She shuf-fled to the shed where the car was. She was looking down, watching the ground to make sure she didn't trip. The last thing she needed was to trip and fall in her condition.

About three feet from the edge of the shed, she looked up and saw the open, gaping garage door. For a minute she thought in the dim light that her poor vision was deceiving her. The car was gone. Of course he would have taken the car. He had no other way to leave.

She made it to the side of the shed and then slid slowly to the ground. What would she do now? Her phone was in there, too. She knew, in the shape she was in, she could not make it down the long gravel road and out to civilization. It was a long way to reach another person and help.

As darkness settled in around her, the night air chilled her, making the pain worsen. Her only option was to go back into the cabin. She would try to clean herself up and bind her ribs. If she could rest, maybe even sleep, she might have enough strength to walk the road tomorrow.

Just like Scarlett she thought, as she made her way slowly back to the cabin, she would worry about that road tomorrow.

CHAPTER 14

Senna woke early Sunday morning with anxiety. The closer the time came to go to church with Blake, the stronger the anxiety had grown.

Yesterday had been her day to work at the library. She and Andrea each worked two Saturdays a month with two part-time college students working the other two Saturdays.

Saturdays were usually busy at the library because kids were out of school and they plan several fun projects to get the kids interested in reading. There was still quite a bit to do for the book drive coming up at the school, so the day flew by rapidly for Senna. She'd had very little time to dread Sunday morning.

She and Blake had gone to the park again with another picnic dinner. This time of year was so nice out in the evenings. They both knew that would change soon as the summer heat settled in.

She knew Blake was intentionally avoiding talking about church. She could tell he wanted them to just enjoy their time together, and that was more than fine with her. They'd had a good time and had even wound up playing on the swings as if they were little kids again. She had laughed, and it had felt good.

But that was last night and this morning she lay in bed, sick to her stomach about having to face this. What if she found she could not do this? She knew she would lose Blake over it. This was too important to him.

Then there was Andrea. Though she knew her friendship with Andrea was not based on going to church, Senna couldn't help but think it would hurt her, and that was the last thing she wanted to do. When it had never been brought up, it had not been an issue. Now she would either accept or reject and both Blake and Andrea stood to feel any rejection personally.

And she knew what it would be. Senna knew beyond any shadow of a doubt that she would reject it. She knew this was only a formality. She would go this one time so that she could say she had gone, then reject further invitations.

Her soft bed felt good to her and, as she rolled over, she wished she could just stay there. She was sad because she knew today was a pivotal day and that things would never be the same again. In her heart she was already mourning the loss of the friendships she had just made and was about to lose.

Senna laid in bed until her phone rang. It was Blake confirming the time he would be by to pick her up. No avoiding it any longer, it was time to get dressed.

There was one suit she had bought recently while shopping, she really didn't know why, but it had caught her attention. In her experience, it was always necessary to dress as formal as possible for church. So she pulled out that suit and dressed.

She pulled her hair back into the tight bun she had continually worn only a couple of weeks prior and left off any sign of makeup. When she looked into the mirror, she felt as though she were heading to her execution.

The doorbell rang, and she went to open the door. As the door swung open, she was surprised to see Blake standing there in blue jeans and an untucked shirt with his sleeves rolled part way up, and tennis shoes. Maybe they weren't going to church after all.

"What's going on?" Senna asked Blake as she let him in.

"What do you mean, *what is going on?*" he asked. He looked at her dressed severely the way she used to dress when he first met her. But what concerned him was the sadness on her face.

"Why aren't you dressed for church?" Senna asked.

"I am," Blake replied.

Senna was really confused. She just stood and looked

Blake over. He was dressed to go to the park, not to church. She felt like a cruel joke was being played on her and she felt heat glowing on her cheeks.

"You don't have to dress up at our church. What you wear isn't important. Everyone is just themselves," Blake said.

Senna was trying to reconcile what Blake had just said with what she knew church to be, and she couldn't. More contradictions that frustrated her.

"We have plenty of time. Why don't you go back into your bedroom and change into something else that you will feel comfortable in?" He brushed back a stray hair that had escaped the bun, "And if you don't mind, would you wear your hair down? I really like it that way." He smiled and bent down to kiss her.

Oh my, he had such a way with her, she thought. She went back into her bedroom, shut the door, and threw off the suit and pulled the bun out of her hair. She didn't understand, but she would not argue about this.

Fifteen minutes later, Senna emerged with a cute spring dress and her hair down. She had even taken the time to put on a little makeup. When she walked out of her room, she knew by the look on Blake's face she had made the right choice.

Anxiety and confusion surged once again when they pulled up into the parking lot of a very large building that looked nothing at all like a church. Blake's casual demeanor went a long way to helping calm Senna's nerves, but waves of nausea kept washing over her. She had wondered what rituals they demanded that she wouldn't know.

Right before getting out of the car Senna reach across and stopped Blake from getting out. "I won't know what to do," she said with worry, almost in tears.

"You don't have to do anything, just enjoy it. If I think there is something you need to know, I'll tell you. I don't want you to feel uncomfortable," Blake said and smiled.

As they walked up to the door, there were others going in. As Senna watched them quietly, they all seemed happy and greeted each other with hugs and pats on the back. There were two people standing at the door welcoming everyone in. When one grabbed her hand and shook it, she felt awkward, but mumbled "hello".

She felt Blake's hand on the small of her back. It was reassuring as it guided her where to go. They stopped just inside the sanctuary door. Blake scanned the room and when he saw Andrea, they headed that way.

Andrea was excited to see Senna and scooted down to provide them easier access to the two seats she had saved. Andrea was dressed in blue jeans, too. Suddenly Senna felt overdressed.

Senna was enthralled by the room and the people in it. She resisted the urge to just gawk around at every-thing. There were people milling about and chatting. They were dressed in various ways. There were a few people dressed formally, yet others even had shorts and

T-shirts on! No one seemed to care. It didn't seem to matter to them.

One thing they all seemed to have in common, though, was that they were all smiling and seemed very happy; not only that, but happy to be here.

The lights dimmed slightly and out on the stage walked a few people who picked up various instruments and microphones. She didn't realize there would be a performance, *no it wasn't a performance, they were the song leaders,* she thought.

TV screens above and on each side of the stage lit up and music played. Everyone stood and sang the words to songs she had never heard, the words of which were displayed on the screens. Some people were clapping, and some were raising their hands. Senna gripped the back of the seat in front of her so tightly that her knuckles became white. She didn't know these songs.

Senna felt Blake's hand slip around her waist from behind. She knew he wanted to comfort her. She tried to sing along, quietly, since she didn't know the melodies. By the third song she had relaxed somewhat. The words and the music felt good. They were positive words about a loving God, not unlike the hymns she had sung as a child, but these were sung so differently by this congregation.

She concentrated on reading and thinking about the words of that third song.

...You've known me forever and loved me even longer

You sing to me... You sing over me... You are my lullaby,
Your loving light brings warmth to my soul.
You breathe life into me... You breathe life over me... You
are my breath,
Your loving light brings warmth to my soul.
When I fail... When I fall short...You've already
caught me...

The words spoke of God as a loving Father who had known her from before she was born. When the chorus portion began tears involuntarily flowed down Senna's cheeks. The words and music spurred such emotion inside of her that she was not able to explain it or contain it.

...Oh how my heart aches with your love, you're like honey
to my soul
You left all for me, for I am the one, not the ninety-nine.
I failed, and you pursued me, I fell and you caught me,
You left it all for me, for I am the one, not the ninety-nine...

She thought she had never really felt God's love before and questioned it's existence. All those times she had sung about it when she was young it was just lip service, singing about a God she had never really known.

...You left it all for me, for I am the one, not the ninety-
nine...

Her whole life she had been working hard to earn it, validation, love, acceptance from God and man. From her father. This song says that He pursued me even when I failed, He loved me from the beginning.

It occurred to Senna it might be embarrassing Blake that her face was wet with tears, but, surprisingly, she didn't care. She couldn't have stopped them even if she'd tried.

But then the music was winding down and as she sat down, she saw Andrea's hand reach across Blake to her handing her a box of tissues. She noticed there were boxes everywhere underneath the seats. Suddenly she wasn't so embarrassed any more.

She wiped her cheeks and sat down. The musicians had left the stage and a nice-looking man in blue jeans, walked onto the stage. He talked some about the songs they had just sung and how true the lavish love of the Father truly was. He welcomed the pastor to the stage and sat down.

The only father she had ever known was a mean and hard man. If she were to compare and call God Father, then how could she want a God like that? The only love she felt she had known was her Gran's love. Was it possible that it was God's love coming to her through her Gran?

The pastor looked to be in his forties, Senna thought. He, too, was dressed casually. He had a good natured way about him and it was easy to listen to his words. He spoke about God in a way that Senna had never heard. He said that God had come to give life to us and that above all else He desired a relationship with us.

Senna was surprised when he said Jesus had come to

destroy religion such as the Pharisees and Sadducees practiced. He explained how religion was an enemy of God and prevented a relationship with His people, His children.

Throughout the entire sermon, Senna sat transfixed until near the end when she felt nauseous and then had a sharp pain pierce through her gut. It was so intense that it took her breath away. As the pastor continued to speak, it stabbed harder and harder.

In just a few seconds Senna slumped over and passed out. Blake was immediate in his response with Andrea there by his side. The ushers were discrete as Blake tried to revive Senna. When she would not respond, he picked her up and carried her out to the foyer and laid her on one of the sofas.

After several minutes, the paramedics which had been called pulled up and Senna had still not awakened. Her pulse was good and all her vital signs were on target. They loaded her up and rushed her to the nearest hospital. Blake went with her in the ambulance with an agreement from Andrea that she would meet them at the emergency room.

All the way there, Blake held Senna's limp hand and prayed as tears fell from his eyes.

THE FITFUL NIGHT had done nothing to ease Carrie's pain. The lack of pain meds or ibuprofen locked her into a painful existence. The morning light did not find her feeling refreshed, only more battle worn.

The night before, she had found that taking a deep breath and holding it in would allow her just enough stability to attempt to tear an old sheet into strips with minimum pain. It was the best she could do to support her broken ribs.

Even though there was no electricity, there was water, so before wrapping herself she stripped down and took a shower. The hot water tank which was fueled from gas in the propane tank, gave her hot water which felt soothing against her skin.

Carrie would have liked to have scrubbed her entire body but the inability to move forced her to be satisfied with just standing under the fresh hot water. It felt like heaven to her. She gasped as she squeezed the old shampoo bottle in an effort to relinquish a tiny blob of the gelled substance into her hand.

The hot water ran out way too soon. Carrie shut the water off and pulled a bath towel around herself. Exhaustion surged through her and she felt dizzy. Sitting on the edge of the toilet seat with the mental fog fully gone from her mind, bits and pieces of the night before claimed her memory. As she sat there, fresh waves of shame and guilt washed over her.

It was chilly in the cabin so she pulled the towel

tighter around herself and walked slowly to the bed. Sudden unexpected pain would shoot through her about every fifth step and she would have to stop and recover until it passed. Needless to say, her progress was slow and painful.

Drying herself off the best she could, she picked up the sheet she had torn into strips. It was challenging trying to wrap herself. The pain made it hard to breathe, and the exertion exacerbated the pain even more.

Finally she was done and was dressed in an old sleep shirt she'd kept there. She wanted more than anything to just curl up in the bed and sleep for days on end, but she knew tomorrow she would need her clothes and she didn't want to wear them soiled as they were.

So she mustered a little more energy and took her clothes into the kitchen to wash them in the sink. Having filled one lantern when she'd come back in from the shed she carried it with her from room to room.

In the kitchen, she did her best to clean up the broken glass, not wanting to cut herself yet again. As she gently squatted to look for dish soap under the sink tears rolled down her cheeks. The peaceful solace this cabin had once held was now obliterated with fresh and painful memories.

With as little movement as she could manage, she hand-washed her clothes in the kitchen sink. She didn't have the strength to ring them tightly but did what she could and draped them across the backs of the kitchen chairs.

Finally done with all she felt she could do, she'd gone back to the bedroom and gently laid her body on the bed. Exhaustion consumed her more than it had any other time in her life. The exhaustion was complete, not just consuming her physical body but her soul as well.

Carrie reflected on all that had happened as she woke up that morning. It was Sunday and no one would be looking for her and there was no place she had to be. She realized that the work she'd done for so many years in order to isolate herself from others had been thorough. There was no one.

Part of her wanted to stay hidden in this little cabin away from everyone, away from the shame and humiliation that now enveloped and consumed her.

To come out into civilization meant having to face her demons. She would have to tell others how she came to be in such a mess. She had never felt so broken and alone, literally. Fresh waves of shame and guilt washed over her yet again.

Lying on the floor last night she'd had to make a decision to live, or had that decision been made for her? She hadn't died even though she lay there willing herself to do so. So what did that decision mean? In order to live, she knew she had to make drastic changes in her life and she knew she couldn't do it alone.

But the truth was, she didn't have anyone. Her partner

Randy was the closest person to her and he could barely stand her right then. Her parents were gone and with no siblings, there was no family.

Since her parents' death she had made it a practice to never make true friends. She would befriend people only to keep them at arms-length. It had just felt safer that way.

There was always AA. *Was that true recovery though?* she wondered, or just kicking the inevitable can down the road? Those she had known who had gone to AA never seemed truly free, and she didn't know if she wanted a place where she was always talking about the problem. She wanted a way to get past the problem.

It was still early and Carrie decided she would get some more sleep. She doubted her clothes would be dry yet, anyway.

It seemed no easier to swing her legs over the side of the bed and raise herself up. As she worked her way to a standing position, she felt the stiffness of having laid still for so long crush her body. She thought that maybe she felt a little better than the night before, but only slightly.

She needed go to the bathroom. She then turned her clothes over to help them dry on both sides. It was then all she could do to shuffle to the bedroom and lie back down to sleep for a while longer. It would be a long walk down the road and it would be slow going in her condition; therefore, she wanted to make sure she left in plenty of time before it got dark again.

Sleep came again, but not before memories of the night before crept in and invaded her thoughts, giving her an even deeper resolve that her life would be different from this moment on.

SENNA'S AMBULANCE made it in record time. She still had not woken up when they arrived at the emergency room. Blake was genuinely worried.

The paramedics had been great. They were efficient and attentive and had asked Blake a few questions to help determine their course of action and what to relay to the hospital who had waited on alert for their arrival.

The antiseptic smell of the hospital hammered home the truth of what was happening as Blake walked through the automatic doors. He was in shock that his vibrant and healthy Senna was being ushered by doctors and nurses into the deep recesses of the emergency room.

Another shattering reality hit him when trying to answer the questions the nurses were presenting him. He did not know Senna as well as he thought he did.

He told them everything he knew, but she'd said nothing to him about feeling bad. She'd just doubled over a few times and then collapsed. It had all happened quickly.

By the afternoon they had her in a room with all types of monitors. She was breathing well on her own so no breathing assistance was required. No one seemed to have any idea why she was not waking up.

The sterile atmosphere of the hospital was wearing on Andrea as she sat with Blake. When afternoon turned to evening Andrea brought up the fact to Blake that Senna had gone to see Dr. Specter on Friday afternoon and wondered if she had said anything to him about it.

The look on his face told her everything. First there was surprise, then his eyes darted searching his memory for something he must have missed, but there was nothing. He was surprised that she'd already had an appointment because she hadn't mentioned it at all.

"I can't believe she didn't say anything about it to me," said Blake.

"She's very self-conscious about it," replied Andrea. "You know she is a medical doctor, a psychiatrist, but a medical doctor? Do you think there is any light she could shed on this?" asked Andrea hopefully.

He wiped his hand across his face and sat back in his chair. He had no idea. He didn't see how she could, but he was willing to try anything. Andrea still had the doctor's information in her email on her phone. She flagged down Senna's nurse and gave her the information. The nurse agreed to tell the doctor and put it in her file.

When evening came with no change, Blake and Andrea were bored and at a loss what to do next. They had taken turns getting coffee and taking bathroom breaks. Neither one wanted to leave her completely alone, but both were growing more exhausted by the moment.

Around nine o'clock, a nice-looking lady knocked quietly before entering the room. "I am Dr. Marion Specter. The hospital called me. Can you tell me a little about what happened?"

For what seemed like the millionth time Blake and Andrea gave a detailed account of the day's events to the doctor. She sat taking notes and listening quietly.

"I can't share what Senna and I discussed in our session, but honestly it was very little since it was only our first hour. You have both shared much more with me about Senna than I knew before.

"It seems from what you have told me that a lot of her father's abuse stemmed from his strict religious beliefs. It may just be possible that while she was in church, it brought back such a wave of emotional pain and conflict it traumatized her all over again. If that is the case, I believe she will wake up on her own again, in time." The fact that Dr. Specter was a compassionate person was evident to both Blake and Andrea. They listened intently as the doctor spoke.

"Did we cause this, this trauma by taking her to church with us?" Blake couldn't have felt worse. The thought that he might have been to blame for Senna's episode was overwhelming.

"It is possible, but you shouldn't blame yourself. With the depths of her abuse, it was a ticking time bomb. It could have happened at any time. Feel comforted that she was with both of you when it did."

"Thank you," said Andrea.

"I will talk with her doctor and see if he has any suggestions. It may shed new light on her situation," said Dr. Specter. "I'll check back in on her in the morning. Let me suggest to you that you both go home and get some rest. The nurse has your contact info, so if she wakes up they will call you. She will need both of you strong and rested when she wakes up."

After Dr. Specter left, Blake insisted that Andrea go on home. He said he would as well, but wanted to stay just a little while longer. Andrea understood. Before she left, she stood by Senna's bed, reached down to hug her friend, and whispered 'I love you'.

Blake spent another hour at Senna's bedside before calling a friend to come pick him up and take him home. While he was there, he talked to her. He shared his heart, his love, and his dreams with her. He told her how she had to wake up, he willed her to wake up, but she quietly slept on.

AT ONE O'CLOCK that afternoon Carrie knew she had to leave. Her clothes were dry enough, and she had no idea how long it would take her to walk out in her condition.

Dressing was painful and slow. She looked through

the cabin one last time hoping that maybe she had brought her cell phone in and had just forgotten about it. But no such luck, it was not there. Her clothes were still damp, and they felt rough and grimy against her skin.

Her good eye was much better. The swelling had gone down enough for her to see pretty well through it. The other eye, though still swollen, was much better and she could see somewhat through it, too.

Sadness overwhelmed her as she stood on the back step looking at the shed. The gaping whole of the open garage door felt like the gaping hole in her soul. She slowly walked toward it and stood looking where her car had been. Through blurred and narrowed vision she attempted to once again search for her phone. She desperately hoped that he had thrown it out before leaving in her car.

Realizing it wasn't there, she resigned herself to yet one more disappointment; she took a deep breath and steeled herself for the long and painful walk ahead.

It was hard to walk on gravel on a good day, but today it was almost impossible. It was constantly shifting underneath her feet jarring her damaged body. She tried for a while walking on the side of the road, but the weeds were high and she had already startled a snake which in turn had startled her as it slid away into the woods.

Had she not been in the situation she was in, she thought she might have enjoyed the beautiful day.

Thankfully, it was not too hot yet and there was a slight breeze to keep her cool.

Stopping several times to catch her breath, she tried to not grumble to herself about how her wet jeans were chaffing her legs and how her makeshift wrap was sliding down, coming undone.

Finally, she was at the road. She looked to her left and thought about the convenience store about a mile and a half to her left. To the right she knew there was a house or two, but couldn't remember just how far away they were. She thought one was closer than the store, but what if no one was home?

Deciding to walk to the store, she turned to her left. She was now facing the sun that was dipping down toward the horizon. She fought to hold her broken ribs, walk, and shade her eyes all at the same time. Maybe she should've gone the other direction.

It took her almost two hours to walk that mile and a half. Normally she could have run it in no time. The miles had taken their toll on her and she was going slower and slower with each step.

Carrie had nothing to do but think as she walked. A lot of thought had gone into who to call once she arrived at a phone. After playing the reel over and over, she realized that the only person she had to call was Randy.

There was only one car at the store when she walked into the parking lot. With what seemed like her last ounce of effort, she pushed the door open. The look on the clerk's face when he saw her face told her she must look as bad as she felt.

He was quick to help her get a seat in one of the padded booths they kept for diners. He brought her a large bottle of water and asked if she wanted something to eat. She hadn't eaten almost forty-eight hours but wasn't sure she had the strength.

With a quick nod he presented his cell phone to her, and she made the call. Randy picked up on the third ring. He hadn't answered in a bad mood but she was sure that would change as soon as she told him her story and what she needed.

She took a deep breath and began.

CHAPTER 15

*R*andy was standing by Carrie's bed the next morning when she woke up. He'd rushed her to the closest hospital as soon as he picked her up. She had vetoed all of his suggestions to call an ambulance the day before, stating that if she could've walked the miles she walked in the condition she was in, then she could withstand waiting on him to drive her to the hospital.

The findings were: three broken ribs, a broken bone in her hand, a cut in her hand from the glass, a broken collarbone, a sprained ankle from the walk down the gravel road, and countless contusions and abrasions.

Multiple tests were done to check for internal bleeding and brain injuries. There had been initial concern that the broken ribs make have caused some internal damage, but that was not the case.

Relief flooded her when she was told that there appeared to be no lasting damage to her eyes or her brain from the beating she had taken. Her field of vision continued to grow as the swelling decreased.

That was the easy part, thought Carrie. The hard part was still ahead of her.

"Now we have to get down to the details." Randy had out his notepad. The one from Sandy with his initials on it. He was in full work mode. He was now ready to hear the full story, with Carrie leaving nothing out.

She didn't care if the guy was found. The car, well that was a blow. She had bought it with her inheritance, but her last few days had shifted her priorities. If the car was never found, then that was fine, too. Honestly, she wanted to maintain some shred of dignity with her partner.

When she hesitated, Randy reached out and laid his hand on hers. "It's all right. I know I've been hard on you lately. My life has been a pile of crap. But, Carrie, aside from Sandy, you're my best friend. In many ways you're a closer friend than Sandy. Nothing you say will shock me. Trust me, I've imagined that you were doing the worst things possible on your nights out. The truth can't be any worse than what I've already imagined, can it?"

Tears flowed down Carrie's abraded cheeks. Then sobs followed. Randy stood, laid down the pad, and reached to hold his friend.

Randy tried to hold her as long as she needed, but this

type of raw emotion really made him uncomfortable. After what he hoped was an acceptable period, he let her go and pulled his chair closer.

Carrie reached for the tissues and looked down at her hands. She wasn't sure where to start, so she started with the most recent evening which had led her to this.

It took her approximately an hour to tell her story. As Randy took notes she paused for him to catch up. To her surprise, he never said one condemning word, one snide remark, or one 'I told you so'.

As he wrote, Randy's heart was breaking. Once she had finished with the events leading up to her hospitalization, she took him back to other times. When she had finally wound down, Randy chided himself that he had been so wrapped up in his own life that he hadn't seen any of what his partner had been going through. But then she'd hidden it well.

"I don't know what to do," It came out of Carrie's mouth with a sob. "Things in my life have to change, but I have no idea how to make that happen."

Randy didn't either. His life was only going slightly better than Carrie's. His wife couldn't stand the sight of him, he felt like a stranger to his kids, and he had no idea what to do about it.

"I don't know either Carrie, but we'll get through this together," he tried to reassure her the best that he could. Maybe they could help each other. He knew he would be kinder to her from now on. She had never deserved what he had dished out. And neither had Sandy nor his kids. He had to find a way to do better, be better, too.

"Does Bracket know?" asked Carrie. That would be another painful conversation.

"He does. He's a kind man, Carrie. We are fortunate to have him," Randy knew he was sincere. Bracket had been the one person Randy had confided in lately. He himself was not a perfect man, and he was compassionate when others failed.

"I have to go for now," Randy said as he stood to go. He reached out one last time and patted Carrie's good hand. It will be okay. I promise.

"How can you promise?" asked Carrie.

Randy looked at her, then away, and left the room. She was right. How could he make such a promise?

BLAKE WAS at the hospital early Monday morning. He had not slept well at all. His heart and his mind was on Senna.

So by 6:00 a.m. he was on his way. His mind was retracing events from Sunday in an attempt to find a clue, any clue of what could have caused Senna's collapse.

Why had she not told him she'd been able to get in to see the psychiatrist on Friday afternoon? And moreover, why had she not told him it was a psychiatrist rather than a licensed counselor?

Blake was sure it was too personal for Senna. She may

have been embarrassed by the whole situation and was just too uncomfortable to talk about it, even to him.

He tried to not worry. He was not a worrier by nature, but with Senna, how could he not worry about her?

Blake remembered her lying in the bed so still, with her hands to her sides. She had looked so peaceful. Her skin had been pink and he could see no outward sign that would keep her asleep.

The drive to the hospital seemed to take forever even though it had only been about twenty minutes. He quickly found a parking place and soon was entering Senna's room.

Turning the corner to her room, his hopes were crushed when he could see no noticeable change. He went straight to her bed and picked up her hand. It was so soft, but limp. He bent down to kiss it.

The chair scraped loudly as he pulled it up to Senna's bed, but she didn't stir or flinch. Could she hear anything at all, he wondered? His mind searched for suggestions of what he could do to help her.

"Senna, I'm here," Blake began. "It's Blake. Baby, I want you to wake up for me now." Panic tried to set in and he choked up from her lack of response.

The morning continued to come alive inside the hospital. Soon the noises increased in the hallway. He knew he needed to go to work, but he couldn't make himself move.

Blake had called his partner Charles yesterday and explained to him what had happened. Charles was adamant that he take as much time as he needed. Things were covered at the office.

But Blake had a sense of duty to his clients and was torn. He felt completely helpless here watching Senna sleep, but how could he leave her?

The nurses were coming and going, checking her vital signs. They were patient and kind. Two hours after he had arrived, Dr. Specter knocked quietly on the door frame as she entered the room.

Blake rose to greet her with a handshake. Pulling up another chair on the other side of Senna's bed she asked, "Any change?"

All Blake could do was shake his head. He took a deep breath and let it out. "I don't know what to do." His voice sounded hopeless. He had waited for so long to find the right woman, the right woman for him, that is. He was thirty-three and just when he was not sure if he would find someone he wanted to spend the rest of his life with, suddenly there was Senna.

"Blake, could I have some time alone with Senna?" Dr. Specter asked.

Surprised, Blake agreed. What could she possibly do?

He decided to go get some coffee. He knew the walk would do him good.

As soon as Blake left the room, Dr. Specter closed the door and stood close to the head of Senna's bed.

"Senna, I know you can hear me. This is Dr. Specter."
She picked up Senna's hand and sat on the edge of her
bed. Leaning in she said, "I know you are there. You need
to come back to us now."

Senna's countenance showed no response; however,
the monitor showed an elevation in her heart rate. Dr.
Specter continued. "Senna! Come out and talk to me."
She said with slightly more force.

As Blake pushed the door to enter Senna's room, Dr.
Specter was rushing out, and they nearly collided.

"Sorry!" she exclaimed. "I-I didn't realize how late it
was. I really have to run."

Blake nodded and watched her hurry away. How odd,
he thought. She'd appeared calm and cool to Blake, but
she was definitely flustered for some reason. Maybe it
was just what she'd said, late for an appointment.

CARRIE WAS RESTLESS. She'd tried hard to rest in the hard
hospital bed. Moving still hurt even though the morphine
drip helped greatly. The doctor had told her that, due to
the severity of her injuries, they wanted her to stay in the
hospital at least three days, maybe four. They also wanted
to continue to monitor brain activity to make sure they
had not missed something there.

She wanted to go home and sleep in her own bed. But
she couldn't do anything for herself, even get up and go

to the bathroom, so she knew she was better off where she was. Had she been at home there would be no one there to help her.

Sometime after lunch, the nurse agreed that it would be good for her to take a walk down the hall and back. Carrie was stiff, and the pain was still so intense that she almost begged to crawl back into bed, but she knew movement would help her recover.

Her nurse walked with her for several feet down the hall. When she saw that Carrie was doing well, she left her to walk by herself assuring her that she was close by. The going was slow. She clung to her IV pole and took short slow steps.

Carrie thought the hallway was long, but she was determined to make it to the end and back. Once at the end, she stopped to gaze out of the large window. It was another beautiful spring day.

She leaned her head on the window watching the traffic on the highway below. The glass was cool on her skin and felt good. Still feeling broken emotionally, she thought how she had failed herself, and those around her.

Finally she was in dire need of lying back down, but still had that long hallway to traverse, so she started back. As she walked back, she glanced into the rooms she passed. Most had their doors open and were filled with patients.

It was quiet, however, in the hallway. The nurses had

done their medication rounds and were now busy behind the desk completing paperwork and charting.

Two rooms down from her room a figure of a young lady laying on her back deathly still caught her attention. She stood in the hallway looking into the room for a moment. Something about her seemed familiar but Carrie could not associate her with a place or time in her memory.

The nurse came to check on her and asked if she was okay. "I am. I think I know this patient but can't remember where from. What's wrong with her?" asked Carrie.

"I'm not supposed to discuss other patients with you, but honestly no one knows what's wrong with her." The nurse was subtly routing Carrie back to her room.

Getting back into bed after a bathroom break caused the bed to feel good rather than hard. *It's all relative*, she thought. The bed is certainly better than the hard cold floor of the cabin.

That property had been in her family for years. Her grandparents had willed it to her, and she remembered playing there as a child. It had been a fun spot for them to get away from the busy city.

There was a small lake in the woods behind the cabin, beyond the shed. She and her dad had fished there for hours growing up. Her mom would fry the fish once dad had cleaned them and they would enjoy a good meal.

She had once heard someone say you can't spoil a

child by loving them too much, but she thought she'd had some of both. Her parents had doted on her. They loved her and they showed her that they did. They had also not denied her whatever she had wanted. Then...

Then she got that call. She had just been selected to join the OSBI and was to start the following week. Her life was perfect. She had a great guy, the job she was starting was her dream job, and a family who loved her dearly.

When the phone rang, it was like any other day. She was riding high on the joy of all things going well. "Is this Carrie Border?" Why should those words feel so ominous?

Four simple words. If you're getting a telemarketing call, that is what they say, and you chalk it up and hang up. For almost any occasion, those four words would not stop your world from spinning. But that day it did. It was his tone. It stopped her cold, and she knew, just knew those words would proceed something horrible.

"Yes, this is Carrie," her breath caught. She waited for the blow to hit.

"Can you come to Hope Memorial Hospital? Your parents have been in a car accident."

There it was. The worst possible news. But hope still lived. If they were at the hospital, then they were only injured and they would recover. But somewhere deep inside she knew better.

She simply hung up the phone without responding.

She'd jumped in her car and fought the icy roads to get to the hospital. Her grandparents had both passed years ago. It had been very traumatic, but they'd had long-term illnesses and, when they had each individually passed, it had been no surprise. If her parents died she would be alone, completely alone. Well, except for Billy that was.

When she arrived at the hospital, Carrie rushed into the emergency room. Before long, she was met by the doctor whose face told her what she didn't want to hear. Before a single word was said, she knew and collapsed on the floor.

They had to find her a bed and sedate her. The funeral was a vague memory as was the first few weeks at her new job. She was never the same after that phone call. She'd hardened herself to ward off hurt. She threw herself into her job and told herself she needed no one.

Billy had become a casualty of that change. He had tried to be there for her and to comfort her, but nothing he did helped. She made it clear, repeatedly, that she was shutting everyone out, including Billy, so finally he was forced to leave her, too.

For years, she had told everyone and especially herself, that she loved her job so much that she didn't need another relationship. But the truth was, she did.

As she lay on the hard hospital bed, she was forced to answer the question, is it more painful to shut everyone out or to experience the pain of loss? She had experienced both, but now she knew she was ready to risk the pain of loss over the pain of isolation.

Carrie fell asleep as tears slid down her cheek, and her sleep was fitful. Dreams of the fight at the cabin kept terrorizing her. She knew she'd brought it on. It had all been her fault.

She was aggressive, but would not let the tables turn. There was no way she would tolerate him being the aggressor. So they had both gotten violently angry. It was as if years of pent up rage was spewing forth from both of them.

There was no way to tell what had led him to that moment. He'd been brooding at the bar when she sat down. In hindsight, he'd been a powder keg ready to blow, and he had.

Carrie didn't remember the end of the fight or him leaving. By that time she was out cold on the bedroom floor. When she woke that morning in the cabin, she had felt more alone than that day at the hospital when she received the news of her parents' deaths.

ANDREA MADE arrangements to leave the library at three that day when the part-time students came in to work. She was out the door the instant they walked in.

All Andrea had thought about during the day was

Senna. She was so confused about what had happened and what was wrong.

Finally, Andrea was at the hospital. The anxiety she was feeling made the ride up the elevator seem to take forever. She hoped to walk into Senna's room and see her sitting up awake, alive, and happy.

But that was not the case. Senna was still asleep. Blake was asleep as well on the foldout chair. She quietly sat down in the chair next to Senna's bed. Looking her over from one end to the other, she could see she was just the same. Her cheeks were pink and there was no sign she was in pain.

Blake stirred and rubbed his face and hair. He blinked hard at Andrea. "Hey there," his voice gruff from sleep. I guess I really passed out.

"Did you leave at all last night?" asked Andrea.

"Yeah, about midnight," he said. "Then I came back about six this morning."

"Blake, I'm here to stay for the evening. Go home and get a shower and eat a bite. I'll be here with her." Andrea knew he needed a break and was more than willing to sit with Senna.

Blake sat with his elbows on his knees for a while trying to get fully awake. "Okay. I think I will since you're here. I hate to leave her, but I know if you are here, she's not alone." He stood and stretched, then yawned.

He walked over, kissed Senna's forehead, then walked out the door.

Andrea had brought a few magazines and a book with her. She thought if she read to Senna it might help her. She read the first magazine, a popular one about celebrities and other people of notoriety. When she'd finished that last article she shut the magazine and looked at Senna.

"Senna, I'm here. Please wake up and talk to me." The change in the monitor caught Andrea's eye. She looked over to see what appeared to her an elevation in Senna's heart rate. She jumped up and ran to get a nurse.

By the time they had gotten back to the room, the heart rate had gone back down to where it was originally. Andrea tried to convince the nurse what she had seen. The nurse agreed that might be the case and encouraged Andrea to just keep reading to her.

Andrea sat down, excited that there had been at least a slight change and began to read the second magazine with fervor. After every two or three paragraphs she would look up over the top of the magazine to see if Senna was awake.

When there had been no change after the two magazines, Andrea got up and walked around the room stretching. She walked over to the window and looked out at the sun dropping lower on the horizon. Deep in thought, she almost didn't hear the slight movement coming from the bed.

Andrea whirled around where Senna still lay, but her hand was not in the same position. She was ecstatic and once again ran to get a nurse. The monitor showed a consistent, slightly higher heart rate, and the nurse noted the new placement of Senna's hand.

Leaning in closer to Senna, the nurse lifted an eyelid and shined her penlight into it and then quickly flicking it away. Senna's head jerked to the side to avoid the light, and she squinted her eyes. She was awake!

The nurse talked to Senna to wake her fully. She raised her bed and fluffed her pillows to help her sit straighter.

The entire time, Andrea was pacing at the other end of the room. She was so happy that Senna was awake and couldn't wait to talk to her friend. Finally, she thought to call Blake.

When she pulled out her cell phone, the nurse motioned for her to take the phone outside. Begrudgingly, she did.

Blake's phone was ringing and ringing. He wasn't picking up. He must be in the shower, Andrea thought. She wouldn't leave a message. Hopefully, he would see she'd called and would call her back.

Finally, after about ten minutes he did. "Blake, Senna is awake. The nurse is in with her and when I started to call you she motioned for me to leave the room. I haven't gotten to talk to her yet."

"I'll be right there," Blake said. He was so excited and hated that he had left.

"Drive safe. We don't need you in the hospital too," cautioned Andrea.

She hurried back up to Senna's room. The doctor was in there with her so Andrea waited in the hall. She was trying to listen in but could barely hear anything. Finally, they all left and shut the door behind them.

As soon as they were a few feet down the hall, Andrea slipped in. It appeared to her that Senna was back asleep as she had been before, but when the chair slid as she sat down, Senna opened her eyes.

Andrea jumped up and grabbed her friend. "Senna, I'm so glad you are awake. How are you? What happened? Why did you collapse? Are you okay?" She couldn't help asking every question that had run a track through her mind the entire previous day and evening.

Senna looked at Andrea. Her brow was creased in concern for her friend. "I'm okay. I honestly don't know what happened. The last thing I remember, I was listening to the pastor preaching. Then waking up just now."

Andrea sat next to her friend and picked up her hand. This time Senna squeezed back. For a few minutes they just sat there smiling at each other.

Blake came rushing through the door, breaking the heartfelt gaze between the two friends. Relief poured from Blake. Andrea stood to give Blake her space. He scooped Senna up in his arms and just held her for the longest time.

Then when he thought he might be holding her too tight, he released her enough to look her over. "How are you?"

Senna laughed. "Ask Andrea. She just asked me ninety-nine questions, none of which I could answer."

The rest of the evening was spent with the three of them sharing about the events of the previous day. Nurses came and went and then just before visiting hours were ending, the doctor came in.

He strongly suggested—insisted really—that both Blake and Andrea go home for the night and allow Senna some time alone. They reluctantly agreed.

Once they had said their goodbyes, the doctor sat on the edge of Senna's bed to have a long talk with her. He sincerely hoped that she could remember enough of what had happened to shed some light on her condition because as of that moment he had no clue.

CHAPTER 16

*S*ince the doctors could find no physical reason to keep Senna, they let her go home. Her doctor had visited with her for quite a long time the night before, but she had no memory, other than listening to the Pastor and then waking up there in the hospital.

Blake had come to take her home. He was quite relieved, but still concerned since they still had no idea what had happened.

On the ride home, Blake nervously fiddled with the radio flitting from one station and song to another. He wasn't sure what to talk about. His natural urge was to shelter her and protect her and he didn't want to open a discussion that might upset her. Each word he thought to say was filtered through a veil of concern about how it would affect her.

Senna seemed quite fine. She was quiet, but seemed eager to get back home and then back to work at the library. It was as if a slice of her life had just been removed and she was right where she had left off on Sunday.

"Senna..." He started to ask yet another question, but stopped. What more could he ask that had not already been asked?

"Yes," she replied.

"Nothing. I'm just so confused and concerned about what has happened. Not knowing what caused it has made me concerned that it will happen again."

The entire thing made Blake curious and he had no basis on which to even develop a theory. He finally decided that there was nothing he could do, but just love her and be there for her. But he had made a mental note to watch a little closer to see if there were signs he had missed before. Signs of something else going on that had just been simply missed.

Senna stepped out to the back porch, closed her eyes and breathed deep. The scent of her neighbor's fresh cut grass was invigorating, and she took her time to soak it in.

"I love spring," Senna said.

"I do, too," replied Blake.

Was it just him or did she sound different? One would

have always described Senna as sweet, maybe almost too sweet. He had surmised that her timidity had caused her to repress adverse emotions, so no one ever saw anything but her sweet nature.

"You can go now," Senna said point blank at Blake.

Her tone was different from just a few seconds earlier. "Are you sure?"

"Yes." There was certainty in her tone and, was he wrong, or was there an edge to it that he had never heard from Senna before?

"I just want some time home alone. I don't have to go back to work until tomorrow so I just want some time alone to rest." She held his gaze. Her eyes did not waver. There was something very strong there that had not been there before.

Blake was hesitant to leave her alone, but finally with insistent reassurance from Senna that she was fine, he left.

As soon as the door closed, Senna felt a huge relief. She didn't know why, but she had to back away from this relationship with Blake. It was just a feeling, not something she could tangibly put her finger on. There had just been a sudden resistance to being with him.

That would also eliminate the issue of having to go back to church with him. Yes, at the moment it had felt wonderful and soothing, but now it was a faint memory. It had to all be a mastery of manipulation, she thought to herself. She returned to her old resolve to set religion aside.

Andrea was another thing. Senna knew Andrea would not push her to go back to church. She felt no risk in continuing to be friends with Andrea and was glad. But there was an unsettled feeling where Andrea was concerned as well.

Was she just too happy? Yes, who was really just that happy? It suddenly left a sour taste in Senna's mouth.

She pondered recent events and kept going back to her last memory. Why had she blacked out and lost an entire day? Her doctor had said she had no physical signs of anything abnormal in her body.

So, was he saying it was a mental issue? The thought angered Senna. As she lay on her sofa, the quiet of the room left her to meditate on that thought. Soon she was grinding her teeth and feeling betrayed and judged.

Did Andrea and Blake also feel she was a mental case? After all it was Andrea who had given her the info for the psychiatrist. She began weaving threads together to build a case against herself that didn't exist, and she became angrier.

Resolutely, she decided she didn't need any of them. Maybe they were all truly like her father and were only concerned about changing her into what they wanted her to be. She had some decisions to make, some changes to make.

Pacing the floor, she wrestled with a whirlwind of

emotions ranging from near violent anger to tearful sorrow.

Stopping her pacing as a new thought struck her; she could move from Kachina and get another job. Then she wouldn't have to see Andrea and there would be no chance of running into Blake. Maybe that was it, a totally new start somewhere else where no one knew her. A devious smile crossed her face. Yes, that would fix it all.

Her thoughts lost steam eventually and, as she lay there, sadness gently pushed the anger aside. She felt broken, betrayed, and alone. Finally, consciousness faded and pulled Senna into a deep sleep where there were no thoughts of anything, only blackness.

"I'm going crazy in this hospital," Carrie said to Randy on the phone. "What's going on with the case?"

"I'm not sure that talking about the case will help you rest and recover," said Randy.

"Grrrr," Carrie growled. "Talk to me. Tell me what's going on."

Randy laughed. Carrie was well on her way back. "The tarp sales were like a needle in a haystack. You can get them anywhere off of Amazon or in any home improvement store. If we find a tarp, then forensics can probably match it to the fleck they have.

"The ATV was a different story. Sales nationwide on

that specific model was considerably smaller. I have been working my way through the list."

"Any suspects jump out at you?" Carrie's investigative senses were growing excited.

Randy took a deep breath. Should he shut her down now and insist that she rest, or did he dare let her in at this point? Having worked with her as long as he had, he knew nothing would stop her from bugging him until he did.

"Okay, but here's the deal, if I talk to you about all of this, you have to promise me you will not try to get out of the hospital or go against the doctors' requests at all, in any way." Randy was very stern.

Giddy with glee, Carrie agreed. She had a huge smile spread across her face. She knew Randy wouldn't resist her.

For the next hour, they discussed the leads he had been slogging through. It was true that so much of investigative work was laborious and detailed. Most of the time they were hip deep in a haystack looking for that needle.

When the nurse came in to change Carrie's dressings and give her a sponge bath, they had to hang up. Randy promised he would keep her apprised of anything new in the case.

Carrie wouldn't relinquish the phone completely until the nurse gently removed it from her hand, told Randy goodbye and laid it on the nightstand.

"I feel much better, you know," Carrie told the nurse.

The nurse cocked her eyebrow up at Carrie, quite amused. She knew where this was going. "I bet you do. You are still on a strong morphine drip. But the doctor has given orders to cut that way, way back today. You'll need a little time to readjust."

Carrie frowned. She had to show them she was getting better. She decided that she would walk the hall every few hours to build her strength back up. When they saw how mobile she was, they would know how well she was doing and would release her.

As soon as the nurse left from her ministrations, Carrie slowly swung her legs over the side of the bed. A pain lurched through her mid-section stopping her cold. Determined still, as soon as the pain had subsided, she continued moving to get down off the bed and into a standing position. As soon as she did, she realized her IV pole was on the other side of the bed.

She shut her eyes and shook her head at her stupidity. Holding her arm out over the bed, she carefully walked around the end of the bed to the other side. She grabbed the iv pole and removed the clip from her finger which relayed her pulse to the monitor. Immediately an alarm began beeping.

Ignoring the beeping, she proceeded toward the door. When she met the nurse heading in to turn it off, she watched to see what buttons she pushed. It may be necessary information for future use. The nurse was expressing encouragement about walking as Carrie was leaving the room.

By the end of the day she had walked up and down the hallway three separate times. She felt exhausted, but knew it was going to help her in the long run. While she walked, she had thought.

When she passed the room where she'd seen the lady, she noticed that she was gone. The thought that she knew her but couldn't remember where from, really bugged Carrie. She could never just blow something off like that. Her mind would gnaw on it until it revealed itself to her.

As she walked, she did a mental inventory of all the places she frequented and then thought of the people, she encountered there. It was frustrating because she could be a clerk at a convenience store or a fast food worker. But she didn't think that was quite right. Those thoughts just didn't seem to fit.

No matter what, she just could not remember where she'd seen that lady. By the end of the day, she was exhausted from the walking and the reduction in pain meds failed to mask the pain of her injuries. Once again, that hard bed had never felt so good and she committed herself to it for the remainder of the evening.

Randy missed Carrie even though lately they had been at odds with each other. She was a good partner, and he valued her intuition and insight. Sometimes he wanted to scream when slogging through massive amounts of data, but it was vital and necessary. She was always encouraging, and she seemed to make it go smoother.

He'd been able to eliminate, or temporarily set aside, all the out-of-state ATV owners. Yes, they could have moved here or some other such thing, but he felt it best to focus on local owners first.

Ironically, the Big Horn Ranch had one just like that. He sat and stared at the name on the list thinking. Was it a coincidence? They'd honestly abandoned that line of thinking when the new, actually older, bodies had turned up.

The dumping ground of those bodies was several miles from the Big Horn. He couldn't quite buy into that connection, but he wrote it down on his list to investigate further.

Once through the list of local owners, he had five he felt he needed to visit and interview. He called Mike and Rick and they agreed to split the list. The owners were all over the place and it would certainly be more efficient to work together.

He kept the Big Horn on his list since he was familiar with it. The route to the ranch naturally took him past the hospital where Carrie was recovering. He decided that he would stop on his way back. He could fill her in on what he'd found. She would love that.

Arriving at the Big Horn, he noticed that things were just as he remembered. Today, though, there seemed to be much more activity. He drove back to the main barn where he knew Pinky's office to be.

He walked into the barn and on through to where Pinky's office was located. There was no answer when he knocked. The huge double barn doors on that end of the building were wide open and Randy stood looking out from them at the activity.

A ranch-hand walked by and Randy stopped him to ask where he might find Pinky. The hand pointed toward a large corral and continued on. Randy made his way to the corral.

It was made of welded panels joined together and it was huge. Inside were maybe a fifty cows, not fully grown, but not brand new either. Randy didn't immediately see Pinky, but was engaged in what he was watching.

"What are you guys doing?" Randy asked one of the hands standing nearby.

The hand looked up at him and simply said, "Workin' cattle." He looked back down at the rope he was coiling up feeling his explanation had been sufficient.

Randy frowned and mulled over the phrase, 'working cattle'. What on earth did that mean? Walking farther around to where the hub of the activity seemed to be, he saw a chute leading from the corral to another, smaller corral.

As he stood and watched, he saw a man single out a cow, no, a young bull Randy realized, and pushed it into the chute. The chute was an odd contraption about the length of a cow. It had steel bars on the sides and levers that moved the sides in to squeeze the cattle firmly and another lever which closed a door in the front around the animal's neck.

In what seemed like lightning speed, one ranch-hand injected the bull with a hypodermic needle, another one clipped a tag on his ear, and another hand was... What was he doing, Randy couldn't quite see.

Randy's stomach flipped as the ranch-hand stood up after a swift movement with a strange-looking knife and came away with testicles. The chute was opened and another ranch-hand ushered the once-bull out to another, larger corral.

Randy stood slack-jawed watching this process. They were all working in tandem, quickly and efficiently. He noticed not all were bulls, and those only received vaccinations he assumed, and tags, if necessary.

"What cha want?" It was Pinky's voice that broke Randy's fascination with what he was witnessing. He turned around to find Pinky standing there, frowning.

"Oh, hi, Pinky," said Randy. "This is fascinating."

"Good to know. What cha want?" Pinky was not

happy that his work had been interrupted. "This ain't really a good time to talk."

"Yes, I can see that. I really have only one question." He pulled out a picture of the camouflaged colored ATV and showed it to Pinky. "Do you guys have one of these?"

"Did have. Got stolen."

"Was a report filed?" asked Randy.

"Yep," Pinky was trying to hurry this along so he could get back to work.

"We called Darren, filed a report. That's all I know, now I gotta get back to work." Pinky turned and walked off.

There wasn't really much else he could ask Pinky. He would visit Darren to see when the ATV was reported stolen and see if there were any other details that might help him with their current case.

He walked back to his car, still visualizing the entire 'working cattle' process. Once back in his car, he shuddered, and was thankful he was not a ranch-hand or a bull.

"Yep, about a year ago, I think," replied Darren to Randy's inquiry about the ATV theft. "Let me pull that for you."

Darren shuffled through a series of files and pulled one out. His chair squeaked loudly as his large frame sat down. He had opened the file and was thumbing through it as he sat.

"Seems like there were several things stolen. The ATV for sure, then some other small equipment." Darren looked up and handed Randy the file open to the list of stolen items.

Randy read through the list of about twenty items. Most items he had no idea what they were. Another item caught his eye in addition to the ATV. "I see here that a castrating knife was stolen." Randy looked up to see Darren's reaction.

"Hmmm, I'd forgotten about that," said Darren. Randy could tell he was thinking and remembering back to taking the report.

Randy shut the file and thought for a moment. Tell me about a castrating knife. He had just witnessed first-hand how sharp they must be in order to castrate a bull's testicles in one swift movement.

Darren leaned forward placing his forearms on his desk. "Well, they are generally made from tempered high-carbon steel, incredibly hard and rust-proof. They're very sharp and hold their edge. I think the ones the Big Horn uses are custom made from a knife making company. I was told the one that was stolen had a blunt tip and a trigger guard to protect them from getting cut when they used it. The guard keeps a person's hand from sliding down onto the blade. The Big Horn's knives all have their brand on the handle."

Randy sat and thought for a minute. "Could that type of blade have been used to cut a throat like in our murder victims' cases?"

Thinking for a minute, Darren then replied while nodding his head, "Yep, I don't see why not. The medical examiners would be the best judge of that."

"I need a knife like the one stolen from the Big Horn. Are all their knives the same?"

"I don't know. They probably have some old knives they used way back, but I am sure they have more than one like the one that was stolen," Darren said.

"I need one of those knives to take to the medical examiner. I was just out there, though, and they were working cattle. I hate to rile Pinky any more than I already have today. Would you go out there as soon as they are done and get me one?"

Randy really didn't want to have to go back out there right then. He knew it would be best to wait until they were done with the cattle.

"Sure thing. I'll call Pinky this evening when they've cleaned up and see if I can head out to pick one up. I'll call you as soon as I do."

Randy stood to go and heartily shook Darren's hand. He felt energized. Going to the big Horn to see about an ATV was turning into a much bigger possible lead. Just as Randy reached the door to Darren's office he thought of something and turned back to look at Darren. "Did you ever have a suspect?"

"As a matter of fact, we did. There was a ranch-hand that went missing about the same time. We hunted all over and never could find him or the stuff. We never could figure out where he might have gone off to," replied Darren.

"Can I have the file you have on him?" asked Randy.

"Sure." Darren pulled out another file and motioned for Randy to head to the copier with him.

Once the file was copied and Randy was headed back out the door. Pieces were falling into place in his mind and he couldn't wait to tell Carrie.

WHEN RANDY ARRIVED at the hospital, Carrie was sleeping. He stood there for a while, not wanting to wake her. He was eager to share with her what he had found, but knew she needed her rest. He finally decided to sit down for a bit and wait.

In about fifteen minutes, a nurse walked in. "She's pretty out of it," she whispered. "She was determined to walk the hallway today until she recovered. I think she quickly realized it would take more than her sheer will to make that happen. It was good, though, to see her walking. It does speed up recovery if one doesn't overdo it." The nurse was checking the IV drip and the monitor as she spoke.

Carrie stirred and opened her eyes some. She felt like

she had been hit by a truck. Maybe she had overdone it. Seeing Randy though, sitting on the chair behind the nurse brightened her spirits.

"Randy," Carrie said. She raised the head off her bed and attempted to scoot herself up, wincing in the process.

"You overdid it, didn't you?" he asked.

"I just want to be well and out of here. You know I can't sit around, I have to be doing something." The disgruntled look on Carrie's face made Randy smile.

He grabbed his chair and pulled it up close to the side of Carrie's bed. "Hey," he said in a conspiratorial voice, "I have something." He pulled out the file he had gotten from Darren and his notepad.

"You won't believe this but I've been back at the Big Horn Ranch today." He stopped to let that sink in.

Carrie's face screwed up. "Huh, why?"

"They were on that list of ATV owners. There were five total I felt should be followed up on. I took the Big Horn Ranch and another that I will go to tomorrow. Mike and Rick took the others.

"Go on," Carrie was eager to hear more.

"Seems like their ATV had been stolen before the first of the five bodies were found. And before you ask, yes they filed a report with Darren. I went by his office and he copied the file for me.

"That's not all. There was a list of items stolen at that time, one of which is a castration knife," he paused and looked up to see Carrie's reaction. He chuckled at her round eyes.

"Just so happens my timing was just right to witness one in action today," said Randy. "When I got to the ranch, they were working cattle." He felt slightly proud that he had gained the ability to sling that term around, hopefully impressing Carrie.

"Working cattle..." Randy began.

"I know what that is," interrupted Carrie.

"You do?" Randy was surprised.

"Of course. I'm surprised you don't. How long have you lived in Oklahoma? For-ev-er, and you don't know what working cattle is?"

"Well, anyway," Randy continued deflated, "Darren agreed that it was a possibility that the knife would be sharp enough to slit a man's throat the way our victims' throats were cut. He didn't want to say for sure and we both agreed the medical examiner would be the one to confirm or deny.

"He's going back to the Big Horn this evening to get another one just like it so we will have one to compare it to. But that isn't all," he was gaining excitement again.

"They had a suspect in the theft," Randy paused to get Carrie's response.

"Well, go on," Carrie was excited to hear.

"A ranch-hand at the Big Horn went missing about the same time as the thefts occurred. They never found him or the stolen items." Randy let that sit there and stew for a minute.

Carrie's mind was churning. She was assimilating all the new pieces into what they already knew. Randy let the process play out because it usually produced productive results.

"You know, we have never gotten an id on the fifth victim. We were checking missing person reports, but if he left the Big Horn and it was assumed that he left because of the theft, no one would have filed a missing person report," Carrie's eyes glowed.

Randy hadn't put that together quite yet, but it made perfect sense.

"Do you have info on him?" Carrie was reaching toward Randy to hand her what she already knew without asking that he had. He handed it over and she eagerly read.

"Randy you have to get this into the system and see what turns up. The age, everything fits with the other victims."

"I know, but I want to run right back out to get the knife from Darren as soon as he has it and so I thought spending time here at the hospital with you was the perfect solution since it's about half-way between Kachina and our office."

Carrie nodded, deep in thought. Ideas were rolling around in her head and for the next hour, she and Randy tossed around theories and possibilities to explore. When

Randy's phone buzzed in his pocket, it startled him. It was Darren.

Hanging up the phone he stood and gathered the paperwork they had been reviewing. "I've got to go, but I will keep you in the loop."

Carrie wanted more than ever to get out of that bed and go with him.

CHAPTER 17

*A*ndrea felt a slight chill when Senna walked in to work the next morning. "Hey, there, how are you feeling?" Andrea was sincere in her inquiry. She cared deeply about Senna and hoped that she was better.

Senna's smile was tight when she said, "I'm fine. It was all just a really big fuss for nothing." She quickly put her things away, her purse in the drawer and her lunch in the fridge, and went straight to the overnight deposit box and began sorting.

Confused as to what to say or do, Andrea left her alone and went back to her work. She couldn't shake the uneasy feeling that she had inside. Something wasn't right, and she didn't know what or how to fix it. Patience, she thought, patience is the key.

It was the day before the book fair at the school and having worked efficiently up to that point, there was very little left to do. Andrea got the boxes of books together by the back door where they would load them when it was time to head to the school.

Lunchtime came and even though Senna had always brought her lunch before, they had fallen into the habit of getting something and eating together in the office. The fact that Senna had brought her lunch today disappointed Andrea. She thought she was making a mountain out of a molehill, maybe Senna's budget was getting tight.

At precisely eleven twenty-nine, one minute before her scheduled lunchtime, Senna went to the fridge, got her lunch and headed for the door. "I'm going to lunch now," was all she said as she left. The front door swung shut at exactly eleven thirty.

Andrea had such a sick feeling inside. Since no one was currently in the library and Senna was out, she thought she would call Blake.

Blake quickly answered. Andrea told him how the morning had gone and of her concerns.

"When was the last time you spoke to her?" asked Andrea.

"Last night. I called her about seven to check on her. She seemed fine. Quiet, but fine." Blake concentrated on replaying the call in his mind. Had she really been fine?

"You know, now that you mention it, she did seem a

little off. I just chalked it up to the stress of the ordeal. She sounded tired, so I didn't keep her on the phone long so she could rest."

"I'm assuming she's gone to the park to eat her lunch the way that she always used to do. If you aren't in the middle of something maybe you could check on her," said Andrea. She stood behind the counter fiddling with the pencil in her hand.

Blake moved to his office window that overlooked the park. "Yes, she's there. I'll go check and let you know how she is." Blake was already heading out the door when he hung up the phone with Andrea.

As Blake crossed through the park to the bench where Senna sat, he was hopeful that he and Andrea were wrong. But passing out like she had done was not normal, and neither did this seem to be.

He slipped onto the bench next to Senna. "Hi there," he smiled at her as she turned her head to look at him. She did not smile back.

"How are you?" Blake asked with concern creasing his face.

Senna looked back out into the park. "I'm fine. You know Blake I really think we shouldn't see each other anymore."

Blake wasn't sure he'd heard her correctly. "Why?" He was crushed. Her statement seemed so cold and hard. He'd never heard her speak so matter-of-fact and to the point.

"I just can't do it. I don't want to do it," she said still looking out across the park.

He sat with his elbows on his knees and looked down at his hands. This was a blow out of left field and he had no idea how to handle it. What had he done? Was it church? Had taking her to church rekindled the trauma, setting her back, erasing all the strides she'd made?

"I don't understand," he said quietly.

"I don't care if you understand," she said. Her voice was curt and short.

Blake's head snapped around to look at her. What he saw was a cold and indifferent Senna, not the sweet and charming lady he had fallen in love with. But to love meant you loved all of a person no matter the mood or emotion they were dealing with. He did love her and he had to find a way to help her.

She turned her head to look at him and said, "Seriously Blake, you need to leave me alone."

Her cold eyes bore into his and he quietly nodded in agreement. He knew this was not the time to try to convince her otherwise. He stood up and started to remind her that he loved her, but stopped himself. He knew right now it wouldn't help.

He turned and walked back toward his office, stunned, broken and bewildered.

"IT's a day earlier than I had planned on releasing you," the doctor said, "but if you'll promise me, you'll take care of yourself and follow my instructions, I'll let you go home." He looked at Carrie over the tops of his reading glasses. She felt like she had many times in the past when her SAC had scolded her.

"I promise I will," Carrie overzealously agreed. Her mind was racing ahead to what she needed, well wanted to do. First she would call Randy to come get her.

The doctor was writing on her chart and then on a prescription pad. "I'm prescribing you some painkillers, but I want you to try not to take them unless you absolutely must. Take ibuprofen if you can get by with that. If you only moderately exert yourself, you shouldn't need them.

"I better not see you back in here because you have re-injured yourself." It was a stern warning and Carrie fully understood the repercussions. She nodded her head in sincerity. There was no way she wanted to wind up back in the hospital.

As soon as the doctor left, Carrie was on the phone with Randy. "Come get me."

"Now?" Randy asked surprised at the immediacy in her tone.

"Yes. The doctor has released me and I've got to get out of here. But I need clothes. What I came in with are a mess. I can tell you where to go get some stuff at my house."

"What if I just stop at the Dollar Store and get you some sweats? I don't want to go digging around in your undies looking for clothes for you."

Carrie almost laughed at Randy. "That's fine. I think the *undies* I have are fine. Hurry up."

"Okay, Okay, I'll be there soon," Randy said. He was glad that Carrie was being released, but he had a sneaking suspicion that she had not been released to go back to work, only home.

By the time the wheels that churned, had churned out the hospital release paperwork, Randy had arrived with a beautiful pair of purple sweats.

"Really?" said Carrie when she looked in the bag. "Are you kidding me? Purple?" She looked at Randy and she thought she almost saw a smile creeping in.

"Never mind, I would wear a pink tutu just to get out of here." She was heading to the bathroom still shuffling a bit. Soon, she emerged like a purple gumdrop.

"Don't say a word," she warned Randy.

"I say nothing," he said as he moved his fingers across his lips mimicking a zipper.

"I'm just going to wear these rubber bottomed socks out of here. My boots are a mess and I'm not sure they go with my outfit," Carrie smiled back at Randy. "I'm ready; let's go."

The euphoria of being released from the hospital gave her the strength she needed to ride down to the car in the wheelchair and get into Randy's car. She wanted to will herself to be at one hundred percent, but she just couldn't.

She knew she'd made considerable progress when she thought back to when she was first injured. That was only four days ago. In another four days, she would be even better.

Randy drove her to the pharmacy to fill her prescription and then straight home. She didn't want to admit it, but the jostle of the car ride was rough on her. Randy helped her into her house and got her settled on the sofa in her living room. She popped a pain pill without water and gently laid herself down.

Randy nervously looked around not knowing what to do next. "What can I do for you before I leave?" he asked.

"Sit down and let's talk about the case." Carrie was raring to go, but she knew right then all she could do was talk.

"Nope. I'm going to leave and you are going to rest. I promise that after you've rested, we can talk. You aren't fooling me. The car ride was hell and you need to rest."

"Well, I'll call you when I wake up," said Carrie. "Wait, I don't have my phone. Did you guys try tracking my phone?"

Randy tilted his head at her with his eyebrows raised. "Really? You had to ask? It was dead. No signal and no trace."

"What about the last place it showed it was on?" Carrie was eager to hear.

"The cabin," said Randy. "I'm guessing he busted it or took out the card and tossed it in the woods on his way out. I bet if we go looking we'll find it out there somewhere.

"The forensic team went out on Monday and went through the cabin getting fingerprints and bagging anything they felt might be a clue." Randy had not told her that until now. He knew what her reaction would be.

She groaned. "Oh, no. I don't want them out there!" She was distraught. "Randy, there are going to be so many fingerprints, it will take them decades to go through. I don't want everyone knowing all about my life." She wanted all this to stop.

"Too late. They've already come and gone." His matter-of-fact attitude irritated Carrie.

"Found the car yet?" She raised the elbow that she had slung over her eyes to look at him.

"Not yet," he said. "You really kept that hidden from everyone."

"For obvious reasons. A law enforcement official on a government salary driving that.... Not only would I have never heard the end of it, but Internal Affairs would have been all over me wondering where the money came from."

"I get it." And he did. He was antsy to leave though. He was excited about the new leads and wanted to pow-wow with Mike and Rick, and even Darren. He felt they were finally really getting somewhere.

"Okay, well, I'm out of here, if you're sure you don't need anything else." He stooped down and awkwardly planted a kiss on her forehead. "Please don't get up and do anything stupid."

"I will."

"You will do something stupid? Or you will not get up?" Randy asked.

"I will take it easy and rest. I promise," she said.

"Oh, hey," Carrie suddenly remembered, "I have a doctor's appointment tomorrow afternoon at three. Do you mind taking me?"

"Nope, not at all." Randy gave her a wink and headed out the door. Carrie watched him leave and heard his car pull out of her driveway. She should've asked him to bring her laptop to her, she wanted to order a new phone, but she also wanted to do some research. She was just as eager as Randy to learn more.

Resigning herself to lie where she was for the time being, she allowed herself to drift off to sleep. The facts of the case were floating in the back of her mind and a face drifted by, and then she was out.

"DID YOU HAVE A GOOD LUNCH?" asked Andrea when Senna came back. Blake had called her the minute he was back at his office. He had described to Andrea what Senna had said and the changes in her. He'd been devastated. Andrea would have liked to say she had been shocked, but from what she had seen that morning, she wasn't.

"It was fine." Cool and aloof. Andrea had absolutely no idea what to say or do. Her gentle offering of friendship had worked before. Maybe she would just slide back into her bubbly self and win Senna over again.

"What did you think of church on Sunday?" Andrea asked. She held her breath waiting for a reply. She had told herself she would stay away from that topic but she couldn't stand it any longer.

"Honestly, I won't be going back. They have an intoxicating way of manipulating people's emotions with lights, music, and an eloquent delivery. I saw right through it." Senna was working at the counter looking at the overdue book list.

Andrea just stood looking at Senna. From what she had witnessed on Sunday she couldn't fathom that Senna felt that way. What Andrea had seen was a genuinely emotional outpouring from a broken woman. *What on earth could've happened to her that day?* pondered Andrea.

"I'm sorry you feel that way. I've attended that church for years. I know most of the people who go there. It would break their hearts if they knew someone felt that they were being manipulated. I know their hearts and they have a genuine love and concern for people," Andrea was choosing her words carefully.

Senna turned her now cold eyes on Andrea and said, "How can you know anyone's heart—truly know?"

It left Andrea speechless. She simply shook her head and walked away. It was true, how could anyone truly know what was in the heart of another person.

WHEN CARRIE AWOKE, she felt much better. She'd slept for over two hours on the sofa. It felt like more rest than she had gotten in several days. She had the urge to check her cell phone for messages, but of course no phone, no messages.

She slowly got up from the sofa, went to the bathroom and then realized she was hungry. She decided to order a pizza online with her laptop. Pulling the chair out at her desk she sat down and turned on her computer. The first order of business was to order a pizza, then a new phone. The confirmation code said her phone would be delivered the day after tomorrow. Good enough.

She was interested in the castration knife that was on the list of stolen goods from the Big Horn. She'd known what 'working cattle' was, but there were several tools used in castration. Her grandfather had always used a Newberry-style castrating knife. That type of knife was a tong type apparatus with curved ends, one side with a sharp blade pointing in towards the other curve. The other side had a slim v-shaped end for the blade to slide safely into when cutting. It certainly wasn't something that could easily be used to slit a throat with.

After researching and reading for the next thirty minutes her doorbell rang. It was the pizza delivery. Her wallet had been in the car, but she kept some cash stashed at home, thank goodness. She ate almost half the pizza ravenously. It tasted so good after eating hospital food that she had no restraint.

Carrie could feel herself getting antsy. She wasn't exactly house-bound; she had her old Honda Civic which she drove to the office each day, but her doctor had said no driving. Honestly, she didn't feel like leaving, anyway.

She wanted to call Randy and felt very frustrated that she had no phone. For lack of anything better to do, she sat on the sofa and turned on the TV. She flipped channels until she found a movie and settled in to watch it and wait for Randy.

The movie finished, and he still hadn't come by. Tired of the TV noise, she shut it off and laid back down on the sofa. Her mind was clearer than it had been in days and she was eagerly analyzing the facts of the case.

The missing ranch-hand could be victim number five. If that was true, then he was not the killer. Maybe victim number five was not the missing ranch-hand, but just another victim and the ranch-hand was the killer of all seven.

So if the thief was the victim what could have happened? He stole the stuff and then it was stolen from him? Someone had him steal the stuff, and then they killed him? Someone paid him to steal the stuff? What was the most likely scenario?

She heard a car pull up and realized it was Randy. Thank God he was back. She'd thought she would go stir crazy.

"Do you want some pizza? I got pizza," Carrie offered.

"Sure," Randy replied.

They sat in the living room and Randy pulled a slice of pizza out of the box which was still sitting on the coffee table. "That's so good, even cold. I'm starved."

"So what have you got?" Carrie just couldn't stand it anymore.

Randy attempted to chew the huge bite of pizza he'd just bitten off and swallow it down. "Okay. Okay. Got anything to drink?" he asked.

"A beer in the fridge," Carrie half-heartedly motioned towards the kitchen. She let him settle back down and finish the slice he had started. She was forcing herself to be patient when it was the last thing she wanted to do.

Randy wiped his hands on a paper towel he'd also retrieved from the kitchen. He sat back in the chair and took a long swig. "None of the other ATVs panned out. As of right now, the Big Horn Ranch's stolen ATV is the closest bet.

"The missing ranch-hand slash thief's name is Anderson Cooper. They called him Andy. We have requested his dental records and they'll be here by tomorrow. He was thirty-nine years old, about 5' 10" tall and 160 pounds. He was slight of build just like Justin and Keith.

"I took the knife to the medical examiner and Henry said he felt strongly that knife or one just like it could have been the murder weapon. He still has it and is doing further tests, but on initial examination, he felt like it would be a match."

Carrie was filing away each detail mentally as Randy gave them to her. Her mind was categorizing them with great efficiency. Then something occurred to her.

"Randy we've been searching for a male killer all this time. We've assumed that because men were the victims that it would've had to have been another man to move the bodies.

"But if the men were slight of build and a woman was strong and fit, she could've nearly had as much strength as a man. It could also be possible she could devise ways to move a body."

Barely slowing down, she continued, "What if a woman enticed the man to drink with her in a remote place where she already had the blue poly-tarp, let's say the top of Crown Rock Mesa. Then when he passed out in the car seat from the ketamine, she could place the tarp on the ground outside the passenger door, open the door, and tilt the body out onto the tarp.

"Once on the tarp, she could use the castration knife to slit his throat. Then she could roll the body up like a burrito, blood and all inside, and move it to the edge of the cliff. Holding the edge of the tarp, she could unfurl it tumbling the body to the ground below."

"Okay," Randy was listening. "What about the first body we found? There was no tarp. The body was killed right where he lay."

"I've thought about that. Why move the body at all there? It was a remote area and maybe she had to improvise. Maybe it was spur of the moment and she didn't have the tarp with her."

"In that case she could've left the body on the top of Crown Rock," said Randy.

For a few minutes they both sat thinking. "Let's go back to the first five bodies. They were all five done the same, from what we can tell. I'm guessing she used a tarp, rolled them up and then used a wench on the ATV to drag the body up onto the bed in the back. She then drove out to the woods and dumped it with the lift on the bed. That model has a hydraulic bed which can be used to dump dirt, gravel, and such. Easy peasy." Carrie snapped her fingers for added impact.

"How did she cover her tracks at the two scenes in Kachina?" asked Randy.

"I don't know. You have to figure part of this out," Carrie said with a wink.

"It still could be a man," said Randy.

"Could be, but to me it feels like a woman. She could entice a man to do about anything she wanted if he was drinking. Trust me, I know."

CHAPTER 18

*I*t was the day for the book fair and the library was closed with a sign on the door. There had been little time for Senna and Andrea to talk while carrying books and setting up tables.

Andrea wasn't sure what to say, anyway. She felt, for now, it was best they just work together as cordially as possible, while hoping that Senna would recover and feel better about things, eventually.

"I forgot to tell you, I have another appointment this afternoon with Dr. Specter," declared Senna, matter-of-factly.

"Oh, that's good," Andrea replied. "What time do you need to leave?"

"I'll leave at two o'clock."

There was no courteous request or asking if the

library would be staffed, just a simple statement of what she was *going* to do. Andrea tried to not get angry.

"I thought you would be seeing her on Fridays," said Andrea.

Senna looked at her and said, "Why would you think that?"

"Well, because your appointment last week was on a Friday. I just assumed...," replied Andrea.

"That was because there had been a cancellation." Andrea had never heard Senna be so condescending. "She's decided her best available spot for me is on Thursday afternoons at three o'clock."

"Thank you for letting me know," Andrea couldn't help showing her frustration. She was seething.

The book fair ended at one o'clock and Senna and Andrea loaded the leftover books into the boxes and drove back to the library. Neither one spoke a word the entire time.

Once the books were unloaded, Senna grabbed her purse and said, "I think I will leave now."

Andrea looked at the clock. "But it is only one thirty. I thought you weren't leaving until two?"

"I know, but I thought I would leave a little early." Senna was so flippant that it stunned Andrea yet again. She watched Senna walk out the door and wondered what on earth could have caused this drastic change in her?

As she went back to unpacking the books and getting

ready for the after school group to arrive, Andrea's heart was heavy. The only one she felt she could confide in about Senna and what she was feeling about all of it was Blake. She decided that when she could, she would give him a call. She knew he was hurting even more than she was and maybe she could be a comfort to him as well.

ARRIVING EARLY to the medical complex where Dr. Specter's office was located, Senna decided to sit in her car for a while. Something had changed inside of her and she had no idea what. Less than a week ago she'd been happy, really happy. She'd pushed Blake away, and she was pretty certain that she'd pushed Andrea away as well. She had hurt them both deeply and yet couldn't seem to stop herself.

Senna hoped that seeing Dr. Specter today would help her sort some of this out. It would be nice if someone could just flip a switch and everything be fine, back the way it had been last week. She knew, though, that recovery was always slow. She had felt such hope with the progress she'd made, but now she felt like she had digressed to a worse state than she'd originally been in. She felt discontent, irritable, angry, and unstable.

Her car was parked near the entrance of the complex with the front door only a few feet in front of her. The man and woman walking toward the entrance caught her attention. She knew that woman. She recognized her face but couldn't remember from where.

The woman was looking straight at her, and it made her feel uncomfortable. Seeing recognition on the woman's face, she realized that the woman knew her, too. She diverted her eyes to her lap and slid down slightly in the seat. She did not want her coming over to the car.

Randy had picked Carrie up for the doctor's appointment and they were right on time. As they were walking up to the door Carrie spotted the woman she'd seen in the hospital. She knew that woman and suddenly she remembered where she knew her from.

Once inside the door, she motioned for Randy to move to the side out of direct view of the lady's car. "I know that woman out there in the car," said Carrie.

Randy was looking at her waiting for more. He dipped his head slightly and raised his eyebrows hoping to prod her along, "And so..."

"She was the woman two doors down from me in the hospital," Carrie paused.

"And once again, so..." Randy didn't want to be impatient, but he knew he was certainly missing something.

"It's been bugging the thunder out of me to try to remember where I knew her from. Yesterday right after you brought me home when I was falling asleep on the sofa, I was thinking about the case. All the clues and people were rolling around in my mind, and I was trying to make sense of it all. I remember now right before I fell asleep that her face came to mind," Carrie was speaking low, but her voice was excited and urgent.

"I know her from the Darkside, she was there almost every time I was there. Boy was she a player, too. She had the men pawing all over her. I saw her leave with a different man each time I was there and she never left without a man. I thought it odd. I never saw her with the same man twice.

"I never told you, but I found the Darkside a long time ago and have been going there off and on for over a year." She paused to let that sink in, waiting for a reprimand.

Randy didn't want to appear shocked, so he didn't respond to her last statement. "Could be a coincidence," he finally said. He thought he knew where she was going with this, but was also trying to decide if her theory made sense.

"Were you ever there when Justin and Keith were there?" Randy asked suddenly concerned his partner may be more involved in their deaths than she was letting on.

Carrie's face creased in concentration. "I don't think so. I wouldn't have jeopardized the case by holding back that information. If I'd seen them or thought I had any information that could have helped, I would've told you." Carrie was looking intently at Randy. She wanted him to know she was sincere.

"I know," Randy said. "I've known you long enough to know your priority is always the case."

"Ike was being very discrete when we interviewed

him. He knew I'd become somewhat of a regular there, but that is one reason I liked it so much, everyone's business stays their business."

Randy nodded. "So, let me make sure I'm following you. After our discussion last night, you think that a woman could be our killer, and you highly suspect that the woman out in the car could be the woman at the bar?"

Once Carrie heard it come back out at her, she seemed skeptical of her own theory. "Sounds a little out there, doesn't it?" Carrie asked, hoping he would say, 'no Carrie, certainly not!'

Randy stood looking out the glass front of the building towards the woman's car. He could barely see her through the car window. They were back far enough in the building that he was sure she couldn't see them. Could it be possible? He wondered. Maybe. It was as good as any other theory they had, but they didn't have enough reason to even bring her in for questioning.

"Let's say you're right," Randy began, "what do you suggest we do at this point? We have no evidence linking her to the crime. We need to find out who she is and do some digging, see if anything validates this theory."

"Her car tag. Hang back while I go up to my doctor's appointment. When she comes in, hopefully, or even if she starts to drive off, get her tag, make, and model of her car." Randy had already thought of that while Carrie stated the obvious next step.

Carrie went on up to her appointment and Randy found an out of the way place to sit where he could watch the lady in the car without drawing attention to himself.

Within ten minutes she got out of her car, locked it up, and headed towards the door. She was dressed very conservatively in grey slacks and a simple navy top. She wore almost no make-up and her hair was tied back in a loose low ponytail. She certainly didn't match the description Carrie had given him.

He'd had his phone ready with the camera app open and held it where it looked natural to an observer, but where he could easily take pictures of her coming through the door.

She rode the elevator up. Once the doors had closed, Randy made a beeline out to her car. He quickly took a photo of her tag and stepped back to take an overall pic of her car. It was a five-year-old silver Prius.

He glanced casually in her windows to see if he could see anything unusual. Nothing at all was in there. Clean as a whistle.

He had shared everything he and Carrie had discussed the night before with Mike, Rick, and Darren this morning at a joint meeting they'd had in the war room. They had thrown out a few additional thoughts and suggestions, but were excited about what they had been able to put together so far.

He sent the pics of the lady and her car to all three plus Carrie, in a group text and asked if anyone knew her, particularly Darren. Then he asked if one of them would run her plates and gave a limited explanation of what Carrie had said earlier.

Almost instantly Darren responded to their group text. "I know her," it said, "She's the lady that works at the library here in Kachina. I can't remember her name right off."

Randy about choked, the library? A couple of cute snide comments came through from Mike and Rick, but Rick agreed to run her plates. Randy texted everyone a thank-you as he walked back into the building. He went back to where he had previously been sitting. If the lady came out before Carrie, he wanted to be able to observe her without suspicion.

But it wasn't to happen that way. Carrie came out after about forty-five minutes and he'd seen no other sign of the lady. Randy wanted to hear about Carrie's visit and Carrie wanted to hear about the lady. They agreed to go sit in Randy's car after moving it to where they could strategically observe the lady leaving. Once there, Carrie would tell him all about her appointment.

"Doctor said I was fine."

Randy looked at her like, *really?*

"Okay, but really I am healing well. He checked the stitches in my hand and said they should come out in a few days. No signs of infection. He looked where my ribs were broken and said there were no signs that indicated additional damage or that they weren't healing correctly. I am to come back next Tuesday at three."

Satisfied, Randy gave Carrie the events from while she was in with the doctor. "Seems like a long shot to me," said Randy. "You should have seen her. She looked like a librarian. I guess that is because she *is* a librarian." Randy laughed at his joke.

"You're right. It doesn't jibe with what I know. Could be a twin. Could be that she is boring by day and daring by night. Could be I was totally wrong, but I doubt it." Carrie was once again throwing out possible scenarios the way she loved to do.

It was after four o'clock before the lady emerged from the building. She did not look around and therefore did not notice Randy and Carrie sitting two rows behind her car under a shade tree. Even if she had looked up, it would have been hard to see them with the shade and reflection on the front car window.

"I'm almost positive it's her. She's a dead ringer for the lady I'm talking about, but her body language is totally different. The lady in the bar walked around with confidence and an air of owning whatever space she was in. This lady is an obvious introvert and mousy. She looks like a feather blown the wrong way would scare her to death." Carrie kept trying to formulate an explanation in her mind.

"Did you happen to see what floor she went up to?" Carrie asked.

"No. I was sitting out of the way so I could see her enter the building and then get on the elevator, but I couldn't see what button she pushed once in there.

As the lady pulled out of her spot, they did the same following behind at a safe distance. Randy's phone pinged. "Take a look at that for me. It may be info from Rick."

Carrie picked up Randy's phone. It was indeed from Rick. 'Lady's name is Senna Carter. No record. No flags of any kind. Didn't want to dig deeper until we know more. Address: 632 Pine Grove, Kachina'.

She texted back, 'Tailing now. Will advise'.

The tail was uneventful. They followed her back to Kachina and then to the address that Rick had sent in the text. Randy drove past and then circled the block. Her house was on a corner lot so he circled and came back at a right angle to the street they had driven in on. He stopped well back, but close enough to see her house.

It was a small white clapboard house, and it looked to be about nine hundred or so square feet. The exterior was tidy and well maintained. There was a large detached garage at the back of the lot situated at the end of the driveway. The lady pulled her Prius up close to the garage, put it in park, and got out. She went to what they assumed was her back door, losing sight of her as she walked behind the house.

They discussed leaving, but were so curious they felt compelled to stay. She was the closest thing to any kind of suspect they'd been able to generate. After about an hour, the lady came back out. She was dressed in jeans and didn't have her purse so it didn't appear that she was leaving.

After punching a code in the keypad next to the garage door, it began to go up.

"Oh my goodness," Carrie exclaimed. "Do you see what I see?"

Randy sat there dumbfounded. There in that little clapboard garage sat a bright red Ferrari. "Sweet! Can you see the model?"

"No, her Prius is parked too close."

Randy had grabbed his duty camera from the backseat and was using it to zoom in and take pictures. The model and tag were still hidden behind the Prius.

"I've never seen a Ferrari like that," said Carrie. "Could be something special."

The lady had gone into the garage and was doing something at the back where neither Randy or Carrie could see. She was only in there about ten minutes then left, closing the door behind her before going back into the house.

Randy sent the pics of the car to their group text, 'What kind of Ferrari is that?'

Mike, being a car guy, knew exactly what it was 'A Ferrari 488 Spider, depending on options lists new at close to $400,000'.

Randy and Carrie let out a consecutively shocked huff

of air. They were dumbfounded and speechless. If the thought of a Ferrari being in this little tidy detached clapboard garage had taken them back, then this exclusive Ferrari that cost more than six times the cost of that house, rendered them beyond thought and speech.

"Well, there is definitely something wrong here. The tag isn't visible in the pics." Randy quickly texted back to see if any other vehicles had come up under that lady's name. 'Nope. None' came back. 'Check for stolen Ferraris' and 'Did. Found none' came back.

"We need probable cause for a search warrant," Carrie thought out loud. "I want in that house and garage." Her mind was inventing plausible reasons to gain entrance.

"Me too," said Randy just as his phone pinged again. 'Only two sold. One to a Sienna Carter'. Randy quickly typed back 'typo?' to which the response was 'no'.

Adrenaline was surging through both Randy and Carrie. They sat for the next hour discussing theories and plans with no movement in or around the house.

Not long after Senna had left for her appointment, Andrea was able to find the time to call Blake.

"I hope I'm not interrupting you," said Andrea.

"No. I can't concentrate on what I am supposed to be doing," replied Blake. He sat back in his desk chair and rubbed his eyes. The stress of it all was wearing him down and he felt old and tired.

"Have you talked to her; since yesterday at the park that is?" asked Andrea. She was nervous and paced behind the library counter, and she currently couldn't resist an old habit of chewing her cuticles.

"No. I think it's best to give her time," Blake said. "I'm trying to figure out what's going on. I love her, Andrea. Well, I loved the Senna I knew. She doesn't seem at all like the same person now. I waver from being hurt to indignant that she would treat me this way, I'm so totally confused. It's been a cycle like that all yesterday afternoon and today."

Andrea told him about how Senna had been at work that day and the things she'd said. "She actually left early for her doctor's appointment, which alone is strange, but she didn't even give me the courtesy of saying she would be leaving, or acting as if she cared if it was an imposition on me." Andrea felt renewed frustration.

"I know this may sound odd, and I completely understand if you can't or don't want to, but could we meet for dinner? I really need to talk and you are the only one I feel like I can talk to about this." Andrea held her breath, hoping. She knew it was forward, and she hoped Blake didn't read more into the request than she had intended.

"I'm pretty beat from all this, but I agree with you. I need to talk about it, too, and eat. Let's go to the diner and have a burger, if that's fine with you."

Relieved, Andrea readily agreed to meet him at the diner at six fifteen. Andrea would be done at the library at six o'clock so that would give her more than enough time to shut things down and get to the diner.

Blake was just walking up to the diner door as Andrea was crossing the street. Their normally friendly greeting was dampened by their downcast spirits. The diner was busy and all the booths were full. As they were standing there, the group sitting at the booth in front of the window got up and left.

The waitress buzzed by with a promise to clean the table for them. She was quick and efficient, and in just a heartbeat, they were seated.

They ordered from memory and sat for a while with nothing to say. They were both, individually, lost in thought. They attempted some small talk and then their meals came.

Blake ate his burger, but Andrea only picked at her chicken sandwich. They wanted to talk about it, but honestly didn't know where to start or what to say that hadn't already been said.

Once the waitress came and cleared their food away, Blake said, "Andrea did you see any of this, any clue that she…" he choked up and couldn't finish.

Andrea just sat quietly shaking her head. She was looking down at the paper napkin she was tearing into tiny little shreds. Then she looked up, and seeing the pain on Blake's face, reached across the table with both of her hands and covered his.

"Blake I'm so sorry. I know I'm hurting, but I know it is nothing like what you're feeling." They both sat with Andrea's hands covering Blake's, looking at each other face to face. Both were oblivious to the fact that Senna had just driven by and had seen them clearly through the window of the diner.

Senna had left her house after Randy and Carrie had decided to leave. Randy and Carrie had had no reason to believe Senna would be leaving or doing anything that would further the investigation. They were also not yet authorized for a stakeout, so they had left.

It was just as well because Carrie was feeling exhausted. Her body needed rest. Randy took her home and then said goodbye.

About thirty minutes after they'd left, Senna got in her Prius and drove away. She'd had no idea she had been watched. She wanted to go to the grocery store and fill her tank with gas.

From the street, Senna had seen Blake and Andrea in full view. They were sitting in an intimate position in the front booth of the diner. Blake and Andrea were leaning in with their forearms resting on the table. Andrea was covering both of Blake's hands with both of hers. They were face to face, obviously completely engaged in intimate conversation.

Nausea engulfed Senna. She drove on past and found

herself doubling over in pain. She quickly pulled the car over and parked just before passing out.

IT HAD BEEN hard to talk about the situation with Senna at first, but soon Blake and Andrea were sharing their hurt and hoping for resolution. They found that, once they had opened up, time had flown by. One thing was certain though, they both cared deeply for their new friend and wanted to do whatever they could to help her, and also hoped to restore their relationships.

It was well after nine and dark outside by the time Andrea was pulling into her driveway. The little house she lived in did not have a garage, so she always parked on the gravel driveway next to her house.

She stepped out, locked her car door and headed to her back porch. It may not have been necessary to lock her doors in Kachina, as small and safe as it was, but she always did.

Once at the porch, she was trying to find the right key on her key ring. She wished she'd thought to turn on the back porch light before leaving that morning, but she rarely came home after dark this time of year, so the thought had never occurred to her.

Suddenly, she felt something grab her from behind. It was some type of strap that pinned her arms down to her sides. She began to scream, but as soon as she opened her mouth it was filled with a soaked rag.

Her eyes began to water and burn and she found she'd lost the ability to fight back. Soon darkness overtook her.

Sometime later she began to wake. It was dark wherever she was and her mind was foggy. As realization of what had happened hit her, panic immediately set in. She began to struggle against the bonds that kept her arms tight against her sides.

She began to scream, realizing that the rag was no longer in her mouth. As soon as she did, a lantern was lit in the corner of the room and light slowly filled the space. She was in a cabin of some kind. There was a small side table where the lantern sat. And... and the rocking chair that Senna sat in next to the table.

Confusion completely consumed her mind. "Senna, what are you doing?" Andrea asked.

Senna got up and came to stand in front of Andrea. She squatted down right in front of her. "I'm not Senna." The voice was not Senna's. In fact if Andrea had heard that voice independent of seeing Senna in front of her, she would not have known who it was.

Andrea just sat, confused and frightened. The lady stood up and walked back to the chair dragging it closer to where Andrea was. She sat down and leaned back. It was an old wooden rocking chair that creaked when she rocked. The lady leaned back, crossed her legs, and began to slowly rock.

The binding was holding her arms down so tightly that Andrea's arms were in excruciating pain. "Can you loosen this tie? I'm in so much pain, and my arms are numb." Andrea was hopeful that she would comply.

The lady just continued to rock slowly.

"Who are you, if you are not Senna?" Andrea asked.

Still, the lady just continued to rock back and forth which only escalated Andrea's fear. Hot tears of despair rolled down Andrea's cheeks. She was too terrified to say any more. The lady looked exactly like Senna. But her body movements were totally different. Andrea couldn't put her finger on it right then, but Senna never held that kind of posture or moved in that way.

And Senna would never dress like that. She had on tight, low-slung skinny jeans with a little tank top that didn't quite reach to the top of those jeans. A logo on the front was of some kind of biker emblem or something, Andrea couldn't quite tell. And she wore high heeled black sandals. Senna was barely out of flats.

But it was her demeanor that was the most different. Without saying a word, she caused Andrea to be alarmed. Even if she had not been abducted and tied up, she knew in this woman's presence she would feel terrified. It felt like pure evil radiated from within her.

"You're trying to hurt Senna." It was a matter-of-fact statement, condemning Andrea of something she had not done. "I saw you with Blake at the diner tonight."

This lady knows Senna. It has to be a twin. But Senna

never ever mentioned having a sibling of any kind. Andrea's mind raced.

The chair stopped rocking, and the lady very slowly and deliberately uncrossed her legs, leaned forward, and placed her arms on her knees. "I'm Sienna," she said carefully pronouncing her name, as she stared into Andrea's eyes. As the lady spoke, Andrea felt her hair rise up on end. Andrea had to look away because she could not bear to look into those eyes. They chilled her to the bone.

"I will never allow you to hurt Senna." The lady, Sienna, stood and walked over to Andrea, reaching down to slightly loosen the wide strap that held her. Andrea realized it was a nylon ratchet tie-down strap. She was grateful for the slight release, but her arms surged with pain as the blood flowed back through.

Not only did the strap wrap around her entire midsection and both arms, but also around some type of pipe running from floor to ceiling behind her. The strap kept Andrea firmly pressed against the pipe. She moved slightly to see if the pipe had any give to it, but it held firm and steady.

The wooden floor squeaked and cracked as Sienna walked over to the other side of the room, picking up another strap exactly like the one that was already on her. She came back and wrapped the second one around her as well.

"There. No wiggling out of that." The top strap ran just above Andrea's elbows and the second strap ran slightly below her elbows. Her arms were firmly tied down with her elbows tucked tight into the narrow recess of her waist. She was sitting firmly on the ground and knew she wouldn't be able to get her legs up under her, but with Sienna sitting there, she wouldn't even dare try.

Sienna casually sat back down in the chair and began to rock again, watching Andrea in the dim light of the lantern. Andrea sat still not wanting to antagonize her.

They both sat in silence for some time, Sienna gently rocking back and forth and Andrea sitting deadly still, terrified. Her mind was racing, trying to pull pieces and explanations together to help her understand what was going on.

This lady, Sienna, obviously Senna's twin, was the exact opposite of Senna in every way. Maybe she had not grown up with Senna, but when she was born had been adopted to another family and Senna never knew about her.

Did that theory fit with what she knew about Senna and her life? Andrea wondered. Possibly. Had this lady ever reached out to Senna? Did Senna know about her and had just never said anything to Andrea about it? How could one twin be so sweet and innocent and the other one be the epitome of sheer evil? The questions raced in between threads of fear and panic.

"Why did you take me?" Andrea finally had the courage to ask Sienna.

Still, the lady just rocked quietly watching Andrea.

"What are you going to do with me?" Her voice was thick with panic.

Sienna had control and was in no hurry to respond. She was a master of manipulation and control, and if she decided to answer at all, it would be on her terms and in her way. But then like a cat with a mouse she thought it might be fun to engage with Andrea.

"You were hurting Senna and I couldn't let that happen."

"Blake and I are friends. We had dinner tonight because he was hurting and concerned that Senna had pushed him away, and I was just there to talk to him. He loves Senna," Andrea was pleading with Sienna to understand.

Then in a flash, Andrea remembered how Senna had been treating both she and Blake since coming out of the hospital. "Besides, Senna has treated both Blake and I horribly since she came home from the hospital. She's pushing both of us away." Andrea was trying to keep her anger pressed down as she remembered the change in her friend.

"True, she was getting too close to the both of you. I had to stir her up a little so she would pull back. Senna loves Blake, but I won't allow her to put herself in a position for him to control her, or for you to control her either."

"We don't *want* to control her!" Andrea was shocked at that statement. "We care about her."

The rocker was quiet except for a slight creak against the old wood floor. Andrea listened to see if she could recognize noises outside. Where was she? All she heard was noises from the woods.

"If you don't want me to come between Blake and Senna why did you stir her up so she would pull away from Blake? It doesn't make any sense." Andrea was tired of this game. She hurt, and she was angry. If Sienna had the ability to cause Senna to pull away from them, then Senna must know her, Andrea thought.

"It's simple. She loves him. He makes her happy, but I will never allow anyone to control Senna," she paused for effect. "An equilibrium had to be established. Senna pulling away will cause Blake to be so desperate to have her back that he will acquiesce to whatever Senna wants."

"He would have done that, anyway. Love doesn't force itself on a person. Love is giving and kind," responded Andrea. She nearly spat the words back at Sienna.

"Hmmm, not the kind of love I have known. I think you are confused." Sienna was matter-of-fact.

"You don't want anyone to control Senna but you!" Andrea said.

Anger flared in Sienna. "I have to control her for her own good!" Sienna could feel herself losing control so she willed herself to calm and she began to rock again.

Andrea was dumbfounded. This was so twisted that

she couldn't even begin to figure out what the truth of it all was.

"So you tell me, why did Senna need to pull away from Blake and me?" asked Andrea.

"Mainly that church crap you guys were pushing on her."

"Senna went to church of her own free will. I never even asked her to go. Blake asked her to go, but made it clear that if she was not comfortable going, then he was fine with that. Neither one of us wanted to push Senna to do something she did not want to do," said Andrea. It was hard to mask the disdain she had for this lady in her voice.

"True, but she was at a place where she would've done anything for either one of you, so I merely shoved a tiny wedge in between so she would pull away, giving her time to come to her senses about a few things. I'll let her warm back up to Blake when it's time." A smile was on Sienna's face, but not one that would warm a heart or extend a greeting. It was the kind that sent cold chills down Andrea's spine.

Realization dawned on Andrea that this person loved Senna, but not enough to give her freedom. It was as if Senna were a bird in a gilded cage that she pampered, but controlled.

"I need to go to the bathroom," said Andrea. It was a fact and not a ploy to escape. Her bladder was full and hurting.

Sienna calmly reached her foot behind her hooking a flat pan with the toe of her shoe and slung it towards Andrea. It slapped up hard against Andrea's leg. It appeared to be like the type of pan someone would use to drain oil from their car, but it was clean and looked new.

Andrea looked up at Sienna. "What do you expect me to do with that?"

"Figure it out. I have to go now, but I'll be back." Sienna turned off the lantern, and the room filled with pitch black darkness. She could hear her walk across the room to the door and open it.

"Wait! Help me go to the bathroom," Andrea was panicked that she was leaving, even though being in the same room with her felt like being in the same room with a demon from hell.

There was no response as the door closed.

AFTER SIENNA LEFT, Andrea tried to think of how to go about using the pan to relieve herself. She was sitting flat on the wooden floor, her arms straight down to her sides. The pipe which was in the very corner of the shed, ran straight up the center of her back causing her to sit tight in the corner of the room.

Andrea knew that she first had to get enough room underneath herself in order to slide the pan under her, but with her legs straight out in front she wasn't sure how to do that.

As she sat thinking, she began to systematically move parts of her body to see just how much mobility she actually had. Beginning with her legs, she found she could cross them sitting in what was called Indian style, and she could also pull her knees up fully with her feet flat on the floor.

Her arms were pinned with her elbows tight against her small waist. This prevented the straps from moving up over her wider shoulders or lower over her hips.

She pulled up her knees and tried to push herself straight up. After several tries she had been able to slide up an inch or so, only to almost immediately drop back down again. With her arms down at her sides, her hands could only bend at the wrists. She pushed with her hands when she pushed with her legs, but that was no help either. It seemed impossible.

The temptation to give up, was overwhelming. But she resolved herself to be determined. She was angry, and she wanted to use that anger to fuel her tenacity.

She realized that she could slide the lower part of her arms behind her slightly. With the pipe so close to her she could grab it awkwardly with her hands. So now what, she thought. Well, she could push down on the pipe while pushing up with her legs.

So, she pushed and held, pushed and held. The ground gained was so slight each time that it took her fifteen minutes or more to get to the place where she could push herself up. Once there, she realized she could actually stand, and did so to allow her legs some relief from sitting so long. However, in the process she had exhausted herself and her body ached all over.

The problem of using the pan was still ahead of her though. She slid her arms and hands back to her sides again and could just barely reach to unfasten her jeans sliding them down slightly. Once she had done that, she moved back down the pole. She had been able to move the pan underneath her with her foot while standing.

Once done, she did the reverse to move the pan away and fasten her clothing. She was relieved that she had been able to tackle that problem. Exhaustion threatened to take her under, but she refused to allow it to do so.

If she could maneuver the way she had just done, then surely she could figure out a way to get out of here. The main problem was the straps. Sienna had only slightly loosened them earlier.

The straps' ratchets were behind the pole, between it and the corner of the shed. She tried to move back and forth slightly to see if she could work the ratchets around, but they were lodged there and no amount of wiggling seemed to move them out from behind the pole. Being wedged so tightly in the corner also greatly limited her mobility.

She worked for the next hour or so trying different movements in order to try and shrug or wriggle free from the straps, but made no progress. Her captor had thought this through thoroughly.

Settling in for the night seemed the best option for the moment; as if she had the strength to continue, anyway.

Would Senna think to look for her when she didn't show up for work the next morning? She hoped that Senna wasn't so angry with her that she would be unconcerned about why she hadn't shown up.

CHAPTER 19

The next morning, the sun came through the old wooden boards like daggers. Through the night, Andrea had slept for small bits of time in between working to break free of the straps. Everything that seemed logical to do in her mind prior to attempting it, proved to be a dead end.

She wondered what time it was. It was difficult to tell inside the windowless cabin. The cabin was a rudimentary one room structure with only an old wooden floor, a pitched roof, and a small cluster of cabinets on the far side of the room.

The outside appeared to be covered only by wooden boards which were butted up against each other. Inside, the two by fours which framed the wall were left exposed. The lantern, a small table, rocker, and pan were the only contents she could see.

Andrea suddenly wondered what on earth the pipe was for. There were a couple of cabinets but there appeared to be no sink. Maybe this pipe had been the beginning of adding plumbing to the structure at one time.

Andrea thought of Senna and wondered if it was time for her to be at work yet. What would she do when Andrea didn't come to work? Would she call her? Would she call someone else to report it? Would she care? The thought that Senna, in her current state, may not even care enough to try to find her grieved Andrea. How on earth had things gone so wrong?

A slight sound reached her ears. She sat stone cold still with her eyes shut attempting to concentrate on the sound. Maybe it could tell her something that would later be of help.

Then the door swung open and in walked Sienna. She walked in with elbow length rubber gloves on, carrying a thick industrial black garbage bag. She laid the bag on the floor, held it open, and slid the pan inside. She then picked up the entire thing and walked outside, shutting the door behind her.

How odd, thought Andrea. Two things occurred to her. One, what would she use now that the pan was gone. Two, was she not going to need the pan and what did that realization mean?

She'd tried to get a look through the door, but all she could see was dense thick woods. There was nothing unusual at all about them.

Andrea continued to sit and contemplate what it all meant and what was going to happen to her when the door opened again. And then in walked Sienna. The gloves were gone, and she had a brand new pan, which she sat next to Andrea before going to the rocker and sitting down.

Andrea ground her teeth. That rocking was enough to make a person go crazy. She was sick and tired of being a specimen in a jar that this psycho played with. Then a feeling came over her of complete peace and calm in the midst of this dark evil cabin. She welcomed it and let it wash over her.

As if prompted by this newly felt calm, she said, "Why do you want to push Senna away from church?"

"Oh sweetie, it isn't from church *per se*. She grew up in church and all it did was lock her up so tight she could never be alright. Church itself isn't a threat." She sat smiling and rocking.

Andrea was momentarily confused, but the calm reassurance she felt prompted her on. "So why did you want to keep her from church if it isn't a threat?"

The look on Sienna's face became dark, and the creaking of the rocker stopped. Sienna leaned forward. "Church has no power. It is the people inside the church." She shook her head and shrugged, sitting back again. "Do you know that most churches house people whose only god is control through legalism? They are so locked into a form of what *they* perceive is godliness that they are clueless to the bondage that they themselves are actually in."

"But..." Andrea prodded her on. She obviously wanted to talk.

"But there are those churches who know it isn't about a building, but about something else. They've tapped into some unseen source and they are dangerous." Sienna's even stare penetrated Andrea.

Andrea knew what she was referring to. She herself had grown up in a church where they did the same thing, followed the same rituals, sang the same hymns every week. It was all fine, except there was no power carried back home with them to live a different life, and there was certainly no joy.

Many years later, Andrea had found a body of people who desired God in a new way. Once she had, she'd never looked back. She knew the difference, one was void of power and the other was full of power which enabled them to overcome anything that life threw at them and to live an abundant life.

Andrea realized that Sienna saw what so many didn't see, just how powerless and useless those religious institutions were. No one ever needed religion, they needed an encounter and then a relationship with the one true

God. There was nothing else, no traditions, or rituals that could replace it for now or for eternity.

Sitting calmly, Andrea was just watching Sienna rock. She continued to feel at peace, knowing who was in control here, and it wasn't Sienna. But what was this all about and what was the endgame?

Then suddenly a vision popped into Andrea's mind. She saw the reports of the murders and then she saw blood dripping from a finger and then she knew Sienna had murdered those men. It jarred and unsettled her at first, but she was able to allow peace to restore and calm her once again.

"Why did you murder those men?"

Sienna had momentarily looked away, and at those words, jerked her head back to look at Andrea. A sinister grin grew across Sienna's face. "What could you possibly be talking about?"

"I know it was you," Andrea knew saying those words could guarantee her death. She knew Sienna would not allow a loose end, and that is what Andrea would be. But she had to confront her. She was speaking now from some other source, not her own.

"What did you need so badly from those men?" Andrea asked, not backing down.

"I needed their blood." Cold empty eyes stared back at Andrea.

"Why do you need the blood?"

Sienna looked away and, for a minute, Andrea

thought she saw raw emotion trying to overtake the evil that dominated Sienna's soul. For several minutes Sienna didn't say a word, only looked off into an unseen distance. "I need the blood to make me whole."

"Sienna," said Andrea with compassion, "we all do."

CARRIE WAS PUSHING for partial duty back at work. She was trying to convince Bracket she could do light desk duty at least part time. His refusal was firm. He had no intention to grant her request. But, after her continued pleading and reasoning with him, he knew she would work the case behind his back. If she were here, he could at least keep an eye on her.

Bracket stood and looked at Carrie. His gaze held her focus, and she squirmed in her seat. The chair in front of his desk betrayed her nervousness with its squeak. Randy had given in to her request to stop and pick her up on his way in to work that morning. He couldn't resist her either.

Pale yellow covered her face now with only hints of black. It was much better than the solid black and blue when she had first been admitted into the hospital. She had done well hiding it all with makeup. There were still stitches in her hand that would come out next week. He would have to make sure she protected that hand. It was the one that also had a broken bone and it was in a splint.

The brace under her shirt to stabilize her ribs was barely visible.

Against all his better instincts, he said, "You have not been cleared for duty. But, you may sit here in the office and discuss the case with the team. You may not, I mean *absolutely not*, leave this building except to go home. I promise you that if you do not comply completely—or even if you are complying and I feel it is in your best interest—I will send you home and you will not argue."

Carrie knew he would let her stay. She wanted to jump up and hug him but that wasn't possible in her condition. Her ribs still felt like knives grinding and piercing her insides. The doctor had said it would take quite a while for them to mend completely and that sudden movements could re-injure them. She would go crazy if she waited for that to happen before coming back to work.

She settled for a simple, "Thank you. I promise..." he was already waving his hand at her, knowing he would probably be sending her home before the end of the day, no matter what promises she was about to make.

With a huge grin on her face, a grin of victory, Carrie stood and left the SAC's office. Randy was at his desk and looked up when she came toward him.

"You won, didn't you?" Randy knew how it would go down so he wasn't surprised.

"Light desk duty only," said Carrie.

Randy smiled. He knew she would push that limit the

first chance she got. "Uh huh. Sure." He looked back down at his desk to the report he was reading.

"So what have you found?" Carrie asked.

Randy stood, gathering the papers he had and said, "Let's go back into the war room and see where all this fits in."

In the war room, the boards were full with information. The gray faces that once held question marks now had photos of the actual victims, including the missing ranch hand from the Big Horn. They had been able to confirm his identity. About three years ago he'd had knee surgery and the device that had been implanted had a serial number. It was him.

Mike and Rick had been great at tracing the victims' steps leading up to their deaths, but there were still huge gaps. Carrie sat and looked at the board for the first time in several days. After having time away and seeing it fresh today, it gave her an ability to spot things she had grown used to seeing before.

"Common threads," she began. "These men were all slight of build. They were all from five feet, eight inches to five feet, ten inches and all were around one hundred sixty-five to one hundred seventy-five in weight. That fits with our theory that a woman, could have been the killer. She was targeting men who would be easier to move."

She continued, "Then, even though these men worked all over the place and had different lives, some married, some not, they all had a habit of occasionally going to a bar late in the evening to get a drink. That's where she's picking up these men."

"How does that fit with the librarian?" asked Randy. "I just can't see her going to a bar."

"I think she likes to unwind and play at night. She is a master of deception, wanting the world to see her as meek and mild while she hunts at night." Carrie paused again to let that sink in and see where it landed.

Randy was still skeptical. "It's a stretch. I can't see it."

"Okay, let's shift gears. What about the stolen items from the Big Horn? We need to see if any of them have turned up in pawnshops or elsewhere," said Carrie.

"We can, but I think it's another long shot. The items were just common, small ranch items, except for the ATV. They weren't worth anything to anyone but another ranch."

"Quit being a negative Nelly," said Carrie. They were back in the flow of the way they worked. She was good at generating theories and action plans. Randy was good as poking holes and bringing them back to earth. When they had first started working together, this had upset Carrie. She took it personally and fought back. But she had grown to see the strength their partnership held when they worked this way. Randy's comments kept her theories grounded, and they were not personal.

"What about phone records? Both Justin and Keith

had phone calls from a burner shortly before their deaths. What about the others?" Carrie asked.

"The first victim Anderson Cooper did. He had several calls back and forth. But that was the only time that number shows up and as you can guess, it was also a burner phone," answered Randy.

"What about serial numbers on the phones? Were they bought at the same time or in a batch?" Carrie loved it when her mind would rapid fire with thoughts. Adrenaline would surge through her and gave her a high. Right now that adrenaline was better than any pain killer she could have purchased.

"Not bought in a batch and neither did they have consecutive serial numbers."

Carrie got up and walked over to the first white board. They had rearranged the victims in order of death once they had received the medical examiner's official report. The missing ranch hand was first. He had been killed almost a year ago which aligned perfectly with the theft at the Big Horn and his disappearance. It had been too long for there to be an exact day and hour for a time of death, but it was close enough that it all fit together.

He had priors. The ranch where he had worked in Colorado fired him for stealing. They had pressed charges, and he had spent a year in the county jail. There were other petty thefts and incidents in his past, but nothing as severe as murder or manslaughter.

Carrie's question was: did he steal them, then give

them to the perpetrator, or did he steal them for the perpetrator? With the existence of several calls back and forth to the burner phone it felt to her like the whole thing had been planned by someone else.

"The dates on the burner calls for the first victim, I'm assuming, coincide with the thefts," Carrie was stating what she felt were facts, but also asking, hoping for Randy's input.

"Yes, the last burner call was an outgoing call from Anderson Cooper the same night that the items were stolen." Randy had double-checked his notes to confirm.

"So, let's say this woman, whoever she is, manipulated him to steal the items from the ranch. He complied and his last call was to tell her he had done it and was successful. Then they met, exchanged goods, and she killed him." Carrie turned to look at Randy.

He sat mulling it over. "I can see it. It fits. But I still can't see that lady we followed yesterday being the one. I don't want us to get so locked into her that we miss someone else."

"True, I know," Carrie agreed, turning back to the murder board. "But there is that car though," she said turning back around to him, her eyes aglow.

"But you had a Porche," said Randy.

"Yes, but my Porche was bought used and was the least expensive model to begin with. It didn't cost anything near what this car did," Carrie explained. "It's a perfect example of a normal everyday woman working at a low-paying job, having an expensive car and a separate night life."

Randy knew she was right, but what were the odds? He couldn't deny the fact that this librarian had a Ferrari in her garage.

"Maybe it's a boyfriend's, sister's, or a friend's," offered Randy.

"It could be," Carrie mulled that over in her head a bit. "Odd about the registration being a S I E N N A and her name is S E N N A. What do you make of that?"

"Could be a sister, a twin. That would explain the look-alike. She looks just like the librarian, but doesn't act anything like her," said Randy.

"True. What does it say about Senna, any siblings?" she asked Randy.

He shuffled some papers, then read from one, "Mother: Francis Elaine Carter, formerly Williams, Father: Edward Thomas Carter, no siblings shown."

"Adoption?"

"None recorded here, but could be," replied Randy.

"What do we have on a Sienna Carter?" asked Carrie.

"Nothing."

"If she was adopted out to another family, then her last name would not be Carter," said Carrie.

"But the car's registration is under Sienna Carter," replied Randy.

"Address?"

Randy once again shuffled through the file and came

up with an address completely different from Senna
Carter's address.

"We need to check that out," Carrie was heading
towards the door.

"Hold on there, champ," said Randy. "You're benched."

THE LOCKED library door jiggled but held firm in
Darren's hand. He peered through the glass door to see if
he could see anyone inside. The dim interior light made
it hard to see, but it was clear that no one was in there.

He stepped back to see if there was a notice of some
kind stating they would be closed that day, but he saw
none. The breeze felt good on his head as he lifted his
Stetson to wipe his brow, but even better when it was
reset firmly back on his head. He stood on the sidewalk
looking around and up and down the street. This was
highly unusual.

The fact that Randy and Carrie had seen fit to have
him talk to Senna, and now the library was closed in the
middle of the day for no reason, didn't seem like a coincidence to him.

He went back to his car and called Randy.

"Hey Darren," came Randy's voice over the phone.
"What have you got?"

"Nothing. The library is closed. There are two
primary ladies that work there, and neither one is there. I

think they have some part-time students who work there, too, but the place is locked and there are no lights on. The only time I've ever seen the library closed was for a few hours when they do the book drive at the elementary school and that is usually only for a couple of hours, and they just did that yesterday."

Randy sat and thought for a minute. "Seems like an odd coincidence to me," said Randy.

"That is exactly what I thought," agreed Darren. "What do you want me to do?"

"Why don't you go by both of those ladies' homes and see if they are there and if they can give you any information? Let me know what you find."

Darren agreed, turned on his car and headed to the first address. The closest house was Senna Carter's house which was just a couple of blocks from the library. He drove by slowly once, then turned around a couple of blocks past and came back. He parked along the curb in front of her house. Only the sound of the birds chirping filled the neighborhood. The silver Prius sat in the driveway.

No one answered Darren's knock on the door. He remembered from the group texts yesterday that the Prius was the car registered to Senna Carter, but he was eager to try and find the Ferrari they had talked about in the group texts the day before.

Curiosity getting the best of him, he wanted to peek into the garage to see what he could see. He didn't have a warrant but it wouldn't hurt to just take a look in the garage, he thought.

Darren walked off of the porch and onto the gravel driveway. He watched the neighborhood as he walked, but saw no sign of anyone out, or of anything suspicious. A ripple of nervous tension ran across his skin, knowing he was doing something potentially unlawful, even dangerous.

The garage door did not have any windows. He continued on around the side of the garage that faced the street, again no windows. There was no fence or other boundary enclosing the yard or the garage, so he continued on around to the back.

Another garage door just like the one on the front was there. It was a through-and-through garage. He realized how someone could easily pull a vehicle into the garage, open the door on the other end and pull on through to the alleyway. Disappointingly, that door had no windows either.

Making a full circle around the garage, Darren found no windows anywhere and nothing suspicious. The backyard and the back of the house looked normal and nothing seemed out of place.

His car was hot when Darren crawled back into the front seat and he began to sweat the instant he was inside. But he wasn't ready to pull away from the curb just yet. He knew he wasn't the sharpest tack in the box, but he liked a good puzzle. As he sat there wondering what was going on here, he decided to head on over to Andrea's house. Maybe that would shed some light on things.

The patrol car engine roared to life quickly, and he proceeded to the address of Andrea Wells. It was farther across town than Senna's house was. Again he drove by, slowly looking the neighborhood over and then turning around, parked in front of the house as he had done before.

There was also a car in the driveway just like at Senna's, but this house didn't have a garage. He went to the front door, but once again there was no answer. It appeared by the presence of cars in their driveways, that both women would be home, but no one answered at either place.

Darren walked over to the car, a fairly new blue Chevy Cruze. Walking all around the car he noticed that the doors were locked and there was nothing of note he could see inside the car.

He looked back at the house and could see the back porch. An odd sensation told him to look closer that something wasn't right. He cautiously walked over, scanning every inch of the ground before him. Then he saw that a set of keys had been dropped in the grass next to the back porch. There was a Chevy key on there and various other keys which could have been house keys.

He breathed deep and a sick feeling settled in. Adrenaline surged through his body and his law enforcement training kicked in. He looked around for anything else odd or out of place. Time was of the essence now.

It could just be nothing, but it didn't feel right. He felt certain those keys were the keys to the car sitting in the driveway. He stepped up on the back porch and tried the door. It was locked.

This lady could have been trying to unlock her back door when something happened to her. The grass did not look disturbed as if there had been a struggle and there were no signs of a purse or other items.

The lawn was recently mowed which made it low enough that it didn't readily show footsteps. There was nothing else except the dropped keys. He left them where they lay until he could get someone out to take photos and dust for prints. He didn't want to disrupt the collection of evidence.

Quickly, back at his car, he called Randy. He filled him in on his visit to the two houses. "I think I can get a warrant to check out Andrea's house based on the locked library and the dropped keys with her car in the driveway. The judge here will grant it."

"Can you get inside the library too?" asked Randy. "I doubt there is anything there, but you never know. It's odd that both women didn't show up to work."

"Will do. Hey, did you find anything at Sienna Carter's address?" asked Darren.

"Headed that way now. I'll keep you posted," said Randy.

~

THE HOUSE that Sienna Carter had on her vehicle registration was northwest of Oklahoma City. Driving there
would have gone faster, but these were two-lane streets
marked off in one-mile sections, a stop sign at each one,
and a speed limit of forty-five miles per hour.

When Randy pulled up to where his GPS had taken
him, there was a large acreage. A long and winding drive
led to the main house which was tucked back into the
woods. The house was magnificent.

As Randy got closer, his surprise grew. The yard was
clearly maintained by a professional landscaper. There
was a four car attached garage and another large barn
that matched the design and details of the house. Behind
and to the side of the barn was a large corral.

It looked like a ranch, but there were no horses or
cows on the land or pasture that Randy could see. There
was also no sign of people or cars. He couldn't smell any
large animals either, only the floral smells from the lush
flowerbeds.

Honeybees swarmed the bushes as he walked by, stir-
ring them to life. That was the only sound Randy could
hear.

He walked to the massive double door, and rang the
bell, and then waited. After several minutes he realized
that no one would be coming to the door. The doorbell
was a security doorbell, and he knew the owner would be

able to see him from wherever they were and could also speak to him if they chose.

After a few more attempts of ringing and waiting, he walked off of the porch. He wasn't having any better luck than Darren was. Once back in the car, not in a hurry to leave, he called Carrie.

"Tired of sitting at your desk?" Randy asked.

"No, because I have been doing more digging," there was a hint of excitement in her voice. "I pulled the tax records on that property that Sienna Carter had listed, where you are now. The owner is Williams Stables, Inc. Williams is the maiden name of Senna's mother Elaine, so I dug further. This is her mother's parents' home and ranch. They have both passed away."

"It still doesn't tell us who Sienna is," said Randy. "This property is expertly maintained. It looks like someone is living here, but it doesn't appear to be a working ranch right now. The corrals and barns are kept up, but there isn't any sign of a horse or any other animal."

"Randy, I just have the feeling that the answer to all of this is right before us, but, man, for the life of me I can't see it!" Carrie's frustration was agonizing.

Randy told Carrie what Darren had found in Kachina. "Darren is getting a warrant for the other lady's property who works with Senna at the library."

"What if that Senna is the killer, and she has abducted her co-worker and is going to kill her?" asked Carrie.

"Naww that's a stretch. This killer only kills men. It doesn't fit. Something else is going on with that," said Randy.

Carrie sat quiet a minute thinking. Randy was right, killing a woman was totally out of the realm of this killer's MO. "Well, what now?"

"I guess I'll head back to the office. See you soon."

"Okay, I'll keep digging."

SIENNA DIDN'T RESPOND to Andrea's comment at first. She remained lost in thought. But then it seemed as if Andrea's words had somehow finally penetrated her thoughts. Sienna looked at Andrea. Her face was sad, not angry or intimidating.

"What do you mean?" she asked Andrea. Sienna had leaned forward with her elbows on her knees.

Andrea wasn't sure where all of this was going to go. She felt something deep inside of her compelling this conversation forward. She was still afraid, but took a deep breath and courageously kept going.

"Sienna we are all lost and hopeless. In the very beginning, when Adam sinned in the garden, it divided us from God," Andrea began.

"Stop right there!" Sienna was waving her off, not wanting to hear anything more. She leaned back in the rocker and looked away.

"No, wait, listen to me, Sienna," Andrea's voice was soft and non-threatening. "The only answer to sin is the blood. Before Christ, they continually sacrificed bulls and goats to temporarily cover their sins, much like what I suspect you've been doing. But it wasn't good enough, so they had to keep killing and killing and killing." Sienna looked back at Andrea once again interested.

"Finally, Christ came. He was the son of God in human form. He was sinless, and it was His perfect holy blood that spilled out once and for all so we could be whole and in a relationship with God again."

Sienna sat and listened to Andrea. She was tired of killing, very tired. Could it be true that there was a blood that could make her whole once and for all? She just looked at Andrea skeptically.

"You can't get to this blood by killing mere human men. You can only get to it through Jesus."

"Nonsense," declared Sienna standing up. She wiped the wetness that had formed under her eyes and stood up. "I have to leave now." And just that quickly she was out the door.

Andrea was crushed. The ache in her body was overwhelming. She was tired, sore, and hungry. What was to become of her? Resignation that she was going to die settled over her like a thick fog. This lady had killed many times and she would not likely leave Andrea alive.

Tears rolled down her cheeks. She'd never felt so alone. The day passed with no more sign of Sienna and no one had come to rescue her. Soon she didn't even need the pan any more. She had not had anything to drink for a very long time and was quickly becoming dehydrated.

Her entire body strained to gather any clue as to where she might be. There were no sounds of civilization anywhere that she could hear. She smelled only the deep woods, no exhaust fumes or other city smells.

She dozed in and out and then finally realized the light was fading between the cracks in the wood. Night would soon be here. Sobs wracked her body. Would anyone come? Anyone at all?

CHAPTER 20

$\mathcal{D}$arren had been able to get a warrant for
Andrea's home and car. The district adminis-
trator for the library system had granted them approval
to search the library, and she had met Darren and Randy
there early Saturday morning with a key.

Cool, dark quiet greeted them when they entered the
library. There was nothing unusual there—except for the
fact that it was closed on a Saturday—nor at Andrea's.
Neither Andrea nor Senna had surfaced.

Blake had tried to call Andrea, and had left a message
a couple of times, but she never returned his call.
Concern choked his mind. That was not like her.
Looking out his office window, he saw Darren's car and a
few other cars through the trees. He couldn't see the

library from his window, but he could tell by where they were parked that it was where they were.

Something bad has happened. He knew it, he could feel it, and anxiety surged through him. Jumping up, he was out of his office, down the stairs, heading for the library as quickly as he could maneuver the stairs.

His blood was pumping, and he was trying not to panic, but it wasn't helping. What if something horrible had happened to Senna and Andrea? He pushed the thought aside, choosing to believe the best, not the worst.

When he reached the library, Darren was just coming outside. "Darren, what's wrong?"

"Hi, Blake. The library's been closed for two days in a row. No one has seen either lady who runs it. We were searching for anything that might help us find them or what might have happened."

Blake's face went white, and he looked around for something to lean on, feeling lightheaded. *It was true. Something has happened to them*, he thought. Leaning on the hood of Darren's car, he tried to comprehend what Darren was telling him.

Darren, immediately concerned, asked Blake, "Hey, are you okay? Did you know these ladies?"

"Yes. I was dating Senna, and Andrea and I are friends," replied Blake. He was in shock at what was happening.

Randy became immediately interested in their

conversation. "When was the last time you saw Senna Carter?"

"I haven't seen her since Wednesday at around noon. She was sitting on the park bench having her lunch and I came out and sat with her for a few minutes. She wasn't herself. I didn't stay long and went back to work," said Blake. His senses had returned, and he felt an urgency to do whatever he needed to help them find Senna and Andrea.

"When was the last time you saw Andrea?" asked Randy.

"Thursday night. Senna was not the same when she came out of the hospital on Tuesday. She was pushing me away and was being abrasive with Andrea. It was extremely unusual and Thursday Andrea called to ask if I wanted to have dinner so we could talk about it. We had a burger over at the diner."

"That was the last time that anyone has seen Andrea." Randy knew he and Carrie had seen Senna at the medical complex and then at her home on Thursday. To his knowledge, Thursday was the last day that either of the ladies had been seen.

Randy called Rick to fill them in on the details of the search. We need to find these ladies' cell phones. Can you guys trace them and see if you can get a location? Mike agreed and was quickly off the phone.

"Senna doesn't have a cell phone," Blake said.

Both Darren and Randy looked at Blake, immediately interested. "She's a little old-fashioned. She only has a landline in her house," said Blake.

Randy sent a group text to Mike regarding the lack of cell phone for Senna. "Well that makes things more difficult," said Randy.

"Darren, do you think that you can get that judge to give us a warrant for Senna Carter's house, garage, and car? I know it is a stretch, but at this point, I'm not sure what to do next. I'm concerned they are both in danger," said Randy.

ANDREA THOUGHT she had literally passed out. She had no recollection of falling asleep and was growing weaker by the moment. She'd had no food or water since Thursday night at the diner with Blake and had only picked at her chicken sandwich then. What she wouldn't give to have now what she'd sent back with the waitress that night.

Pain was her closest companion now. She was attempting to move as much as possible and each movement brought with it new levels of excruciating pain. The awkward position she was bound in quickly cut off blood supply in multiple places in her body.

She had perfected standing up. She could also move her arms slightly to her back as she did when grabbing the pole to help herself stand, but not forward. It just made no sense to Andrea. She knew she should be able to get out of these straps and kept trying.

The movement had not loosened the straps though. They were a tough, thick, woven strap made to hold tons of weight. Each time she'd had a new thought about how she might wriggle out of them, or dislodge them, it was quickly dismissed once failed. All the movement was succeeding in was rubbing her skin raw.

The thin, short-sleeved top was no protection from the abrasion of the straps. They had rubbed through one sleeve and it felt like her skin was raw and possibly bleeding. The straps and her top were blood-soaked on her right side.

The door opened with a loud swish across the floor, startling Andrea. She thought it was well into the afternoon of maybe Saturday and she was in no mood to talk. The comforting peace she had felt the evening before was gone. Despair was the only thing she could muster up.

It was Sienna, of course. But she carried food and water with her. Dare Andrea hope that she was going to feed her?

The little bundle Sienna carried plopped to the floor next to Andrea where Sienna dropped it. The smell confirmed that food was indeed inside and Andrea's stomach gnawed to get at it. Sienna squatted down and looked at her. "I'm going to let you go for long enough to eat and drink something. I promise you, though, if you try to escape, I will catch you and I will kill you."

There was no mistaking her sincerity. Her voice was as cold as ever, chilling Andrea to the bone; however, something was slightly different. Andrea didn't quite feel the overpowering evil radiating off of Sienna the way she had before. She seemed a little calmer somehow.

"Thank you," responded Andrea, and she meant it. She had never truly known what it felt like to be starving. She was genuinely grateful for the food and water.

The burger and fries tasted like heaven. The burger was still warm. Andrea felt the juice trail down her arm as she bit into the meat. She didn't care that she was eating like a pig. The rocker creaked as Sienna rocked.

Andrea tried to not choke down her food too quickly or drink the water down too fast. She knew it would make her sick and she would throw up. Was this to be her last meal? She didn't know, but she was going to savor it as if it were.

About the time she was finishing the last French fry, Sienna said, "Tell me more about the blood."

It startled Andrea. She looked up to see Sienna's eyes locked onto her. Once again, Andrea felt a calm, over-powering peace flood her body and the strength that came with it. Eloquent words formed in Andrea's mind as the peace flooded her being. So she told Sienna about the blood.

THEY HAD GOTTEN the warrant for Senna's house. Darren and Randy were there and Mike and Rick were on their way, stopping to pick up Carrie. It was overkill for a warrant on a small house, but they had felt that feeling when you know something big is about to break things wide open. They were ready and none of them wanted to miss it.

Darren and Randy started with the garage. They wanted to see that Ferrari up close and personal, but it wasn't there. Disappointment was followed by curse words. Randy asked Darren to go ahead and start on the house, agreeing he would work on the garage.

It was a very large garage for such a small house. It was as old as the house, mid-1930s, but a second garage door had been added and both doors were up to date with garage door openers and keypads on each end.

The inside of the garage was neat and tidy. When Randy flipped the switch, the room filled with bright light. The two side walls were filled with deep cabinets all enclosed with cabinet doors. He took photos of everything.

At this point, Senna was still an unknown. They didn't have concrete evidence to call her a suspect, but they all felt it in their gut that she was somehow involved. However, feelings didn't win court cases. Randy wanted proof of something. Proof that Senna was a victim or perpetrator.

He began to open the cabinet doors, one at a time. They were very orderly, containing the typical stuff that everyone stores away. He found nothing of note until he came to the last cabinet on the bottom which had a lock on the latch. That's odd, he thought.

He took another photo of it and then used a bolt cutter to cut off the lock. Inside, was a large plastic tub. It was made of sturdy, thick gray plastic and appeared to be industrial in nature. It was about three feet by two feet.

He took more photos before pulling the tub out into the garage. He studied it for a brief second before opening it, his mind was racing trying to anticipate what it might contain.

At first when Randy opened it, he wasn't quite sure what he was looking at. The distinct smell of bleach hit his nose immediately when he lifted the lid. Before he could pull anything from the tub, he heard Rick's car pull up. He stood and waved to them.

Looking at Carrie he said, "You aren't supposed to be here." And he smiled.

"I know. I talked Mike and Rick into bringing me. I'm just going to watch and observe." Her smile matched his.

"What have you got there?" asked Rick.

"Just pulled this out of that locked cabinet. Was about to see what treasures we have here."

"I know what it is on top," said Rick. "It is a pair of

waders. My dad used to have a pair he fished in. Rubber pants with suspenders."

Randy reached in with a gloved hand and gently lifted them out without letting them touch anything else. "We need an evidence bag for these," said Randy.

"You haven't see Senna Carter, but trust me, she doesn't go fishing in rubber waders and they've been washed in bleach. Smell it?" Rick produced a large paper evidence bag and Randy gently guided them in. Underneath where the waders had lain, was a large pair of elbow-length rubber gloves. Those went into an evidence bag as well.

Once those were bagged, they all four stood looking at what was underneath.

There on the very bottom was a blue poly-tarp folded neatly. Actually, as they began to look, there were several tarps all folded and ready to go.

"This is it!" exclaimed Carrie. "It's the evidence we need to bring her in. I knew it. I just knew it."

"We don't know if any of this has anything to do with the murders. I have blue tarps in my garage," said Randy. "Yes, it is all suspicious and yes, it is something to go on, but it is not the murder weapon."

"We have to find her first. We've been looking for two days and can't locate her," said Rick.

"We can get warrants for the house at the horse ranch in the country," said Carrie.

"That may be a stretch," said Randy. "There is no indication that she is in charge of or has anything to do with that property. We'll have to pull the corporation documents and see who is."

Darren soon came out and said there was nothing in the house at all that was suspicious. They showed him the tub and described all its contents. "Wow. I would have never thought. If you knew her, you would know what I mean. She is timid and won't hardly even make eye contact with me. I have a hard time believing it," said Darren.

"Do you think maybe someone is setting her up?" asked Darren. "We didn't find anything else except this one tub that was locked up. What if someone is storing this in her garage so that it won't be found in their possession, but in hers?"

Darren made a good point, but the most simple answer was that she just didn't think she would get caught with it. "We will take it back to the forensic lab and see what they find. We will know more once we find her and bring her in," said Randy.

BLAKE SHUT his office for the day. He had to find out where Senna and Andrea were. He feared that the killer had abducted them both and that their lives were in grave danger. But, he honestly had no idea where to search.

Anxiety sharpened his mental acuity to a degree, as

long as he didn't allow himself to fall into full panic mode. He worked to push away fearful thoughts of the girls' safety and focus on solutions.

He didn't know Andrea's parents. He thought he remembered her mentioning once that they lived in Dallas. Something about having moved closer to her brothers and a new grandbaby.

He didn't want to try contacting them. That was best left to the authorities. Senna had no family and, to his knowledge no friends. He could contact a few of the group from church that was Andrea's age. He had seen her at group functions many times.

A car honked behind him and he realized he'd been sitting at the stoplight when it had turned green. The discomfort in his palms brought the realization that he had been gripping and twisting the steering wheel too tightly.

He drove to his small-group leader, Brandon's home. "Can I come in and talk?"

Brandon motioned for Blake to sit, but Blake didn't want to sit. He wanted to be out there actively looking. Shifting nervously from one foot to the other, he explained to Brandon the situation.

"I've been driving for hours and have no idea where else to physically look."

"What can I do?" asked Brandon. He was on high alert and felt his skin prickle as Blake spoke. He could feel that something was wrong, desperately wrong.

"Andrea's parents live in Dallas, but I don't want to alarm them yet. I have no emergency contact information for Senna. I thought that we could contact those that I know Andrea is friends with in our small group. Maybe she or both she and Senna are just out with friends." The look on Blake's face betrayed what he really thought.

"I think I have a list. We can make calls. I know it doesn't feel as active as driving around, but may prove to be more productive."

They agreed that they would divide up the list between them and make phone calls. Not wanting to alarm anyone, they agreed it was best to keep the inquiries casual.

It took the remainder of the day to finish the list. They had reached almost everyone and where they had left messages, they had received return calls. No one had seen Andrea since the weekend at church when Senna, had her episode.

Full panic had now set in with Blake. He'd run his hands through his hair so many times that it stood on end, further revealing his true internal desperation.

Void of any other ideas about what to do, Blake stayed and ate supper with Brandon. He had nowhere else to go and was out of ideas about where to look.

He appreciated that Brandon wanted to feed him, but when he looked at the plate before him, all he could do was remember all the meals he had shared with Senna.

SIENNA HAD LISTENED to what Andrea had to say about the blood. She did not engage in conversation, only listened. Her face had remained neutral, if not skeptical, which made it hard for Andrea to gauge what she was thinking or feeling.

When Andrea had said all she had felt inspired to say, Sienna gathered the food trash, strapped Andrea back to the pipe and left. That had been several hours ago.

Relief flooded her that she was being allowed to live at least a little while longer. Having had a meal and some water, she was finally able to sleep. She thought the straps may not be quite as tight this time, but they still proved to hold her firmly in place.

When she woke from the nap, she could tell the atmosphere had changed. Having lived in Oklahoma her whole life, one thing she had learned is that feeling when a storm is coming, and not just any storm, but a storm that could bring a tornado.

Great. That is all I need, thought Andrea. Maybe it will blow me loose from this pipe. She snorted a sarcastic laugh, then she immediately regretted her sarcasm, remembering all the devastation that tornados could bring. If it blew her loose, she would in all probability die in the process.

All she could do was sit, wait and pray. Especially pray.

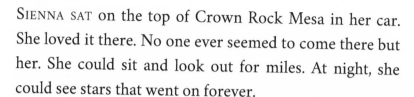

SIENNA SAT on the top of Crown Rock Mesa in her car. She loved it there. No one ever seemed to come there but her. She could sit and look out for miles. At night, she could see stars that went on forever.

She was deeply troubled. She hadn't wanted to hear what Andrea was saying to her, but felt a compulsion to listen, greater than any compulsion she'd ever felt before. It was even greater than the compulsion to kill.

What Andrea had said was confusing to her. She didn't really understand it. But her strong need for the blood, and to feel whole caused some kind of internal affirmation, so she listened.

Where she was sitting on Crown Rock, she could see the storm coming in the distance. She'd felt it long before she had driven up there. The feeling was unmistakable, but rather than moving somewhere safe, which would have been sensible, she'd done the opposite and had driven to the top of the tallest point around for miles.

The sun was out, and the day was bright when she had arrived, but as the hours passed she saw the clouds rolling in from the west. The sheets of dark blue rain that were still miles away were calming.

She was always awestruck by the beauty of the dark, formidable clouds stuffed with shades of green deep inside of them. She knew that meant hail on her car, most likely huge hail and lots of it. But today she didn't care.

Something had broken her today. It was something in the words that Andrea had spoken to her about the blood.

Was it possible that the blood that came from this Jesus when they had killed him was enough to make her feel whole once and for all? And how could she access this blood? It wasn't like she could see it and touch it the way she could when she killed.

For the first time she felt tired, exhausted from it all. She didn't have it in her to keep trying to feel whole any longer. She had reached her end.

The wind picked up and jerked her car. The typical eerie calm that comes right before a tornado was gone. Today that deadly calm had felt just that, deadly calm. But now she felt the wind pick up, and the dust and debris it picked up with it, whipped against her car. Huge random drops of rain began to fall hard through the dust in the wind and made mud balls on her windshield.

Sienna got out of her car. A tornado was coming even though she couldn't see it yet, she could feel it. She was no safer in her car than she was outside of it, but she wanted it all to be over, so she stood. She knew this was her end, and she welcomed it.

The sky drew darker, and the wind whipped harder. Her hair flew and twisted and raged around her head. She didn't even try to tame it.

The wind grew stronger and more violent. It became hard to stand and resist the wind that thundered around her. She lost her grip on the car door and the violent wind blew her up against a short scrub cedar and the branches prickled her skin. The wind pelted her with rain and dust. And then the wind began to roar that unmistakable roar.

She looked up and actually saw the tornado coming for the first time. She screamed out at the top of her lungs, but her words were lost on all but God, and the wind.

ANDREA WAS right about the storm, but all she could do was sit and wait. She felt the atmosphere change. The sky became so dark that inside the cabin it was almost pitch black. It quickly went from eerily quiet, to gusts of wind so violent that the shed shuddered.

Tangible fear ravaged her mind, and she shut her eyes and willed herself to remain calm. Tears streaked her face and repressed sobs threatened her calm.

Then it hit. The shed creaked and moaned. The roar was so loud that only the screech of the nails pulling from the boards could be heard. Andrea braced herself. She had pulled her knees up and dipped her forehead to rest on them. It was all she could do in defense of the storm.

Devastation was immediate and complete. The roof of the cabin was ripped off and exterior boards began to fly away in large planks. As the walls of the building began to twist around and collapse inward, they pummeled Andrea.

Nails ripped through her skin as the wind drug the boards across her body. She was beaten, cut and bruised. Then she lost consciousness, and when she did, her last thoughts were of Sienna.

CHAPTER 21

The aftermath of any destructive tornado leaves residents in shock. But in the midst of the shock, something kicks in to help recover and find friends, pets, and loved ones. Then they survey how their lives have been ripped apart and decide how best to put it back together. With hearts broken they picked up the wind-torn and rain-soaked mementos of their life.

Sirens were heard in the quiet as people were picking up and sorting through the remnants of their homes. While some treated the wounded, fire trucks raced to prevent gas leaks and fires. Police officers assisted in rescues.

The only lights to see by were the emergency lights as all the power had been brought down from twisted and tangled transformers and power lines. Cars and homes and all manner of things had been randomly moved and crushed. It was as though a toddler had dumped out all their toys and began digging through them, scattering the pieces, looking for something they couldn't find.

Blake and Brandon had been at Brandon's dinner table when the storm sirens had blown. It was about seven thirty and there was still some light out, but that quickly changed when the dark clouds moved in.

The sudden darkness brought Blake to life, and he rushed to the front window as Brandon turned on the TV. There he saw the weather and the huge line of colors which ran a broad swath diagonally across the entire state of Oklahoma. The weatherman zoomed in and pointed out large swirls in the colorful line that looked like large hooks, tornados.

With very little time to prepare for a tornado, Brandon and Blake ran to the basement. But almost as soon as they were safe, the tornado had passed and with its passing, came the calm, deadly quiet.

"It sounds safe now," said Brandon.

The only sound was their footsteps on the wooden basement stairs as they emerged.

"Looks like you got off easy," observed Blake.

Brandon breathed a huge sigh of relief. "Yeah, it looks like only a few broken windows, and some shingles out there on the yard."

Brandon's home had suffered. But as they stood on his lawn, they realized just how blessed they had been, for all around them, there was devastation. Random homes were left next to vacant lots where homes had been.

Darkness filled the night sky. The tornado had passed and the stars now shone brightly. It was a beautiful night to behold, had it been any other night.

Workers and residents worked the night through helping each other. The next morning, they were still working hard to do what they could. Blake and Brandon were both exhausted.

Because Brandon's home had suffered minimum damage, he'd welcomed as many people in as he could, for shelter. He had families sleeping all across his living room floor.

The smell of bacon and eggs the next morning woke those asleep as Blake cooked all he could find in Brandon's kitchen. He'd found eggs, bacon, and biscuits, and had also whipped up some pancakes, concerned that there wouldn't be enough food for everyone. Knowing appetites would be low, he did it anyway. Everyone would need their strength for the work that lay before them.

As soon as the smell began to wake the crowd, several people came to offer help. Breakfast was finished, eaten, and then cleaned up efficiently. They were all grateful for the shelter and food that had been provided them.

Brandon and Blake felt grateful to be able to help and

offer what they could, but all Blake could think about was Senna and Andrea.

In the night, Blake had finally been able to make it over to see what had become of his home. He could tell while still two blocks away it wouldn't be good. All the homes as far as he could see were destroyed, some more than others, but none salvageable.

As he approached his home, he realized it had been on the edge of the tornado path, but had still suffered greatly. The roof was gone as were most walls. His life lay in an absurd blanket across his lawn and the surrounding street.

With nothing to be done in the darkness of night, he made his way back to Brandon's in order to help those he could, the only difference being, that he was now one of the homeless, too.

Blake and Brandon had not slept at all. They worked until the early hours of the morning helping rescuers find missing loved ones and pets. Then, once they had settled in to try to get some sleep, sleep didn't come.

They lay on their pallets in Brandon's home office and talked. The entire time that Blake was diligently helping others do what he could, his heart and mind never left Senna. Where was she and was she safe? It was still too hard to maneuver through the streets so he'd not been able to get to Senna's house. Both he and Brandon lived on the far side of town quite a long distance from Senna's home.

He kept resisting the urge to run straight to her house, but the immediate needs of others right before him kept him occupied. Before settling in for the night, he had started in that direction only to have Brandon pull him back. He reasoned that there were others all across town helping their neighbors and someone would be helping Senna, too, if she needed it.

The electric company was still working hard to remove dangerous live lines that were down across homes and streets. It would not do Senna any good if Blake hurt himself just trying to get to her house. He had reluctantly agreed to wait until morning.

He didn't even know where Senna was, nor Andrea. The search Brandon and Blake had been on all day had been fruitless. He knew something bad had happened, and sadness and despair had settled over him. She was gone, and he didn't know where.

Thoughts tormented him when exhaustion should have taken him under. When the first hint of light seeped through the window, he was up and making breakfast. He would do this for those here and then he would set out to try to find both Senna, and Andrea.

The ladies who had spent the night were relieved to have something to do, so they eagerly took over the breakfast cleanup, which released Blake to go search.

He quickly realized that there was still no easy way to do that. Entire homes lay scattered in the streets, roofs and walls, boards with nails, and glass were everywhere.

Huge crews had already begun their clean up, but from Brandon's house, there was no way he was getting his car out and down the street.

So he walked, and as he walked, he prayed. That deep fear in the pit of his stomach would not go away. No matter what he said or did, it remained. There was a foreboding feeling that said, she's gone.

He wasn't quite sure when the tears started. It wasn't a manly thing to do, but his heart was breaking and he didn't care. "Help me find her, please," he prayed. He just wanted to find her now even if she was no longer alive.

To get to Senna's house he had to pass through downtown. Remarkably, the storm had done little damage there. Hope surged that he'd been wrong and that he would find Senna safe and sound in her little house.

Blake picked up speed and began to jog the last couple of blocks to her home. Once there, he turned a corner and there it stood. It was intact and he could see no visible signs that it had been damaged. Her car sat in the driveway.

He ran up to her door and knocked hard. No response. He went to the back door and once again knocked, calling out to her, "Senna, open up. Are you there?" No answer.

He knew where she kept a key to the back door so he got it and went in. Maybe she had been inside and was hurt. He unlocked the door and let himself in, but the house was empty.

The keys to her car were laying on a table near her front door, so he decided to take her car and drive where the streets were clear. Maybe he could find her still.

Blake was forced to avoid the side of town where the streets were impassable. As he drove, he just seemed to drive with no thought whatsoever regarding where he was going.

As if an answer to prayer, he felt an unseen navigation system directing him. He then realized he was heading south out of town toward Crown Rock Mesa.

THE SHORT-LIVED DOWNPOUR had woken Andrea some-time after the storm. She'd survived the tornado, but the shed was gone. All that remained was the old floor and the pipe she was still strapped to.

She began to laugh hysterically as she realized that the sturdy pipe and the straps had anchored her to the ground and were what had saved her. In a tornado, they could just as easily have ripped away and taken her with them, but in this case, today they had saved her.

After the tornado came through, the rain had only lasted for about ten minutes and then the beautiful night sky had appeared. She wasn't sure how long she had been out, but the rain had passed and the night sky was clear when she came to. As she looked up, she knew it was a message of splendor from God to let her know He'd been with her all along, and He still was.

Andrea was wet and the cool night breeze chilled her to the bone, but she had hope. The bruises ached, but she didn't think she had any broken bones. The cuts from the nails were mostly superficial, and the rain had washed away the blood.

As she rested her head down on her knees, she wondered about Sienna. The words she had spoken to her came from somewhere other than her own mental knowledge. She could feel her mouth speaking truths she had known but could have never put to words herself. She knew it had been God speaking through her to Sienna.

When she spoke, she'd felt God's compassion for Sienna, and therefore, Andrea had begun to feel compassion for her as well. She had seen her the way that God saw her.

As she was speaking, she saw in her mind things about Sienna, she could have never known. She knew God was revealing things to her mind, so she could help Sienna.

So while the storm raged, she wondered where Sienna was and if she was all right. Before Sienna had left her for the last time, Andrea had been able to explain to her about the cleansing blood of Jesus. How it had paid the price for all sin, for all time. And all that a person had to do was to come to Him and receive it. She explained that He waited with loving arms to receive any and all.

Andrea had also explained that it didn't matter if a person had tried to be good all their life or if they had only been bad. No one could be good enough to bring wholeness to themselves, only the blood of Jesus could, which had already been freely given. The price had been paid and was hers for the receiving.

Sienna had seemed non-receptive and skeptical, but she listened, and as she listened, Andrea could tell that barriers were breaking down inside of her. Sienna's countenance changed and the evil that was so dominant before just seemed to wash away. What was left was a face wracked with pain and sadness.

Andrea was not sure she had convinced Sienna that no matter what she'd done, no matter how horrible it was, God's forgiveness was already there and waiting for her.

Andrea had told her of murderers in the Bible who had held prominent roles in God's family. Even David, who had a man sent to the front lines of his army to die, so he could take his wife, was later referred to as a man after God's own heart.

Sienna had left when Andrea's words had run out. She looked sad, but more at peace. Andrea hoped that wherever she was now that her words, the words that had been inspired by God, had taken hold of her heart and that she was safe.

BLAKE DIDN'T KNOW why he was driving to Crown Rock Mesa. It made no sense in his mind, but he felt a driving urge to continue. When he reached the top, there were no cars and many of the spindly trees and shrubs were stripped and mangled from the tornado.

He got out of Senna's car and began to walk the perimeter of the area. The mesa itself was several acres, but the area that was clear enough for people to park was only about one acre.

The only vegetation on top of the mesa was a variety of wild grasses, short bushes, and cedar trees. Cedars could and did live anywhere they chose. Most had weathered the tornado, but many had been ripped from the red sand rock and the various bushes had had their new spring leaves stripped from them.

Blake kept thinking and asking himself why was he up there and what was he doing, but he felt compelled to stay. So he walked. He decided to walk the entire circumference of the cleared area.

As he walked, he looked into the vegetation, and where he could, over the edge to the area below. In most places, there were sheer cliffs straight down, and in other places the drop off was a more gradual slope.

Blake had been slowly walking and looking for about an hour when something caught his eye. Out of a tangle of cedars and brush he saw what looked like a shank of brown hair. The color was so close to the red sand rock, particularly now that it was covered in red mud, that he nearly missed it.

He ran over and began to remove limbs and branches. And then he saw her. It was Senna! He had found her. But he didn't think she was breathing. Doing the best he could to check her without moving her in case she was critically injured, he found she had a pulse. It was faint, but it was there.

He immediately pulled out his phone and called Brandon asking him to get help as quickly as possible and send it to the top of Crown Rock Mesa.

The second he hung up, he was brushing mud and leaves from Senna's face. She was scratched from the cedars, but it didn't look like she had any serious cuts.

"Senna," he said. "Senna, please wake up. It's me Blake." She didn't stir. He patted her cheek, stopping short of actually slapping it, in an attempt to wake her. Still no response.

He sat and held her hand. She had a pulse, so he decided he would just wait for the ambulance. It seemed to take forever. He knew they'd all had a long night and that the roads were still not entirely passable. It would take them longer than normal to get there.

Blake reached down once again, and he kissed her cheek. He brushed his hand along her hair and with urgency said, "Senna, wake up! Please. Please wake up." Memories of the past two weeks flooded him. Had it only been a little over a week ago that he'd been urging her to wake up just like this?

Nervous energy caused him to continue to brush her hair and face with his hand. It seemed all he could do since he didn't want to move her and had to resist the urge to pick her up and hold her to himself.

"Senna, I'm here. I will always be here. Please, please wake up," Blake pleaded.

Just when he was about to give up again, he saw her eyelids flutter just a bit. "Senna, It's me, Blake. I'm here. It's going to be okay."

Senna turned her head slightly to look at Blake. She didn't know where she was or what had happened, but when she saw him, she felt relief rush over her.

She reached up weakly towards him with both of her arms. "Oh, Blake!" Senna exclaimed. He accepted her arms and as she pulled herself to him, he cautiously slid his arms underneath her, holding her as if it were the last time.

He sat there rocking her gently back and forth in his arms. "Why were you up here?" Blake asked her. "I've been looking for you for three days. Where have you been?"

"I don't know. I really don't know." And she didn't. She tried to reach back to her last memory, but couldn't seem to find it. It was like a vapor that dissipated each time she tried to reach for it.

"It's okay. It's okay," Blake kept holding her and gently rocking her. "I'm here now. I love you Senna."

"I love you too, Blake."

When the ambulance arrived, they were still sitting there holding each other. Blake gave way to the paramedics who quickly took over with practiced skill, asking her questions and providing medical care.

Blake stood and continued to look around as they worked. *What on earth had she been doing here and how did she get here?* he wondered.

He followed the ambulance to the hospital where they took her immediately into a room at the back of the emergency room. To his disappointment, they requested that he stay in the waiting area since he was not immediate family.

Before he did, he turned back and asked Senna, "Do you know where Andrea is?" She shook her head, no. And she didn't. The last memory she had of Andrea was leaving the library to go to her doctor's appointment on Thursday.

THE DAY WAS QUICKLY GROWING WARMER and with everything soaked from the rain, it was also humid. Andrea thought to herself that it was time to get out of there.

The cabin no longer had her pinned in the corner so she slid to a standing position and then began to work her arms back and forth. She found that she could shrug her shoulder just so and then when she then leaned to one side, the top strap popped up and over one shoulder loosening it. However, she remained bound by the second strap. The success of freeing herself from the first strap gave her new momentum to tackle the second one.

Standing there thinking, she looked up and saw the top of the pipe. It was about nine or ten feet high. She tried to lean forward in an attempt to pull the pipe with her and bend or loosen it. There was barely a wobble.

With the walls gone she could see just outside were the pipe was and realized it was coming from an old water well. It was a galvanized water pipe. Someone must have intended to add plumbing to this cabin at one time, but never had.

She'd tried multiple times to reach back towards the ratchets, but the straps wouldn't allow it. Now that she was standing and had one strap gone, she tried again. The remaining strap had her forearms strapped tight to her waist just below her elbows.

She could move her arms behind her, but was unable to bend her arms in such a way as to reach the ratchets. She realized that she was able to wiggle her arms enough to reach a distance in front of her though. If she could turn herself around inside the strap, she knew she could reach the ratchet.

The pipe prevented her from being able to rotate herself. She then began to slide to the side of the pipe in an attempt to position the pipe next to her arm. Once there, she was easily able to rotate herself.

She grabbed the ratchet and pulled, releasing the strap. She was free! Relief flooded her. She was free, but it had come at a price. She had ripped dry scabs from the wounds that the straps had created when rubbing into her skin. Dirt and sweat stung and burned, but she didn't care, she was free.

Andrea stood for a minute catching her breath. As she did, she looked around. Where was she? Dense woods were all around her. The tornado had stripped many of the trees bare, but there was still a tangled mess of limbs and briars. In front of her where the door of the cabin had been, was the light impression of a footpath through the woods.

This was the only way Sienna could have possibly come through, but it was so overgrown with briars and vegetation she wasn't sure how. It took her about fifteen minutes walking on the path to get to a clearing.

A beautiful rolling pasture spread out before her. Looking around she saw no sign of a house or a road, but she could see what looked like tracks of some kind that led around the edge of the pasture. Andrea looked closer. They looked like some type of motorcycle or four-wheeler tracks and they went off to her right, so she followed them.

Andrea walked for what felt like hours in the hot sun, but it was actually only about twenty minutes. She was severely dehydrated and the hot sun made each necessary movement take twice the effort.

Then there it was, an ATV. She had reached a road. It wasn't like a city street or even a country road. It was more like what you would see on a golf course, but wider. And there sat an ATV.

Adrenaline surged through her giving her new strength. Sienna must have taken the ATV to come to her. She realized that Sienna could have driven a car to this point, then taken the ATV to get closer to the cabin.

Hopeful, Andrea began to search the ATV. "Yes!" she exclaimed out loud. The keys were in it. She hadn't ridden something like this since she was in high school, but she knew she could remember how. And sure enough in no time, she had it started and was heading down the little road.

THE TORNADO in Kachina had been devastating, but close by in Oklahoma City, there had been no damage and life continued on as before. The path of the tornado had taken it through Kachina and then in a northeast direction tearing up much of the rural countryside and homes there.

Of course, first responders from all the surrounding towns and cities had flocked to Kachina in order to help, but those who didn't have an immediate need to be there knew it was best to stay out of the way so that the work could get done. There would be a time to help, but not now.

Carrie woke wondering where the storm had left their investigation. Had it wiped out places they would need to gather more evidence? What would be left? She was glad they had found the tub that had been locked away in Senna's garage. It was odd to her that there were only a few things in there. The knife was not there, and they still hadn't located the ATV.

They had gotten a warrant to search the ranch owned by Williams Stables, Inc., and would be doing that today. Once again, she'd talked Randy into stopping to pick her up on his way.

"We may both get suspended if Bracket finds out you've been out on the search warrants," Randy said as Carrie slid into the passenger seat of his car.

"Well, I suspect he knew all along I would be," said Carrie. "But you are right, he will give us hell over it."

Darren was consumed by the rescue and clean-up in Kachina, but Rick and Mike were eager to be part of the search at the ranch.

"Wow," exclaimed Carrie as they turned onto the drive and the massive house came into view. The tornado had traveled through this area, but the house and barns had fared well.

Mike and Rick were waiting for them as were several uniformed officers. This was a massive search area and it would take several people to conduct a thorough search. They developed a plan and split into teams, dividing the area to be searched.

After several hours and covering the entire house, garages, and barns, nothing incriminating had been found. All the horse tack, supplies, and tools were gone. It was possible whoever was living here had sold it all when taking over. There were no horses any longer, therefore, no need for gear to care for them.

Inside the house, were just normal, everyday living items. The clothes in the master bedroom closet were not clothes that Senna would wear. But they were clothes that the lady Carrie had seen in the bar would wear. In fact, she recognized a pair of boots she had seen her wear. She remembered them because she wished she'd had a pair just like them.

Carrie wasn't sure what she'd hoped they would find, but she really had thought they would find something to tie it all together.

"How big is the entire property?" asked Carrie as she stood outside surveying the countryside.

"It's big. Had we found more to give credence to our search, we could request teams to search the pastures and woods, but SAC Bracket would never authorize that kind of manpower with what we have," said Randy.

Carrie knew it was true. They had to take a step back and see if they could see things from a different angle. That meant they were back to doing research and digging into the corporate documents, waiting to see if the forensic team would find anything on the items they had taken from Senna's garage.

Soon the other officers had gone, and it was only Randy and Carrie who remained. They were heading to Randy's car, thoroughly discouraged when Carrie stopped. "Do you hear that?" She asked Randy. She could hear what she thought was the faint sound of a motorcycle coming from behind the barn.

Randy stood listening, then his face brightened. "I do," he nodded as the sound grew louder. They shut their car doors and walked towards where they thought they heard the sound.

They walked behind the barn on a driveway that had split from the main driveway. It narrowed significantly behind the barn but remained paved with asphalt and was still just barely wide enough for a truck or car. They stood looking across the hills towards the sound and then up popped a lady driving an ATV. It was just like the one they had been looking for.

Both Randy and Carrie instinctively reached for their weapons, but stood still waiting for the rider to reach them. When she got closer, they realized it was not Senna, but did not holster their guns.

Andrea could see the man and lady standing by the barn and she pressed down harder on the throttle. When she reached them she collapsed forward in exhaustion and relief. She was panting for air amidst tears of joy.

Randy and Carrie quickly ran to assist her. "What is your name," Carrie asked.

"Andrea Wells," she said. Then she began to rapidly babble out the events of the last few days of her captivity. It all came in random bits and pieces and totally out of sequence, but she just had to get it out.

They helped her to their car. Randy had already called for an ambulance as soon as they had seen the shape she was in.

Andrea rested her head back on the seat of the car and closed her eyes. Both Randy and Carrie gave her a minute to rest.

Then not being able to wait a second longer, Carrie asked, "So Senna Carter is the one who abducted you, correct?"

Andrea raised her head and looked at them. "No. It was Sienna."

CHAPTER 22

Six months later, life was calmer in Kachina, Oklahoma. There had been no more murders and Andrea was back working at the library.

They had found evidence of blood on the waders, rubber gloves, and tarps. Sienna had used them to keep herself free of evidence. The castrating knife had been found in a cubby-hole in the dash of the ATV, and Sienna's car had been found below the mesa on the Big Horn Ranch, crumpled into a ball.

Carrie and Randy had turned the case over to the district attorney and were on to another crime and another criminal. Things were not back to normal for Senna and Blake, however. With the help of Dr. Specter, the truth emerged.

The trauma that Senna had experienced from the legalistic dictates of the church she'd attended in her youth, combined with the abusive discipline of her father created a psychosis in her.

Through her life, Senna had held on to that brief window of time each year that she was allowed to spend with her Gran. It was the only time she could be free from all the rules and boundaries that held her pinned down. It was her lifeline and her hope.

The deviation caused by her Gran passing away the previous year had created a psychotic split in Senna's mind. She could not, would not, allow herself to break free from the religious legalism that had been forced upon her as a child. Her entire identity had been grounded in it.

But the trauma of her Gran dying created another identity, Sienna who could be free to enjoy life with no boundaries. Senna had no knowledge of Sienna per se, but often felt the emotions and thoughts of Sienna bleeding through to her own thoughts and emotions when Sienna so willed it. But Sienna knew of Senna and felt protective of her.

Senna could tell though once Sienna had released her hold on Senna. Her thoughts felt pure and isolated again with no tug-of-war pulling and tugging internally at her. She knew the moment Sienna had left even if she hadn't known exactly what it had been.

Senna was living in Kachina in her little clapboard house when her Gran had died. Sienna's domain had been the former horse ranch where Senna had never felt comfortable amidst the opulence.

After Senna's grandfather died, her Gran had sold all the horses, tools, and equipment. When Senna was young they had lived in Oklahoma City, but had also owned the ranch where they raised the horses.

Only barns and corrals existed on the ranch until several years earlier when they sold the house in town and built the beautiful home on the ranch. It had been Gran's desire to leave it to Senna one day, for her to live and raise a family in. Gran had designated Senna as the sole shareholder in the corporate business papers.

Gran had also established a massive trust fund for Senna which Sienna proceeded to spend without hesitation. But it seemed that no amount of physical freedom or spending could help Sienna feel whole. The family attorney still handled all the finances of the business and the trust for Senna, never realizing it was Sienna and not Senna who had been the one in charge of the massive spending spree.

Then one day, blood from a neighbor's dog, that had cut himself, changed things. Sienna seeing the rich red blood felt something evil trigger inside of her. The combination of a desire to feel whole and a corrupted need for the blood, had birthed a killer.

In the cabin, Andrea had explained to Sienna that we

all need the blood to be whole, but not the blood of innocent victims. It was only by receiving the precious holy blood of Jesus that any of us could be made whole.

Andrea's words were able to penetrate deep inside Sienna and something had changed. On Crown Rock Mesa, Sienna knew her time was over and that she could trust Senna to her friends and to God. She knew His blood would make her whole once and for all.

In the fury of the storm, Sienna had told God to take her away, that she was committing Senna to Him. When she woke, she was Senna and Sienna never returned.

Senna had no memory of the murders, but it was clearly her physical body that had committed them. Blake never left her side and vowed to defend her in the trial even though he did not have the expertise. However, to their relief, one of his law professors became intrigued and agreed to take it on, with Blake as second chair.

With Senna's agreement, they brought Dr. Specter onto the defense team to prepare for trial. The first that Dr. Specter had suspected anything was amiss was when Senna was in the hospital. While Blake was out, and she was alone with Senna, who had woken briefly as Sienna, she had threatened Dr. Specter to leave Senna alone. It startled her, and she hurried from the room.

When Senna went home from the hospital, Sienna created an unsettling feeling in Senna in order to cause her to pull away from Blake and Andrea. Senna didn't understand it, but she couldn't resist the urge to pull away from her friends.

The fatigue that Senna constantly battled came from lack of sleep. As Sienna, she roamed most of the night while Senna worked all day. The sharp pains and nausea that Senna had experienced at church had come each time the pastor had mentioned the blood that Jesus had shed. Sienna couldn't allow a loss of control over Senna so she rendered her unconscious.

A split-personality defense seemed ludicrous to almost everyone. Their first opinion was that it was a cop-out and an easy way to get out of being convicted. But those who had come to know Senna, truly know her, knew it was all true and that she could never do the things that Sienna had done.

The jury found her guilty but with the recommendation that her sentence be three years in a minimum security psychiatric hospital. She was relieved.

Blake visited her every day, and Andrea almost as often. Dr. Specter, as well, visited once a week.

"Sienna is gone now for good," Senna said quietly.

"How do you know?" asked Dr. Specter.

"Because she got what she so desperately needed."

"And what was that?"

"The blood. But this time, she finally got the only blood that could once and for all cleanse her and make her whole, the blood of Jesus."

Senna looked down at her hands for a moment before

continuing. "And I am finally free, too. I know I must pay for what Sienna did, but no matter what physical prison I must live in, it will not change the fact that for the first time in my life I am finally free, too. Totally and completely free."

AUTHORS NOTE

For my first foray into fiction I decided to make as much of it fictitious as possible. There is no Kachina, Oklahoma and the people and places are fictitious. They also are not based off of anyone that I know.

I am certain that I did not accurately portray police procedure and the working relationships between law enforcement agencies. Remember this is a novel of pure fiction and must be considered when reading.

Not everything is fictitious. I did research on the details of the tarps, knives, ATV's, cars, motorcycles, and various other items.

I guess it was just easier for me to know that Harley Davidson stopped making the Panhead in 1965 rather than all the intricacies of OSBI and police department procedures. If you are a member of one of those prestigious agencies, please forgive my failures in those areas. Thank you!

ABOUT THE AUTHOR

Nancy Jackson is a mother, grandmother, and great-grandmother, and lives in Edmond, Oklahoma.

When given various writing assignments in her seventh grade literature class, she discovered a love for writing. The praise of her teacher fueled her passion and she flourished.

Throughout her life, she worked in various positions where she was responsible for writing policy and procedure manuals, and a steady stream of corporate correspondence.

In 2003 she published Career Quest, a book on how to determine the best career for a person based on their true hearts desire, talents, and skills. Then, how to pursue that career from resume creation to offer acceptance. It also included how to establish a reputation of excellence from day one.

Her creative writing side was somewhat satisfied by writing at home. She later shared many of those various short stories on her blog. But she never stopped dreaming of the day when she would write her first novel.

Working in many different industries in a variety of roles, she was exposed to a treasure trove of people, places, and things that would later serve her well as she wrote her first, and subsequent novels. She continues to write both non-fiction and short-story fiction which she posts on her two blogs.

Before publishing her first novel, she spent many years as a silver/metalsmith designing and making jewelry. As a metalsmith, she taught for several years where she developed teaching curriculums for each class.

She is also a licensed Realtor, in the state of Oklahoma. Her true passion though, is writing and she is thrilled that she is now able to pursue it with the passion she has always had.

Her first novel, The Blood is the first in The Redemption Series trilogy and is now available. The Water and The Fire are soon to follow.

Sign up for her Inside Track newsletter on her website at www.NancyJacksonAuthor.com to keep abreast of newest released including the next in this series, The Redemption Series.

Made in the USA
Columbia, SC
27 February 2023

ABOUT THE BOOK

Truppenführung, the twentieth-century equivalent of Sun Tzu's *Art of War*, served as the basic manual for the German army from 1934 to the end of World War II. This astonishing document provided the doctrinal framework for blitzkrieg and, as a consequence, for the victories of Hitler's armies.

Rather than giving German military leaders a "cookbook" on how to win battles, *Truppenführung* offered instead a set of intellectual tools to be applied to complex and continually changing battle conditions. The keys to understanding the psychology, philosophy, and social values of the German army that fought World War II are to be found here. This first complete English-language translation is annotated to help the contemporary reader understand its military and social context.

Bruce Condell has worked with defense contractors in the United States and Asia and has been involved with the development of numerous military aircraft, including the PC-6 Tactical Transport and the PC-7 Multi-Role Training Aircraft. **Brig. Gen. David T. Zabecki** is assistant professor at the American Military University and editor of *Vietnam* magazine. His numerous works on military history include *Steel Wind: Colonel Georg Bruchmueller* and *The Birth of Modern Artillery*.